TASTE OF

DARKNESS

A DARKNESS NOVEL

Katie Reus

Enjoy!
Best

First printing, 2014

Cover art: Jaycee of Sweet 'N Spicy Designs
Editor: Deborah Nemeth
Copy editor: JRT Editing
Author website: http://www.katiereus.com

Taste of Darkness/Katie Reus. -- 1st ed.
ISBN-13: 978-1500641498
ISBN-10: 1500641499

For my wonderful husband.

Praise for the novels of Katie Reus

"...an engrossing page-turner that I enjoyed in one sitting. Reus offers all the ingredients I love in a paranormal romance." —Book Lovers, Inc.

"Has all the right ingredients: a hot couple, evil villains, and a killer action-filled plot. . . . [The] Moon Shifter series is what I call Grade-A entertainment!" —Joyfully Reviewed

"I could not put this book down. . . . Let me be clear that I am not saying that this was a good book *for* a paranormal genre; it was an excellent romance read, *period*." —All About Romance

"Reus strikes just the right balance of steamy sexual tension and nail-biting action....This romantic thriller reliably hits every note that fans of the genre will expect." —*Publisher's Weekly*

"Prepare yourself for the start of a great new series! . . . I'm excited about reading more about this great group of characters." —Fresh Fiction

"Nonstop action, a solid plot, good pacing and riveting suspense..." —*RT Book Reviews (4.5 Stars)*

"Wow! This powerful, passionate hero sizzles with sheer deliciousness. I loved every sexy twist of this fun & exhilarating tale. Katie Reus delivers!" —Carolyn Crane, author of *Into the Shadows*

Continued...

CHAPTER ONE

Drake glanced at Victoria out of the corner of his eye, trying not to flinch when she ran through another light. Yellow-ish, she liked to call them, when in reality they were already turning red by the time she blew past them. "Perhaps I should have asked someone else to teach me to drive."

She looked at him, her emerald green eyes flashing with confusion. "Why?"

"You might want to keep your eyes on the road," he gritted out.

Her head snapped back to face forward, her long, midnight black hair making a swishing sound as she moved. "You're such a baby," she muttered. "My driving is awesome. I don't know why you want to learn anyway, you can fly anywhere you want."

He just grunted. As a dragon shifter, yes, he could fly anywhere, but he needed to learn to drive because he needed to blend in to this new, human world. After being held captive in Hell for most of his life—over fifteen hundred years—this new world was jarring. Especially all the technology and these stupid vehicles. He would survive a crash but he didn't like the sensation of being trapped in these small metal boxes.

Victoria took a sharp turn, and when he gripped the handle on the door, she giggled. Which told him she'd done it to intentionally rile him up. That immediately relaxed him. He enjoyed their relationship and the subtle ways she teased him. He hadn't experienced innocent teasing since he was a young boy. If he had at all. He didn't have memories so much as impressions that his life had been different once. He'd been locked in Hell for so long that sometimes reality was difficult to decipher.

Four months ago he'd broken out of Hell because an insane vampire—now dead—had done a ritual spell to open a Hell Gate and release Akkadian demons. The male deserved his death for that alone. Akkadian demons were the scourge of Hell and would have ruined this beautiful planet. Drake had managed to escape and in the process helped Vega, a young hybrid vampire-shifter escape captivity. In doing so, he'd been taken in by Vega's pack. And then he'd found his future mate in Victoria.

Of course Victoria didn't know this. No one did. And he wasn't telling her or anyone. She deserved a male who could drive a vehicle and who understood her world.

Not a fucked up loser with no family and no way to support her. That would change soon though. He was smart and a hard worker. He just needed to learn a few more things. Then he would cross the bridge of admitting all the things he'd done in Hell. Maybe. He hadn't decided if Victoria needed to know everything about him yet. Especially since he couldn't be sure she'd accept his darker side.

He heard her phone buzz in her purse on the floorboard next to his feet, but she ignored it so he did too.

"Okay, we're going to start here," she said as she pulled into a parking lot behind the local mall. His first trip to the mall had been disastrous but he didn't want to think about that now. She parked in an empty spot then got out of the truck so he followed suit.

They met at the front of the vehicle as he rounded toward the driver's side. Stopping her, he gently touched her hip, the possessive action as instinctive as breathing. "Thank you for teaching me," he murmured. He'd been too embarrassed to ask anyone else in the Stavros pack, but more than anything he wanted to spend time with her and this had been as good an excuse as any.

Her cheeks flushed pink as they always did when he touched her. So he tried to do it as often as he could without seeming obvious what his intentions were. He wanted to kiss and lick every inch of her. It didn't matter that he'd never been with a woman, he knew exactly what he wanted from Victoria, what kind of pleasure he wanted to give her. That fresh mountain spring scent of hers intensified. It always happened when he touched her and he wasn't sure what it was, but he liked it. It didn't matter that they lived close to the beach, she smelled like the mountains, crisp and fresh. He'd been in the mountains before, although he didn't yet remember where and when. He was determined to reclaim his past, and one day soon he'd remember everything.

"You're welcome." She looked as if she wanted to say more, but she quickly averted her gaze and pulled away from him.

Her dark hair was an inky waterfall down her back, making him fantasize about what it would be like to run his fingers through it if she ever let him kiss her. When his cock started to harden as it always did in her presence he thought of other things to force it down. All he had to do was drag up one of thousands of images or memories from the last thousand plus years of his life and his erection disappeared instantly.

As he slid into the driver's seat, Victoria was already buckling herself in. "First things first. Always strap in. As supernatural beings we're pretty much going to survive any crash, especially you, but the police are more likely to pull you over if you're not strapped in."

"I'm certain they could pull you over for many other infractions," he murmured, doing as she instructed with the seatbelt.

She blinked once before letting out a loud laugh. The sound reverberated through him and something told him that hearing it would never get old. After living so long in the worst place imaginable, hearing Victoria laugh soothed his soul.

Shaking her head, she didn't deny his claim. "All right, funny man, today we're just going to pull out of the parking space and let you get used to using the brake and gas as you drive around in this small area." She mo-tioned with her long, elegant fingers to the empty park-ing area around them.

He swallowed hard and tried not to imagine what her hands would feel like on him. The truck was still idling so he listened as she told him to put his right foot on the brake while he put the gear in reverse. He'd already done some reading on how to drive so he wouldn't completely embarrass himself.

After an hour of driving around the parking lot, she smiled at him as he parked once again. The sight of her so relaxed with him made his entire body tighten with the need to touch her, claim her. He loved seeing her smile. "You're really good. I should have known, consid-ering how fast you pick up things."

When her phone buzzed again, she sighed and grabbed it from her fallen purse. "Ten bucks says it's Ga-briel."

Drake had heard the phone go off a few times during his driving lesson but Victoria had ignored her cell as she usually did when with him. He gritted his teeth, sure that she was correct in her assumption that it was Ga-briel, the pack's Guardian. The male was obnoxious and overprotective of her. The overprotectiveness was his only redeeming quality. Drake wasn't sure why the male was so protective, but he guessed it was because he and Victoria had both joined the pack around the same time. Victoria had been abandoned by her family and Gabriel . . . well, he didn't know his history, but the male didn't look at her in a romantic light at least. The only thing that mattered to Drake.

"I was right. I don't know why he's bugging me when he knows I'm with you," she muttered.

"That is exactly why he's texting." Gabriel didn't think Drake was good enough for Victoria. The male was correct, but it didn't matter, because he would be some day. And she was Drake's. He wouldn't deny what she was to him, what his inner dragon had sensed from even before he'd laid eyes on the beautiful female. Her scent had filled his nostrils then taken over his entire being and he'd been consumed with the single-minded need to protect her. For some reason it didn't matter that she was a wolf shifter. Or werewolf, as she would have been called thousands of years ago. Victoria had told him that was sort of an old-school term, though many in her pack still used it.

She shot Drake a glance he couldn't read before she shoved the phone back in her purse. "Well, he can just wait to talk to me until I get back. I think you've got some good driving time in. Did you want to try the main road? Maybe a couple side streets?" Her expression was so open and sweet, it jarred him. He wasn't used to sweetness. Even four months after his escape he was still adjusting to everything. When she frowned at him and said, "What?" he realized he was staring too hard.

"Yes. I can drive us back to the compound since the thought of your driving is beyond terrifying," he said dryly.

She raised a dark eyebrow, and her lips twitched as if she was holding back a grin. "I've seen you burn trained vampires to a crisp and swat supernatural beings away with your wings as if they were insects bothering you, and *my* driving is terrifying?"

"Well it's not good."

Her brows crashed together. "Then why did you want me to teach you?" she demanded.

"I like spending time with you. And I knew you wouldn't laugh at me." Something he wouldn't have admitted to anyone else in the pack.

But she was a healer and kind to everyone. Her expression immediately softened. "I would never laugh at you, Drake." When her phone buzzed again she let out a frustrated growl and whipped it out of her purse as she cursed Gabriel under her breath. But when she saw her screen her eyes widened. "Uh oh. Vega has a date. With a human boy. Change of plans, I'm driving us back." She was out of the truck before he could move.

They quickly switched seats and before he'd strapped in she was taking them back to the pack's sprawling mansion in the heart of Biloxi. The United States hadn't existed when he'd been thrown into Hell but he was slowly catching up on history and geography. Not that any of that concerned him now. Not when the pack Alpha's daughter had a date. Drake was just as protective of Vega as he was of Victoria. The young girl had been the first person he'd met after escaping Hell, the first one to show him kindness in over a millennia. "Who the hell is this human boy?"

Victoria shot him an incredulous look as she pulled out onto Beach Boulevard. "What is it with you males? She's seventeen, old enough to date. Besides, I'm pretty certain she could annihilate any human who got too fresh with her."

He frowned. "Fresh?"

"Oh, uh, like too handsy. If a male tried to, you know, get physical with her without permission."

His frown deepened at the thought. He'd seen enough violence in Hell like that for ten lifetimes. Vega was definitely too young to be dating. Or he assumed. "How old were you when you had your first date?"

To his surprise she flushed that delicious shade of pink. "Nineteen," she muttered. "And I know it's a little old but it was because of . . . circumstances."

"Gabriel?" Drake was sure it had to be the Guardian. As the designated second and defender of the Alpha he was a born protector and it made sense he would guard Victoria as well. She was valuable to their pack as a heal-er but the male also seemed to view her as a little sister. Which was lucky for him because if he'd looked at her with any other intentions, Drake knew they'd have al-ready come to blows.

"Yes! He made dating or anything else difficult dur-ing my teenage years."

"What about Valentine's Day?"

She shot him a quick glance before looking at the road. "What do you mean?"

Drake gritted his teeth. He was so unused to ordinary conversation that he often found himself jumping from subject to subject without a normal lead-in to a new topic. It was why he tended not to talk around most of the pack. But with Victoria he let his guard down. There were still things he needed to tell her about himself, like the things he'd done in Hell, but he kept finding reasons to hold off. He didn't want her to look at him differently.

He cleared his throat. "I wondered if the human boy had asked Vega out for the holiday." Which wasn't what he'd meant at all, but it sounded good enough.

Victoria shrugged. "Oh, I don't know. That's a couple weeks away."

"Do you celebrate it?" Some of the younger females in the pack had been discussing the day with great importance. So he planned to give something special to Victoria. He'd been working on it for weeks.

"Not really. The history of the day is confusing and dark and bloody. I don't mind the latter, but I don't like to celebrate something that hasn't been recorded properly in history." She sounded almost offended by the idea, which made him smile again. Victoria cared about history. It was one of her quirks and something he loved about her. "Do you have plans for Valentine's Day?" Her voice sounded almost cautious when she asked.

Which confused him. "No. You can be mine."

She laughed, the sound almost nervous. "I can, huh?"

"Yes. It will piss off Gabriel." The thought made Drake smile.

She snorted. "You two are so obnoxious but you're right, it will. If you're going to be my Valentine then I expect chocolates. Lots of them."

He'd already planned to get her some considering how much the female ate chocolate. She was tall and slender and her high shifter metabolism meant she was often eating something sweet. He wondered if she'd taste sweet when he kissed her.

As they pulled up to the gate of the walled-in mansion and acres of property in the historic district, Victoria pressed in the security code then steered her truck through. By the time they reached the end of the long driveway and parked behind a row of pack-owned SUVs, Drake's internal radar was going off at the sight of Vega stalking toward them, tears tracking down her face.

He and Victoria jumped from the truck at the same time, Victoria falling in step with him as they hurried to meet Vega. When she spotted them, to his surprise and horror, she burst into tears and threw her arms around Victoria's shoulders. The two females had the same build, skin tone and hair color even though they weren't related. Victoria was a couple inches taller at five feet ten, and right now Vega seemed almost fragile as Victoria rubbed her back and made soothing sounds.

The sight of her crying enraged Drake. "Who the hell hurt you?" he shouted, fire tickling the back of his throat. He'd fucking kill that human. He'd burn him into a smoking crisp.

Finn Stavros, the pack Alpha wasn't far behind Vega, his long legs eating up the distance to them.

"Do we need to kill the human?" Drake demanded, which made Vega cry even louder.

Finn rubbed the back of his neck as he looked at Vega and Victoria, then at Drake. "Nobody's killing anyone," he muttered. "She's pissed at me."

"You made your daughter cry?" Drake frowned. The Alpha had done nothing but dote on her for the last four months. He hadn't known of her existence until then. Drake was still confused on some of the specifics, but the one thing he knew was that the Alpha wolf and Vega's vampire mother Lyra would die before hurting their daughter. Since the sun hadn't set yet he knew Lyra couldn't come outside, even if she was awake. Otherwise she'd be out here comforting her daughter.

"I told her that she couldn't go out with a human," Finn muttered again, the frustrated tone of his voice unfamiliar.

Drake looked back at the females to find Victoria glaring at Finn.

"That's why she's crying?" Drake asked in confusion.

"You're all assholes!" Vega shouted, stepping back from Victoria and refusing to look at her father. "I don't know how you live like this," she said, clearly to Victoria. "I'm going for a run unless you plan on locking me down." She stomped away before anyone could respond.

"Is Lyra awake?" Victoria asked as soon as Vega had disappeared into a thick of trees on the property. The place was well-guarded so the shifters could run free in wolf form whenever they wanted.

Finn nodded. "Yes, but she doesn't know about this whole date thing. She's training one of the new warriors in the gym."

"So what happened?"

"I might have suggested that it wouldn't be wise to go on a date with a human."

Victoria placed her hands on her hips. "Suggested?"

He winced. "I might have used the word forbid."

To Drake's surprise Victoria started laughing. "Seriously, Finn? You tell a teenage girl you forbid something, that's just going to make her want to do it more. And you didn't wait to talk to Lyra about this? Do you *want* to sleep alone tonight?"

Finn just let out a growl of frustration. He started to respond when Gabriel appeared out of the thicket of trees in human form wearing cargo pants and a long-sleeved black T-shirt. He shot Drake a wary look, nodded once at Victoria then focused on his Alpha. "Just heard on the radio about your little blowout. Lyra knows and she's on her way up from the gym."

Finn rubbed the back of his neck again. "She pissed?"

Gabriel grinned. "What do you think?"

Finn let out a savage curse and strode away from them, tension in every line of his body.

"Where've you two been?" Gabriel demanded, swiveling on Drake and Victoria.

Drake didn't answer, which was his standard nonresponse to the Guardian. He didn't answer to anyone. Except maybe Victoria.

"At the movies," Victoria said, grabbing Drake's arm and dragging him to the house.

Since there was nowhere else he wanted to be and no one else he wanted touching him, Drake shot Gabriel a smug look over his shoulder as he let Victoria take him wherever she wanted.

CHAPTER TWO

"You don't have to come with me," Victoria murmured to Drake as he strode up the stairs of the pack's mansion to Vega's room. They'd grabbed a bite to eat and Victoria had heard through the pack grapevine that Vega was now back in her room. Sulking probably.

"I know. I want to." He shot her an unreadable look with those beautiful gray eyes. Whenever he shifted into a dragon, they turned silver. They also turned silver when he became emotional, which wasn't too often.

She was still trying to read his moods after four months of friendship. Of course she wanted more than friendship.

Way more.

Sometimes he gave off the vibe that he wanted more too. Like the way he always touched her hips, holding her as if he didn't want to let go. Or the whole Valentine's Day thing. But she was pretty certain he didn't mean anything sexual by it. When he'd first defended her in New Orleans from vampires and demons who'd broken out of Hell she'd thought he was attracted to her. He'd been all growly to anyone who came too near. And he still did that now. But the more time they spent together the more she wondered if he just saw her as some sort of security blanket. Otherwise, he would have made a move by now. Right? He was pretty much the only known dragon in the world. There might be others but so far she hadn't been able to locate any.

And she'd been trying. If he had a family he deserved to know where he came from. Since he didn't know much about technology or know anyone, she'd taken over the task of searching.

So he was basically alone after being locked in Hell for fifteen hundred years. He was still trying to figure things out for himself and she was pretty sure he felt safe with her. Which was great because she loved helping him and spending time with him. Sometimes she felt bad for the sexual thoughts she had about him and for the most part she kept that side of herself locked down. Except when he decided to touch her in that deliciously possessive way. It must be a dragon thing though. Or just his way of touching. Gah, she didn't know.

He was six feet six inches of confusing male. Lord, the man was huge, muscular and smelled heavenly. She just wanted to run her nose all over him, inhaling that spicy, earthy scent that made her inner wolf want to jump up and strut around for him. But what if . . . She didn't even want to think it, but she wondered if he'd even been with a woman before. He'd been alone in Hell for so long and in some ways seemed so innocent despite his darker edge. Could he actually be a virgin?

"What's wrong?" he asked quietly, his deep voice reverberating through her, striking all her nerve endings like a hammer hitting a gong.

She blinked and realized she'd slowed her pace as they reached the top of the stairs. She shook her head and smiled, drinking in every inch of his gorgeous face. He looked to be in his early thirties—even though he was way older—and was more striking than handsome. "Nothing. Just lost in my thoughts."

He frowned as if he didn't quite believe her, but didn't respond. They quickly made their way through a couple hallways until they found Vega's room.

Victoria knocked and was glad when the door opened a few seconds later. Vega opened it, looking more pissed than distraught at least. Her unique violet eyes that she'd gotten from her vampire mother, flashed with annoyance as they settled on Drake.

"Are you going to threaten to kill anyone?" Vega asked dryly.

"I won't threaten anyone." Which was the truth. If someone attempted to harm her, he would just kill, not bother with meaningless threats.

Sighing, Vega stepped back. "Sorry I freaked out earlier and blubbered all over you," she muttered as they walked in to her room. Which was more like a small, luxurious apartment than just a room.

All the rooms in the mansion were like that. The place was insanely huge.

"You have no reason to be sorry. I know what it's like to grow up with overprotective males." Though Victoria didn't hate it as much as she guessed Vega did. But Victoria had been abandoned as a cub and saved by Finn and his pack. She was grateful to have a family and didn't mind Gabriel's crazy overprotectiveness. Well, until recently. She wouldn't mind having more alone time with Drake. Sometimes the pack treated her as if she didn't know her own mind, but Drake never did that. He listened to her and actually asked her to help with things, like driving.

Vega snorted and flopped down on her king-sized bed. "It's ridiculous. I can't even go shopping without a freaking escort. I'm a vamp-shifter hybrid, more powerful than some of my packmates, but no one seems to care."

Drake strode to one of the two huge bay windows overlooking the property and looked outside, as if keeping guard, so Victoria sat on the edge of the bed and absently traced her finger over the white floral pattern on the light purple comforter. "It's not that they don't care. They do. A lot. After what happened they just want to keep you safe. And you might be powerful but you're young and you have two powerful parents, which automatically makes you a target."

Vega took a deep breath and looked as if she was going to blast what Victoria had said, but just sighed. "I know. And I understand. I don't want to get kidnapped or shot again, I just . . . I want the chance to be a little normal and I've never even been on a date. I thought my dad would be way more cool about it than my mom. It's why I went to him first. He seriously freaked though. He's never..." She swallowed hard and looked down at her hands. "He's never even raised his voice at me until I mentioned a date. Then it was like I'd said I wanted to join a terrorist organization." She looked back up at Victoria. "How did you manage to date with Gabriel breathing down your neck all the time?"

Victoria shot a glance at Drake but he didn't seem to be paying attention. She cleared her throat. "Ah, it was not easy." Or, even possible really. She looked at Drake again, not wanting to have this conversation in front of him.

He must have sensed that she was watching him because he looked over, his eyes having turned silver for a moment before returning to their muted gray. "Do you need privacy?" he asked.

She nodded and felt her face flush. She didn't want him to leave, but she couldn't tell Vega anything with him there. "I'll be in my room later if you want to come by and watch a movie."

He nodded, watching her so intently it was like he was trying to see through to her inner-most thoughts. She actually wished he could see them because then maybe he'd put her out of her misery and let her know if he even wanted her at all. "I'll text you."

Once he left, she turned back to Vega whose gaze had turned speculative. "Movie night? Is that code for something else?"

"Shut up," Victoria muttered. At twenty-three she was more than old enough to date and do whatever she wanted, but she didn't want to get into a discussion about Drake with Vega.

"Fine, but you'll answer my questions later. Tell me how you managed to date with the scary Guardian around."

Embarrassed, Victoria let out a breath. "I didn't exactly. The one time I managed to sneak out with a human—sneak out at *nineteen*, I should add—it was awful. We'd been talking for months at school and having coffee dates on campus but nothing really intense. I went back to this guy's place and we were uh, fooling around." Oh, god, even thinking of that night made her face flame. It had been beyond embarrassing.

"Fooling around how?"

For a moment she thought about not telling Vega because she was seventeen, but the girl was more grown up than most people decades older. Today's behavior notwithstanding. "He was, uh, going down on me, when Gabriel busted in. And I mean busted in like a complete maniac with blades drawn. I guess he'd followed me and had heard me from outside with that damn supernatural hearing and of course he assumed the worst."

"Oh my god!" Vega shouted, her eyes wide in pure horror. "He walked in on you when some guy's head was actually between...?"

Face red, Victoria nodded. "Oh yeah. Needless to say that guy never called me again. And anytime he saw me, he sprinted in the other direction." And she hadn't really dated since then. She didn't think Gabriel would ever do something so horrific again—because he'd been embarrassed too—but she'd been busy with school anyway and she hadn't wanted to risk anything like that happening again.

That was the problem with shifter males. They were so damn protective and could act like complete and utter barbarians. And not be apologetic about it at all.

"I don't think Gabriel could scare Drake away," Vega said slyly.

Victoria just rolled her eyes. "I'm not talking about him with you." The teenage shifter seemed to always want to grill Victoria about him. Unfortunately Victoria didn't have any answers and it made her feel crappier to admit out loud that she was pretty sure Drake only wanted friendship.

"Have you kissed him yet?"

"No."

"Do you want to kiss him?"

"What do you think?" she snapped with more heat than she'd intended. She adored Vega and didn't want to be rude, but she also didn't want to talk about Drake. It mixed her up too much inside. Seriously, what if he was a virgin and viewed her as a security blanket? She couldn't even go there, not when her feelings for him were so much more intense.

Luckily Vega wasn't offended. If anything, her grin grew. "Hmm, I'll eventually wear you down. But for now, I need to tell you something and you can't tell anyone."

Drake pushed the door to the roof of the mansion open and stepped outside, inhaling the fresh scent of magnolia trees. He immediately knew he was alone. Though the scent of shifters and Lyra and Vega lingered in the air around the property, no one was on the massive roof. He was glad to be alone.

He knew he shouldn't have eavesdropped on Vega and Victoria but he'd wanted to know about Victoria's dating experiences. And he wasn't apologetic about his decision either. Maybe in another lifetime he would have been, but not now. He might not comprehend everything about this modern world, but he understood battle tactics and evasive maneuvering. Otherwise he wouldn't have lasted in Hell for so long. So any leg up he could get with Victoria he would take.

When he'd heard her say a male had been going down on her he hadn't been certain of the phrase at first.

In Hell he'd seen more than his fair share of orgies and rapes, but he tried not to think about that. All the versions of sex he'd witnessed were violent and not something he wanted to relive.

So it had taken a few seconds for it to register that 'going down' meant oral sex. He knew the behavior he'd witnessed in Hell wasn't normal so he'd done an Internet search on his phone to see exactly what oral sex on a female looked like—Victoria had taught him how to use Google.

The pictures that had come up had been exactly what he'd expected. Not violent, just sexy. While he didn't like the thought of anyone but him doing that to Victoria, he grew hard thinking about licking her most intimate area with his tongue, hearing her moan his name. Finding out exactly what she tasted like.

"Do you want to kiss him?"

"What do you think?"

Drake replayed Victoria's last words over in his head. After she'd said that he'd finally left, needing to get away because he'd been getting too aroused. What *did* she mean? He hated that he was still trying to understand social cues and inflections. It was just another reminder how different he was from her. From everyone in this pack.

His dragon nature aside.

Using his natural gift to shield himself from any prying eyes, he stripped off his clothes then called on his inner dragon, letting him take over until he was in his beast form. As always the change was quick, the shift from human to dragon exhilarating, like he'd been shot up with a heavy dose of adrenaline. Things were clearer and sharper like this. He'd never even seen himself in his entirety until recently but Lyra had told him he was beautiful. Victoria had seconded it.

He didn't think males were supposed to be considered beautiful and he was pretty certain he actually wasn't, that they were just being kind. But as long as Victoria liked him in his animal form she could call him beautiful. His wings sparkled like jade emeralds, the same color as Victoria's eyes. More proof to him that she was his. And his body glittered like thousands of diamond scales. His paler body coloring made it easier for him to use his gift of camouflage so that when he flew high above the city, he was basically invisible. If someone was looking directly at him they might think they saw a blurred cloud but that was it.

Using the roof as a launching area, he shot into the night sky, expanding his wings and savoring every second of his freedom. He'd never thought he'd be free. The concept was still foreign and if he thought about it too long he sometimes wondered if he was still in Hell and had finally lost his mind.

For years he'd stayed in his dragon form as the best form of protection from . . . everything. But he hadn't wanted to lose his humanity completely. Hadn't wanted to let whoever had put him in Hell win. Because someone had. He just couldn't remember who. Fifteen hundred years was a long time and so many of his memories were a blur. He'd been young when he'd been locked inside. Twelve or thirteen maybe.

Taking in the salty air, he headed straight for the ocean, enjoying flying over it. Even at night it was a beautiful, seemingly endless scape of beauty glittering under the moon and stars. No fire or desolation or despair anywhere in sight.

He wasn't sure how long he'd been flying but he thought it had only been a couple hours when he finally landed quietly on the roof again. His clothes and phone were still there in a neat pile and he could hear the patrolling shifters moving around the grounds. Some were most definitely aware of him, but others might have missed his landing. He was incredibly stealthy when he wanted to be.

After he'd changed into his clothes, he checked his phone. His heart rate immediately kicked up a notch at the thought of reading Victoria's message. Others in the pack often texted him, but he never reacted to their messages like he did hers. As if his heart would beat right out of his chest.

Victoria: *Vega wants me to go somewhere with her. Promised her I wouldn't tell where. We won't be long. If you still want to meet up I'll text you when I get back?*

Smiling and feeling foolish for the erratic thump of his heart, he started to respond when Gabriel's annoyed voice carried faintly on the wind. He would have ignored him, but he heard Victoria's name. And anything to do with her concerned him.

Moving stealthily, he called on one of his most potent powers and camouflaged himself in human form as he strode toward the edge of the roof. No one would see him now.

With his supernatural hearing he made out various conversations from packmates on the property and a few from packmates inside the compound. He deducted that they must have windows open because the place was well-insulated.

He distinctly heard Finn and Gabriel talking in hushed tones. Concentrating, he leaned over the edge of the house and pinpointed where the voices were coming from.

Vega's room.

That was strange.

"Victoria wouldn't let her do anything stupid," Gabriel said quietly.

"I know, but . . . fuck, where the hell did she go?" Finn snarled.

"Not with the human. I've got him under surveillance." Gabriel sounded smug.

"Is Drake with them?" Finn asked.

Gabriel snorted. "Victoria didn't say in her text. She just said not to worry about her and Vega. Though that fucker probably went with them anyway."

"I'd feel a hell of a lot better if he was with them." The note of desperation in Finn's voice made Drake frown. Victoria wouldn't have let Vega go anywhere unsuitable or dangerous. Even he, with all his lack of knowledge, knew that. Maybe Finn was being irrational because he was a parent.

"Yeah, me too. I just don't like the way he looks at Victoria," Gabriel muttered. "She's always taking in fucking strays and this guy is the worst. We don't know shit about him or if there are more like him out there."

Finn's response was cut off as someone shut the window. Not that Drake cared what the Alpha thought. Not too much anyway. He only cared about Victoria, but Gabriel's words sliced through him soul deep.

Did Victoria see him that way? A strange lump settled in his throat as his entire body hummed with rage and raw energy. Fuck. Was *that* how she saw him? A stray? *Unwanted.* Something to be pitied. Fists clenched, he turned and started to head back to the roof's door but froze when he spotted Lyra leaning against the closed door. He hadn't even heard or scented her, which said a lot about her power.

He immediately let his camouflage fall but something about the way she watched him told him that she'd seen him anyway. Or maybe just the outline of his magic.

Wearing black cargo pants and a long-sleeved T-shirt, the blood-born vampire had her long blonde hair pulled back into a sharp ponytail. Her grayish-violet eyes sparked under the moonlight as she watched him.

She was one of the only people not afraid of him and he liked that. She'd even given him her potent vamp blood when he'd been shot. He had no doubt that she'd only done it because he'd saved her daughter's life, but Drake would never forget that small act of kindness when he'd been injured and vulnerable. Instead of speaking, he just stood there, waiting for her to make the first move.

"Do you know where they are?" Lyra asked, not needing to specify who.

"No."

Her lips pulled into a thin line, but she nodded once, as if she believed him. Something deep inside him felt the need to defend Victoria though so he continued. "Victoria would never let harm come to Vega. She'd die first."

To his surprise, Lyra let out a sigh and half-smiled, the action making her look younger than normal. Because of the way supernaturals aged, she looked to be barely in her late twenties, even though she was close to a hundred. "I know. It's the only reason I'm not even really angry. Finn is . . . well, Finn is being a protective father but he's new to all this and doesn't understand teenage girls," she muttered. "So what are you up to tonight anyway?"

"Heading to the fights," he said without thinking. He hadn't managed to tamp down the rage or humiliation inside him. If Victoria truly pitied him . . . He quickly banished that thought. The only way to let off this energy right now was to fight. Luckily Finn let his pack and other supernaturals in the area brawl at a private fight club, letting out all their aggression and anger. There weren't many rules except no weapons, no shifting during the fight and that shit didn't leave the ring.

Lyra's eyes glowed brightly for a moment before she cursed and took a step forward. He wasn't sure why she'd cursed, but he watched her, trying to understand the action. "Are you flying or catching a ride over there?" she asked.

So she knew he couldn't drive. He shrugged. "Flying, probably." It was quickest.

"I'll go with you. I'll carry your clothes if you want."

Though Drake was surprised the Alpha's mate wanted to go to the fights, he nodded. "Fine. I need to strip." He wanted to give her a chance to turn around. Once she did he stripped and set his clothes and phone on the ground. Not all vamps could fly, but she was from one of the strongest bloodlines and a born vampire, not made, and she had no problem flying a decent distance.

Without a word she grasped his belongings and took flight, shooting into the air with only a whisper of sound in her wake. He quickly followed suit after shifting.

He'd never lost a fight and he didn't plan to tonight. He just hoped there were some actual challengers in the ring because he needed to let out all the aggression burning inside him. He refused to be an object of pity. Victoria needed to see him in a different light. He just had to figure out how to show her.

CHAPTER THREE

"I can't believe you texted my parents," Vega muttered as she and Victoria made their way through the growing crowd of various supernatural beings to watch one of the ongoing fights. The scent of blood and sweat filled the air along with the steady hum of conversation.

The weekly fights in Biloxi were at one of Finn's properties, a warehouse in the middle of a self-storage place that Finn also owned. It was well-guarded and no humans were allowed in. "Deal with it," Victoria murmured, looking around at the familiar faces of her pack members. There were other supernatural beings there including vampires and half-demons.

Considering Vega's power, Victoria's own healing powers, and the fact that so many packmates were in attendance she wasn't worried about keeping Vega safe. It was the only reason Victoria had agreed to let the teenager come. Well, that and she couldn't really have stopped her. Vega had been determined to get out of the mansion tonight and see the fights.

"It's not like they're going to blame you. You saved my mom's life and my dad adores you," Vega continued, grumbling.

"Yeah well, you're their daughter. They need to know you're safe," Victoria said, pinning Vega with her gaze.

The younger female let out a sigh. "You're annoying when you're right."

Victoria grinned and turned away, still scanning the crowd, and hoping Gabriel wasn't there. If he was, he'd definitely tell Finn about Vega's presence. Victoria would have told Drake the exact place they were headed, but she'd known Vega wanted some relative independence from all males and the girl would have gone with or without Victoria. And it's not like she would have told on her so she'd had to accompany the teenager.

"This is crazy." Victoria looked around in awe and saw that some females and males actually had signs made up cheering on their favorite fighter.

And most of the signs were for Drake. She frowned at that. She'd never come to these fights because they bothered her healer nature on the deepest level.

"No kidding. I guess Drake's very popular here." Vega's eyes were wide as she also looked around and Victoria wondered if she'd made a mistake in coming here. Vega was young, but she wasn't a normal teenage girl either. And she was just trying to spread her wings a little.

Before Victoria could contemplate her decision, a male appeared at her side, seemingly out of nowhere. Bo Broussard, tall, muscular, half-demon and a little scary.

He smiled at both of them, but his red-colored con-tacts—matching his red-streaked dark hair—took away from the friendliness. "Victoria, Vega," he said politely.

"Dude, your eyes are freaky as shit tonight," Vega said, then her eyes widened in embarrassment. "I mean—"

To Victoria's surprise, the male laughed and said, "Good. That's what I was going for." Then he held out his arms for both of them. "If you two ladies would like to accompany me, I have a front row seat. And I think you're going to want to see who's up next."

Victoria took his arm but stood in between him and Vega. No way was she letting the half-demon touch Ve-ga, even innocently. Finn would lose his shit if that hap-pened. The male was more or less accepted by their pack as a good male, but no one touched Finn's daughter.

As if he knew what she was thinking, Bo just grinned wickedly and led them through a crowd of people who parted for him. He took them to a bar that looped in front of a fighting ring. It was one of those octagonal types, not a regular boxing ring. There were a few feet separating the ring from the rest of the crowd, but no actual seats.

Victoria looked at Bo questioningly. "I thought you had front row seats."

"No one here actually sits. I just saw you two and fig-ured Vega was only going to be here until one of her parents found out and she'd want to see a fight."

So Bo knew that Vega wasn't supposed to be here. Likely most of the pack here did too. Victoria didn't think many of them would narc her out. At least not right away.

When a cheer went up from the crowd, Victoria turned to see a huge man with bulging muscles pushing the ropes down and stepping into the ring. Maybe huge was an understatement.

"Holy crap that guy's big," Vega shouted next to her to be heard over the cheering.

Victoria nodded, wondering what kind of shifter he was. She turned to Bo. "How violent do these things get?"

He shrugged and leaned close to her. "Not so bad. At least not bad enough for Vega to need to leave. It's usually just shifters getting out their aggression."

Victoria let out a sigh of relief and pulled back from Bo. As she scanned the crowd she saw a flash of silvery-gray. Or she thought she did. A tall man and woman she didn't recognize were moving through the crowd on the opposite side of the ring and Victoria could swear the man had eyes similar to Drake's. Or maybe the male was just on her mind so she was imagining things. The male slid sunglasses on and turned away, taking away her view of him.

As if her thoughts had conjured Drake up, the crowd started shouting his name, especially the scantily clad females holding signs with his name and little hearts painted on them.

Signs. Seriously? She became aware that she was growling when Bo shot her a surprised glance.

Looking for Drake, her breath caught in her throat when he dropped into the ring seemingly from no-where. He'd probably done that camouflage thing he was so good at. It was almost as if he'd come from the rafters, which he very well may have. Shirtless, showing off his incredible physique that made her mouth water against her will as her eyes trailed over every inch of his cut body. He wore simple shorts, just like the other male in the ring. But that male had nothing on Drake's raw sex appeal. Not even close.

The supernatural beings went wild, but he didn't seem to notice their shouting or jumping up and down at all. Turning his head, he looked straight at her, his expression unreadable. When he looked at Bo standing next to her, his eyes went pure silver for a moment, his lips thinning, before he turned away and faced off with his opponent. Since he'd been in Hell she wondered if he didn't like Bo because the male was a half-demon.

Next to her, Vega squeezed Victoria's arm, clearly ex-cited. The energy rolling off the girl was almost palpable over all the other scents of sweat, blood and even sex permeating the air. Looking around, Victoria saw Lyra standing about ten feet to their right, blending in with the crowd. For all of a second, it took Victoria off guard, but it shouldn't have surprised her that the female was there.

When the Alpha's mate made eye contact with Victoria, she held a finger to her lips so Victoria nodded. It made her feel better that Vega's mother was here and seemingly okay that the girl was watching the fight.

Turning away so Vega wouldn't also look in that direction, she focused on the ring. The other shifter, a bear if she had to guess considering the Kodiak tattoo on his left shoulder, started dancing back and forth on his feet loosely, as if he'd done this many times before.

Victoria wondered if this was more of a formal type of fight but then Drake struck out, slamming his fist against the man's face. Because of their height similarity, it was a strong hit, the bear shifter stumbling back before he rolled into the punch.

From there it was on, the two males pummeling each other like the powerful shifters they were. The hits were hard and brutal and even though she was a shifter, Victoria had to tear her eyes away for a moment. She didn't like seeing Drake getting punched even if he could take it. The sight made something inside her cry out in pain.

Bo stepped closer to her, leaning in toward her ear and said, "The only rules here are that the opponents can't use weapons—"

He was cut off as a roar rent the air. Victoria turned back to the fight in time to see the bear shifter flying through the air in the opposite direction from them, clearly having been thrown out of the ring. Drake jumped over the ropes closest to her, his feet slamming against the concrete floor with enough force that the crowd quieted to a dull hum of conversation.

Victoria could feel Bo moving back from her but Vega stayed close as Drake stalked to her. She was glad for the female's presence because she didn't want to be separated from her and right now she couldn't tear her gaze from Drake's electric one as he closed the rest of the distance between them.

He kept coming, but looked away for a moment, glaring daggers at Bo. Coming to stand in front of her, Drake pulled the metal bar apart, snapping it cleanly so there was nothing separating them. He grabbed onto her hip in that territorial way of his and this time she was pretty sure he meant it for exactly as it was. A possessive gesture.

Her mouth was bone dry. Out of the corner of Victoria's eye, she saw and felt Lyra pulling Vega from her. She was mesmerized by Drake though. His eyes had gone pure silver and she could scent fire burning, as if he was ready to fry someone to a crisp. Her heart stuttered.

"Don't hurt him," Victoria whispered, knowing he'd never hurt her so that fire must be intended for Bo.

He didn't pretend not to understand, but Drake looked over her shoulder, presumably at Bo, and bared his teeth. A low rumble of anxiety rippled through the crowd, but the scent of fire died as he looked back at her, his eyes still shimmering that beautiful silver. "You don't belong here," he rasped out, as if talking was difficult.

She might like—okay, more than just like—Drake, but no one was going to tell her what to do. "Why not?" she demanded.

His nostrils flared and he seemed to struggle to form a response. "This is not a place for a female like you."

At his words, something sharp detonated inside her. She tried to take a step back but he refused to let her go. So she smacked her hand against his chest—and resisted the urge to stroke his hard body like her inner wolf craved. "Like *me*?" she asked quietly, not wanting everyone to overhear them. "As opposed to those groupies of yours? Sorry if I'm cramping your style," she snapped and tried to step back again. She had no claim on him and regretted the clear jealousy threading through her words.

Drake just held firm, his eyebrows drawing together in confusion. "Cramp my..." Blinking, he looked around at the females holding signs then pinned her with that electric gaze again. To her surprise, he looked positively smug. "You're jealous? Of *them*?" Smug or not, there was a hesitancy in his voice that soothed something inside her.

Before she could respond, he leaned down and ran his nose against her jaw, down her neck and back up to her ear where he gently nuzzled her. A shiver raced down her spine and hit all her nerve endings. The action was so insanely blatant that no one could miss what he was doing.

He was publicly claiming her.

Maybe he didn't realize what he was doing. He didn't understand so much about this new world, but his actions were unmistakable to anyone watching.

She clutched at his shoulders mostly in an effort to not collapse, though he'd never let her fall. Her legs felt weak and her breasts tingled as her covered chest came in contact with his bare one.

"I want to taste you right now, but I don't want an audience for our first kiss," he whispered against her ear, sending another delicious shiver rolling through her.

"I..." Her voice died so she just nodded. She wanted him to kiss her too, but for how she was feeling she didn't care whether they had an audience or not. In her wildest imaginings she'd never thought Drake would do something like this.

"Do you want to stay?" he asked in a low rumble, the sound vibrating through her and making the tingling worse.

Throat tight, she shook her head. She wanted to feel his lips against hers, to feel the sensation of his bare skin against her bare body. Of course he hadn't said he wanted to do more than kiss her, but she couldn't stop her fantasies.

"Drake." The sound of Gabriel growling his name made them both turn.

To her surprise, Drake practically shoved her behind him as he turned to face Gabriel. There was no way Gabriel would ever hurt her, but Drake wouldn't let her move out from behind him. So she peeked out around his back and saw Gabriel standing there wearing the loose gym shorts the fighters here wore and nothing else.

"Hell no!" she shouted, immediately realizing his intention. She didn't care that the crowd had grown deathly quiet and that everyone had heard her.

Gabriel's gaze shot to her in surprise. His green eyes flashed in annoyance. "I'm not going to kill him."

Drake just growled, but didn't respond.

"You're not fighting him. Whatever your deal is, get over it. I won't have two males I care about fighting." And she wasn't so much worried about Gabriel hurting Drake as the other way around. She'd only seen him fight in dragon form, other than the short fight tonight, but she doubted he had all these fans because he sucked.

Gabriel ignored her and focused on Drake. "You gonna hide behind your female?"

Drake let out a dark chuckle. "I'm glad you acknowledge she's my female."

Despite the tenseness of the situation, Victoria heard Vega giggle behind her and found herself half-smiling. Lord, these two males were ridiculous. "Enough, both of you. Gabriel, Drake and I are leaving. Now." She really wanted to kiss him. Couldn't wait to get him alone to do just that and a whole lot more.

"No. We will fight. He needs to know I am worthy of you." The deadly edge to Drake's voice sent a chill down her spine and not in a good way.

Worthy? What the hell? She clutched onto his waist, her fingers digging into his skin as fear rolled off her so potent she knew he had to scent it. Both males were strong and she didn't want either of them hurt. It was the healer in her. And the truth was, she didn't know who would win. "Please don't, Drake."

He turned and his eyes had turned a flat gray. "You think he will best me?"

Throat tight, she shook her head. "It's not that. I just..." She didn't know what to say. Couldn't find any words to make him stop. The thought of these two males fighting sliced her up. "Please don't."

His jaw tightened as he stepped away from her. "I must."

Just like that. As if her concerns didn't matter. Victoria looked over at Vega and Lyra and found them both watching her. Lyra was hard to read, but it almost looked like pity in her eyes. Which was just too much to take.

Turning away from the females, she made her way to the exit, the crowd parting and giving her a wide berth. She knew Lyra would get Vega home so Victoria didn't feel bad leaving. There was no way she was watching Gabriel and Drake beat the crap out of each other over her. She simply couldn't do it.

As she exited into the cold night air, she scented Finn behind her before she'd cleared the door. She hadn't seen him but he must have arrived with Gabriel or Lyra.

Right now she didn't want to talk to her Alpha or any-one.

"Victoria!" She turned at Finn's heated voice.

Her Alpha's ice blue eyes pinned her in annoyance. "I know you scented me."

She shrugged, wrapping her arms around herself as a cheer from inside went up. Guess the fight had started. Ugh. "Can you bitch at me later?"

Surprising her, he reached out and pulled her into a hug. "I'm not going to bitch at you at all," he muttered against the top of her head. "Thank you for escorting Vega here."

She pulled back from his embrace. "She was coming tonight with or without me."

"I know." Finn's expression bled into one of confu-sion. "I didn't think . . . she's different than you were as a teenager. Definitely more hardheaded."

Smiling now, Victoria nodded. "Yeah. It's just been her and her mom for almost seventeen years and now she's been thrust into a wonderful—but overprotective—pack with more than one parental figure. It's not just you who's watching out for her, but pretty much every packmate and the smothering is getting to her. And I don't blame her."

"That's exactly what Lyra said," he muttered again.

It was odd to see her Alpha out of sorts. The male was normally cool and composed about everything. Be-fore she could respond, he pulled out his cell phone when it started buzzing.

He frowned at the screen. "Spiro was hurt fighting a couple rogue vamps. Nothing too serious. Want to stay here or come with me?" he asked, meeting her gaze.

While she really wanted to make sure Drake was okay she simply couldn't watch those two males fighting each other inside. And she wasn't going to wait around for them to finish like some pathetic female. Like those women with the signs. "I'll go with you. I assume Vega is going home with Lyra?"

Sighing, Finn nodded. "Yeah. Let's go before I change my mind about that."

Victoria started to smile when another cheer went up from inside and found herself cringing instead. She cared so much about Drake but tonight he'd surprised her and she wasn't sure how she felt about it. She loved her packmates but the one thing about Drake that had always been different was that he listened to her. He didn't go all alpha macho overprotective. Well, not too bad. But tonight, he'd been so determined to fight Gabriel instead of coming back to the mansion with her. The knowledge cut deep.

Conall glanced at his sister, Keelin, when she touched his forearm.

"Should one of us tail the female?" She kept her voice low, though it was unlikely anyone could overhear them among the cheers.

He shook his head, not worried about the pretty, slender female who'd just stormed out of the fighting arena. Glancing around, he tugged on his hoodie, wanting to keep most of his face concealed. He'd also slipped on sunglasses a few minutes ago, which might be considered a little odd, but he'd noticed a lot of supernatural beings at the fight wearing them so he didn't stick out.

"Why not?" She shifted from foot to foot, her gaze on the two fighters in the ring. The male known as Drake kicked the other male with brown hair in the stomach, the action savage. Very dragon-like in nature.

"It will be better to follow him." Conall had seen the way he'd more or less publicly claimed her. He wouldn't be letting that female go far.

Keelin bit her bottom lip, clearly unsure that Conall was right. "We should keep tabs on her in case we lose him." Desperation edged his sister's voice. She wasn't used to missions or any sort of violence but she'd insisted on coming with Conall for this tracking mission. He hadn't been able to deny her.

"She has a dragon's essence protecting her," Conall continued.

"I know, but . . . they're not mated. I didn't realize it was even possible for a dragon to give their essence to a non-mate. Maybe there's something else going on." His sister sounded unsure.

His attention never wavered from the ongoing fight. "It's not impossible if one gave it to her willingly. And he definitely gave it to her."

"Why would any dragon give a part of himself to a . . . wolf shifter?" Her question was one of true curiosity, not disgust. "It makes no sense."

"Why do males do anything for females?" Conall knew he sounded a little bitter but didn't care. He had his own demons to deal with, though now wasn't the time.

Keelin's frown deepened. "This might not even be him."

True. But Conall hoped it was. Their whole clan did. A powerful earthquake had rocked New Orleans four months ago, the event odd enough in the area, but their clan had felt the reemergence of a dragon into their world and had pinpointed it to New Orleans.

All related dragons were linked to an extent so if one was born, their clan felt it on a molecular level. He'd been sleeping when he'd suddenly become aware of the existence of another dragon. But it hadn't been a new birth, it had been a . . . reappearance. Keelin hadn't known what the feeling had been until he'd explained it to her. She'd been five when . . . Conall cut off that train of thought.

He didn't want to hope too much, but it was impossible not to. He didn't believe in miracles. Had stopped centuries ago.

As he watched the fighters, he frowned.

"They're both holding back," Keelin murmured, mirroring his thoughts.

He nodded slowly. "I agree. They both have good techniques but it's almost as if they just want to fight, but not actually hurt each other."

"Not long-term anyway," she murmured.

He wasn't sure what to make of it. They'd come here because they'd heard rumors of an undefeated fighter who'd come from nowhere and was now part of a wolf pack—but wasn't a wolf.

Conall didn't understand why any fighter would restrain himself though. It wasn't the dragon way and it wasn't the supernatural way.

He didn't voice his concerns to his sister, but he worried about the female with the dragon's essence. By having it, she could be a threat to their kind.

CHAPTER FOUR

Drake couldn't believe Victoria had left the fight. He hadn't actually wanted her at it in the first place, but after Gabriel's challenge, he wanted her to see that he could defend her, take care of her. And he needed Gabriel to see that he could defend Victoria if necessary. Because deep down he wondered if that was why Gabriel had been pushing him, to force Drake to prove himself.

Victoria seemed to think he would lose to Gabriel. Which sliced at his pride. While he wouldn't hurt the Guardian too much, Drake was tired of the male questioning his worth, no matter the male's reasoning.

Victoria needed to see that he wasn't a stray. And not someone to be pitied.

He knew she'd wanted to kiss him though and he'd been willing to put away his pride for the chance to publicly claim her. He'd give up anything for a taste of the female and that should terrify him. On one level it did, but after having nothing for almost an eternity, he understood that a female like her was worth risking everything for.

He'd wanted to go after her. Until Gabriel had attacked. Now he couldn't follow until he ended this once and for all. His only consolation in letting Victoria leave was that he would get to beat the shit out of Gabriel. He wouldn't hurt him too bad though. Even if the beast inside him craved spilling the other male's blood.

Jumping back, Drake avoided what would have been a hard punch to the jaw. Continuing to dodge Gabriel's fists, Drake moved quickly, using his agility to jump into the ring.

Gabriel followed, the dark-haired male just as agile. He'd left his blades somewhere, clearly understanding the rules of the ring. As far as Drake knew, the male had never fought here before. The Guardian's green eyes went pure wolf as he bared his teeth at Drake.

Watching him carefully, Drake let all his anger at the male subside. He had to let go of his emotion if he wanted to win.

Dancing to the left, he punched out with his right hand, leaving his face open. As Gabriel moved in for the attack, Drake kicked out, slamming his foot into the male's stomach. He didn't attack as hard as he could have, however. Only because it would upset Victoria.

Didn't mean the other male wasn't going home with a lot of bruises. And some blood loss.

After that blow, it was on, back and forth between them, each punching and kicking the other with every opening. Instead of feeling drained, the sharpest sense of adrenaline raged through him, urging him to continue fighting. To destroy his prey. It was difficult to hold back but the thought of truly hurting Victoria kept him reined in.

Barely.

Because it would destroy her if he killed or maimed her friend.

Drake wasn't sure how much time had passed, but the crowd still continued to cheer and shout with each brutal strike. It didn't surprise him considering how many fights he'd been in while in Hell. Everyone had cheered during those fights too.

Of course those fights had been more brutal and he'd usually been in dragon form battling against wyverns or whatever else thought it had the strength to take him on. Regardless, there had always seemed to be an audience for violence. This plane on Earth was no different.

The exception was he wasn't being forced to fight for his life every day. He fought because it let out his aggression and calmed his beast.

"Tired yet?" Gabriel snarled, sweat dripping down the side of his face. His eyes weren't wolf anymore, but pure human as he jumped back from an ankle kick.

"Nope." Not even a little.

Gabriel snarled again, the sound more animal than human as he rushed Drake.

Embracing the other male's hits, Drake returned his own, slamming his fists into the male's kidneys, liver and ribs with a brutal force. Reality rushed back when two strong arms wrapped around him from behind.

At the same time a male from the Stavros pack grabbed onto Gabriel in the same manner, yanking him backward.

Realizing how lost he'd gotten in the fight, Drake allowed himself to be pulled back, not fighting the other male's grip because his beast knew he wasn't being attacked. He'd never lost sight of his surroundings like this before.

Breathing hard, Drake winced as a sliver of pain permeated his senses.

"You two fuckers trying to kill each other for real?" the male holding him shouted above the crowd who all seemed to be talking at once.

Looking back Drake realized the bear shifter from earlier was holding him, his expression fierce. "You can let go."

Warily, the male loosened his grip and took a step back. Solon, the male holding Gabriel, did the same. Drake and Gabriel glared at each other, both ready for another attack.

As seconds ticked past, Drake became more aware of how injured he likely was. His entire body ached and he knew he had a few ribs cracked. At least. He would heal in a couple hours, but pain was still pain and every breath hurt. The only thing that eased it was seeing Gabriel bruised and bloody.

To his surprise, Gabriel held out a hand. "Draw?"

Drake thought that was respect in the other male's eyes, but the Guardian was difficult to read. It made him wonder if he'd been right about Gabriel's reasons for wanting to fight him. Drake nodded, unsure if the male meant about Victoria or simply this fight. He stuck out his own hand and stiffly shook Gabriel's.

"She's like a sister to me," Gabriel continued after they dropped their hands. "I have to know her mate will be strong enough to protect her."

"I am." If Drake had a sister he imagined he'd be the same way. "She would tell you that she could take care of herself though." Even though Victoria was a healer and one of the most non-aggressive supernatural beings Drake had known, she was still a shifter and very capable. It was one of the things he respected about her most.

Gabriel half-smiled, blood trickling from his cracked lip. "I know. Want to grab a beer at Howler's?"

Drake blinked, unsure he'd heard him right. After just battering each other to a pulp, Gabriel wanted to get a drink with him? He might still be learning much about modern customs, but that was something friends did. And Gabriel had never treated him as anything close to resembling a friend before. Almost no one in the Stavros pack had. "Why are you asking me?"

Gabriel shrugged, then winced. "Because that's what males do. We beat the shit out of each other, then go have a beer afterward."

Drake wasn't sure that Gabriel wasn't lying, but he didn't scent the standard acidic smell that usually accompanied an untruth. "Okay. I need to change first." Howler's was the club on the bottom floor of Harvest Moon Casino, owned by Finn, and Drake knew enough that he couldn't go inside looking the way he did. He also wanted to speak to Victoria before he went out with Gabriel. She'd seemed so hurt earlier and he couldn't bear that he was the cause of her pain. He needed to make his intentions clear. She was his.

Victoria's eyes snapped open as she heard Spiro's raspy voice. "You don't have to stay here all night."

Sitting up straighter in the cushy bedside chair, she eyed her packmate who was stretched out on the bed in the medical room. "Are you sure?" Spiro had been stabbed deeper than the pack's doctor originally realized. The vampire's silver blade had made contact with his heart and the internal effect had weakened the male. She'd used her healing gift on him to speed up the process, but had decided to stick around in case he needed her again. If she used her gift too much it would drain her but she'd barely had to use any energy with Spiro.

"Yeah. I'm about to head back to my room. It's so quiet in here it was easy to pass out." His voice was already stronger as he pushed up, the sheets rustling beneath him.

She frowned at him, taking in his pallor. His naturally darker Mediterranean skin tone had a grayish tint to it. Standing, she checked his pulse and blood pressure then met his gaze. "You're BP is really low. You needed the rest and likely need a few more hours of uninterrupted sleep. Have you been cleared to leave?"

He grinned. "Not yet, *Mom*."

Though she was much younger than Spiro, a lot of her packmates called her that teasingly. It was in her nature to care for them both as a nurse and a healer. "Why don't you stay put and I'll find Ophelia."

"You can't just let me sneak out of here?" His voice was hopeful.

Victoria just snorted. "And risk her wrath?" No way in hell. The doctor was barely five feet flat, with long, dark, curly hair she usually wore in a ponytail. She was adorable and incredibly caring for all her patients, regardless of species, but Victoria had seen her on a rampage more than once. Older than Finn by about fifty years, she'd been alive a long time and pretty much nothing got past her.

As if talking about Ophelia had conjured her up, the petite female strode into the room, a warm smile on her face.

She raised her dark eyebrows at Victoria. "You're still here?"

"I'm about to head out."

Ophelia gave her an unreadable look. "That sexy dragon of yours is looking for you."

Victoria blinked in surprise. "He is?" He hadn't called or texted—not that she'd been obsessively checking her phone or anything. And she wasn't sure she liked Ophelia calling him sexy.

"Yep. Heard he and Gabriel beat the crap out of each other and I told both of them not to bother coming to the clinic. If they want to intentionally hurt themselves, they can heal all on their own."

Victoria hid a smile and nodded. "Good for you."

"Is there anything you want to tell me?"

She looked at the female in confusion. "Uh, no."

"Do you know about the mating habits of dragons or—"

She felt her cheeks warm up. "I'm not having this conversation with you!" Especially not in front of Spiro. Sometimes shifters were just too damn open about everything. While she didn't mind talking about sex she wasn't having a ridiculous medical conversation with Ophelia where the female would probably want to draw her a diagram. It didn't matter that Victoria had a Doctorate in nursing science, Ophelia liked to over explain *everything*. Without waiting for a response, Victoria left the clinic and headed for her rooms. It was close to midnight and she wanted to sleep in her own bed.

And not obsess about the fact that Drake hadn't contacted her after that dominant display of his.

When she made it to her wing of the house, she let out a frustrated growl. She and Drake were in each other's rooms so often his scent still lingered outside in the hallway. His set of rooms was right around the corner on the next hallway and part of her was tempted to go find him, but she decided not to.

She still wasn't sure what to say to him and he hadn't tried to contact her after his fight.

As she stepped inside, that pure masculine scent of his wrapped around her, teasing her senses. It took all of two seconds for her to see him sitting at her desk near one of the huge bay windows. She let the door close behind her. A dim lamp was on, the only illumination in the large space.

He immediately stood, clutching something wrapped in a blanket. "I didn't want to wait in the hall and you've always let me in your rooms before so—"

"It's fine, Drake. You're always welcome here." She'd noticed that with her he seemed to apologize for things that didn't need apologizing for, as if he was worried she'd be angry with him or take away her friendship. It broke her heart. Sometimes, like earlier today when they'd been driving, he'd let his guard down and had been his fun, humorous self, but times like this when she could see the wariness in his gray eyes, it clawed at her.

She eyed his face, noting there was just a fading bruise on his left cheekbone that would be completely gone in the next hour. He healed at a rate faster than her Alpha. "Are you badly injured? I can heal you." Because even if he'd acted like an idiot and fought with Gabriel, if she could take away his pain, she wanted to.

He shook his head, but didn't take a step closer, so she closed the distance between them, moving around her bed toward her desk. But she didn't reach out to touch him, still feeling too awkward.

Before she could say anything, he shoved the bundled blanket at her. "I made this for you. Be careful unwrapping it."

"Uh, thank you." Turning to the bed, she laid it on the cushy comforter and unrolled it to find a gleaming small blade—dagger sized—with an intricate design down the middle. A dragon and wolf were intertwined in the middle, making her breath catch. The way they were entangled together made his intentions crystal clear. A small, insecure part of her told her she was wrong, but she knew what he was trying to say. It shocked and pleased her on the most primal level. "Drake..." Her vocal cords refused to work as she met his gaze.

His eyes had turned a shimmery silver. As he came to stand directly next to her, towering over her despite her taller height, he spoke. "I made it for you. I made the blade a while ago but the designs took longer and..." He trailed off, gesturing to it with his hand. "I hope you like it."

She swallowed, aware of how hard her heart was pounding. "I love it. It's unexpected and beyond beautiful." And the dragon and the wolf in the middle pretty much made her heart beat out of control. She was honored that he'd made something so beautiful for her. And if she was honest, she was a little terrified by it. "How did you make this?"

"I . . . I just used my fire to form it. Sort of like the way a spider makes a web." He seemed almost confused by that. "The blade wasn't difficult but it took a while to imprint the design with my fire."

As supernatural beings they all had magic in them so maybe his ability to create it had something to do with him being a dragon or where he was from or . . . something. The significance of the gift wasn't lost on her either. She was a healer and he was clearly a warrior so he'd given her something that she could protect herself with, something that represented him. "I'll treasure this. Thank you again."

He shifted almost uncomfortably and just nodded in that way of his when he didn't want to talk.

Though she wanted to push more about the blade, he seemed too on edge so she decided to ask something else. "So how was the fight?"

"We came to a draw."

She narrowed her gaze. "And?"

"And, Gabriel invited me out for a beer afterward."

He couldn't have surprised her more if he'd been trying. Gabriel must have accepted Drake then. Not that it ultimately mattered. She wanted her friend to accept Drake, but her wolf already had and she knew Drake was a truly good male on the most basic level. She wasn't sure if it was her healer's nature or what, but she never doubted her instinct. "That's good."

"Is it?"

Smiling, she nodded.

"I wasn't sure if he was lying to me when he said males beat the crap out of each other then have drinks together afterward." Drake's posture was stiff and his expression still unsure.

Laughing, she nodded again. "That sounds about right. I'm just glad you two worked out whatever it was you needed to. I wish you hadn't fought him at all though."

"When you left I wanted to go after you, but Gabriel attacked."

That eased some of her tension, but... "I was looking forward to kissing you." She felt her face heat up at the words, but wanted them out there so he understood exactly where she stood. His gift made his intentions clear so she wanted him to know she was on board. She wasn't certain she wanted to mate in the next five minutes or anything, but this wasn't short-term for her.

He swallowed hard, his eyes turning even brighter before he reached out and ran a hand down her side and settled on her hip. When he flexed his fingers around her she shuddered, her nipples beading into tight points. A rush of heat flooded between her legs as she finally allowed herself to be vulnerable with him. Now that she knew the way he was holding her was intentionally possessive, she couldn't stop her body's reaction.

"I . . . can't kiss you yet," he whispered, his voice filled with regret.

The words were like ice water slapping her in the face, sharp and stinging. She was primed and ready for way more than a kiss. "Why not?"

"I'm not ready for you yet."

What? Victoria had just assumed all shifters were the same. When it came to sex they weren't any different than vamps or humans. Well, except shifters and vamps tended to bite during sex, but she'd heard some humans did too. She placed a hand on his chest, slightly digging her fingers into the hard muscles. Now that he'd admitted his feelings for her she felt more at ease touching him the way she'd been fantasizing about. "Not ready?" Disappointment speared through her.

He nodded. "You deserve a male who has more to offer you."

"What are you talking about?"

"I don't have a job, I'm still learning to drive and I depend on this pack for shelter. And I know so little about this new world. I'm not ready yet."

She'd take him without all of that. "Drake." She tugged him so that he was sitting on the edge of her bed and she did the same, carefully sliding the blade out of their way. Taking his hands in hers, she tried to find the right words. "Did someone put this crap in your head?" Because if someone had, she was going to rip them a new one.

"It's not crap," he growled. "And no one has told me this. These are things I understand as a male. You deserve more than what I am and what I have." He tried to pull his hands back from her, but she held tight.

If he'd truly wanted to pull free he could have, but she knew he wouldn't want to risk hurting her in any way so she held on, linking her fingers through his. Her heart ached at his words. "You don't need to do anything to be with me. I care for you, Drake. A lot." Okay, she more than cared for him. "And I want you just as you are. There's no reason we shouldn't be kissing right now."

His jaw clenched in response.

She could see the indecision in his eyes so she pounced on it. "Haven't you wondered what I'd taste like?" She kept her voice low, the question coming out huskier than she'd intended. She couldn't count how many times she'd fantasized about him running his big hands all over her bare body and following up with his tongue. And she wanted to do the same to him, exploring every inch of him.

Swallowing hard, he simply nodded, his eyes like a supernova for a brief moment.

"Good because I've wondered about you too. Just kissing won't change anything." *Liar, it would change everything.* And she couldn't wait.

She could see the finality in his eyes before he said, "I will not be swayed."

Sighing, she dropped his hands. "Are you sure that's the only reason you don't want to kiss? Is there . . . someone or something else?" She really doubted it considering the gift he'd just given her but she needed to know.

"There will never be anyone else." Again with the finality in his deep voice.

Those words went straight to her core. Right then all she wanted to do was wrap her arms around him and tease his lips with hers, nipping and kissing him everywhere he'd let her. She wouldn't rush him though, she just wanted to taste him, to lay claim to him the way he'd done at the fight.

"You've never looked at me like this before." His words drew her gaze from his mouth to his eyes.

"Like what?"

"Like you want me." There was a mix of awe and disbelief in his voice. As if he didn't quite believe her feelings.

She wondered if that was more the root of his issue about why he wouldn't kiss her. "I didn't want to take advantage of you."

He laughed, the sound reverberating through the room. "You are so small. You could never take advantage of me."

Well, she wasn't exactly small. Slender yes, but she was tall for a female. Maybe not compared to him though. "I don't mean physically, I mean, you know, emotionally. You were in Hell for a long time and we became friends so fast I've been worried that maybe..." It felt strange to just blurt everything out.

His lips pulled into a thin line. "Maybe what?"

"Maybe, you latched onto me because I'm safe."

"I don't understand. I don't need you to keep me safe." There was a touch of arrogance in his voice she liked, as if he was very secure in his ability to protect her. Considering the way he had in the past, he should be secure in that.

She bit her bottom lip. She couldn't very well say she was worried that he viewed her as a security blanket. "There are plenty of females you haven't met."

That frown deepened, making him look even sexier. Which should be a crime. "I don't understand that either. I don't want any female but you."

His words thrilled her, but..."You haven't let yourself be open to meeting others." Lord, why was she pushing this? She didn't want him hooking up with other females but she still couldn't stomach the thought of taking advantage of him when there was so much of the world he didn't understand yet.

He sighed. "Fine. I will meet other females if it makes you happy but I only want to kiss you. I only want to be with you. I just need time to be worthy for you."

Her heart squeezed. "Drake, that's ridiculous. You're—"

The door flew open. Finn stood in the doorframe, her Alpha's ice blue eyes pure wolf. "We think we've had a dragon sighting over the mansion. I want everyone to stay locked down in the mansion. Drake, you need to come with me."

CHAPTER FIVE

Drake stood protectively close to Victoria on the roof. Of course the stubborn female hadn't listened to her Alpha and had instead insisted on coming with them. To Drake's annoyance Finn hadn't ordered her to remain in her room after that initial command.

Drake had quickly come to learn the dynamics of the pack and even though Victoria wasn't a warrior or very alpha in nature, at least not in the physical sense, she did what she wanted. He was pretty certain it was because she was a healer and seemed to have a different standing altogether among the pack. Everyone adored and respected her. He just wished Finn would have made her stay put. Because there was no way Drake was trying to order the female to do anything, even if he did want her safe. He didn't want to push her away.

Keeping his gaze on the night sky, he scanned for any dragon sightings. "Who saw the dragon?"

"Rhea saw *something*," Finn corrected. "She isn't sure what it was but when she mentioned you flying, Solon told her you were already in for the night so she alerted me."

"What was the 'something' she spotted?" He didn't look at Finn, not wanting to miss a potential attack, though he wasn't sure anything was out there.

"A shimmer of light then a brief flash of something that looked a lot like fire." Finn's voice was grim. "Could have been something from the Air Force base, but..."

"We would have heard a jet," Lyra finished when her mate trailed off.

Wordlessly Drake started stripping. If there was another dragon nearby he wanted to know about it. It was almost too much to hope that there were more of his kind. Maybe even family. But if he had family, why hadn't they come for him? Why had they let him suffer in Hell for fifteen hundred years?

Next to him Victoria let out a soft sound and he turned to find her watching him with wide eyes. That crisp mountain spring scent of hers was intensified tenfold as she stared at his chest. Her gaze snapped to his and he started to ask her if everything was okay, but it took two seconds for his brain to compute that she liked what she saw. That was hunger in her green eyes.

For him.

He swallowed hard. Now that she'd let down whatever wall she'd previously erected between them, his reality had shifted and he felt like he was catching up to this new, better world where he could have a future with Victoria. "I don't know what's up there. Keep your blade out. It will protect you," he said softly. Drake didn't remember the particulars, but the blade he'd made her was powerful and could kill anything. It had something to do with being forged in dragon fire. There was more to it, but the knowledge was buried deep in his earliest memories. He hated that he couldn't get to that memory and so many others. But he would. He was determined to.

"You just take care of yourself." Her words were barely a whisper and her eyes glinted with worry, making him feel too many emotions. His chest squeezed tight at the knowledge that she was actually concerned for him.

Drake nodded once then finished stripping after turning away from everyone. He couldn't be around Victoria without being physically affected and he didn't want anyone to see that.

Racing to the end of the flat area of the roof, he jumped into the air, calling on his inner beast and letting the change flow through him instantaneously. At the same time he used his camouflage to conceal his body. Every time he shifted he felt stronger, more in control. As if nothing could stop him. Even in Hell it had been like that.

It was very difficult to kill a dragon. He was certain he must have more weaknesses but if so he hadn't discovered them yet. When he'd been shot in New Orleans he'd been weak but he'd also just come from Hell, the transition to this new plane already weakening him. He was pretty sure if someone had decided to cut off his head he would have died. Inhaling the salt-tinged air, he ascended higher, savoring the way the air rushed over his body and wings.

The higher he flew, it became clear that he wasn't alone in the air. He could faintly hear the flap of wings that weren't his own. But he couldn't see anything tangible. If there were more dragons in the world, and he had to assume there were because he'd come from somewhere, they must have the same camouflage ability as him.

On a burst of speed he pushed himself and darted even higher before letting himself descend in a slow freefall, using his wings to slow his descent. He wanted to pinpoint the sound of the wings he'd heard without his own getting in the way.

As he sloped downward, he slammed into a hard body, the impact jarring him and making his camouflage disappear as he flapped his wings and rolled out of the way of whatever he'd hit. He was beyond stunned there was something in the sky with him, even if he'd come up here looking for it.

Moments later a brilliant cobalt dragon with white-gold wings appeared before him, flapping its wings and watching Drake through glittering blue eyes the same shade as its body. Drake wasn't sure how he knew, but the dragon was male.

The sharpest sense of wonder flowed through him even as it battled with his protective instincts. Fire tingled at the back of his throat, but he reined it in, waiting to see what the other beast did. He'd known, or hoped, that others like him existed but seeing a dragon in the flesh stunned him bone deep.

The other dragon didn't make any offensive gestures, just flapped his wings, watching. Possibly waiting. Maybe for backup.

Battle instincts borne out of living fifteen hundred years in Hell settled into his bones. He knew absolutely nothing about this male other than he was a dragon. He had to assume the male wasn't friendly. Drake suddenly swerved away, heading for the ocean. He couldn't stay there staring at this dragon like an idiot and put Victoria and the Stavros pack in danger. A sharp sense of relief punched through him when the animal followed. Maybe he wasn't a danger, but only time would tell.

Flying as if hell hounds were after him, he raced toward the ocean, dipping and flying around the other dragon at a speed humans couldn't see with the naked eye. It was exhilarating and freeing.

Once they were out over the open water, he slowed, the other animal doing the same. He didn't know anything about this animal and while he was so curious about his own kind he ached with the questions burning inside him, he didn't want this beast anywhere near Victoria. Or his friends. Half the Stavros pack might fear him but he didn't care. They were wolf shifters and had taken him in when they could have left him to die. Or tried to kill him anyway.

Turning his head upward, he let out a long stream of fire, the brilliant orange flames lighting up the sky like the fourth of July. A phrase he'd learned from Victoria.

The other dragon screeched and did the same, shooting flames toward the water instead of the sky.

Drake stopped flapping and dove toward the water, sending himself into a freefall before quickly snapping his wings out over the water as he made his way back to land. When he looked over his shoulder he saw the other dragon heading in the opposite direction, the blue of his body appearing almost liquid as he moved.

At least he wasn't following Drake. That was all he cared about. Even more than his burning desire to know about where he came from, he needed to keep those he cared about safe.

Not taking a chance, he kept a tight camouflage on himself and looped up and down the coastline and over the city, keeping as close as possible to the mansion for the next couple hours as he ascertained any other threats. Once he was certain the other dragon hadn't decided to double back, he eventually returned to the mansion, surprised that Finn, Lyra, Gabriel and Victoria were still there.

Maybe he shouldn't have been though. They would want to ensure the safety of their pack. An unknown supernatural being in Finn's territory was not good.

They moved back as he landed and quickly shifted to his human form. Crouched on all fours, he hadn't pushed up to his feet before Victoria crouched in front of him, her delicate fingers cupping one side of his face.

"Are you okay? Did that dragon hurt you?"

Blinking, he shook his head, loving the feel of her touching him. "You saw him?" he rasped out.

She nodded, then flicked a quick glance at Gabriel before she looked back at Drake. Something had passed between her and the Guardian. Drake was sure of it.

"What is it?" he demanded as he stood, taking a step back from Victoria. Hurt flickered in her gaze but he ignored it as he readied himself for what was to come. He looked at Finn. "Do you wish me to leave?"

The Alpha blinked, as if Drake had truly surprised him. "No. Why would I?"

Unsure if the Alpha was being truthful, he looked at Gabriel who also seemed surprised, then at Victoria who just looked sad. "Do you want to leave now?" she asked, her voice seeming small.

His chest ached at the painful thread buried in her words. Seeing her in pain made him want to gather her in his arms but he had to resist if he was going to be kicked out. He didn't care that Finn had said he wasn't going to. Perhaps he was trying to shield him from embarrassment in front of the others. He looked back at Finn. "It is likely I brought this unknown dragon to your doorstep. I don't know his intentions but he didn't seem aggressive. If you wish me to leave . . . I will." Though the thought pierced him soul deep, he couldn't stay if he was unwanted or if he put the others at risk. He refused to meet Victoria's gaze.

Finn rolled his eyes. "You're not leaving. Unless you want to of course." Drake shook his head and Victoria let out a relieved sigh, which he felt straight to his core. Without looking at her, he bent to retrieve his clothes. As he dressed, Finn continued. "I'm guessing you don't, but I have to ask. Do you know that dragon?"

"No. It was male. That's all I'm sure of. And he didn't attack me, but that means nothing. He could be getting reinforcements. My instinct says otherwise. I don't think the male was an enemy."

Finn was silent for a long moment as he watched him. "Victoria could see you and the other dragon when the rest of us couldn't."

Now it was Drake's turn to be confused. His gaze snapped to hers. Still clutching the blade at her side, she watched him almost nervously. He didn't like to see that look in her eyes. He wanted the hunger from before back. "You saw me when I was camouflaged?"

She nodded. "Yes. When you flew high and started that freefall thing, a blue and white dragon appeared out of nowhere. No one else could see you or him but me until you two collided. Then everyone saw."

"Have you done something to Victoria?" Finn asked quietly.

Offended by the question, Drake instantly bared his teeth, knowing it was a dominating gesture to make to an Alpha, but all his primal instincts flared to the surface. "I would never hurt her," he growled.

Gabriel and Lyra instantly took a step forward, blades and claws unsheathed in the blink of an eye.

Finn's lips pulled into a hard line as he took a step forward and waved them both back. His claws remained sheathed and he seemed more exasperated by Drake's display than anything. "I know that. Everyone in this fucking mansion knows that. I mean . . . I don't know. *Fuck.* I don't know anything about dragons. I just wanted to know if you'd given her the ability to see you."

The flicker of another memory shoved at him, stronger than anything else had so far. It was the blade. Something about it. But he didn't want to tell the others and he wasn't sure why. "Not intentionally." Which wasn't a lie.

As he turned to look at Victoria he was aware of Gabriel sheathing his weapons and Lyra wrapping an arm around Finn's waist. But he didn't care about any of them right now. He just cared about Victoria.

"Are you angry at me?" he asked, hating the audience, but he never wanted there to be any misunderstandings between him and Victoria.

The other three quickly made themselves scarce, moving to the other side of the roof. They would still be able to hear, but Drake liked having the illusion of privacy with her.

"Of course not but if you wanted to go with that dragon—"

"I will not go anywhere without you," he barked, the words coming out harsher than he'd intended. "Unless *you* wish me to." And it would kill him if she sent him away. It would be like losing his other half.

Her expression immediately softening, she gently laid the blade he'd made her on the ground before straightening and stepping closer to him. She reached out as if she wanted to touch him, but hesitated. Which flayed him. He wanted her hands all over him. "I don't want you to leave, but now you know there are others like you out there. And I'll help you find them."

He nodded, pulling her into his arms, all his tension leaving him when she willingly wrapped her arms around his waist and laid her head on his shoulder. "Thank you." The truth was, he wanted to know more about dragons, but not if it cost him Victoria.

He would give up everything for her.

He wasn't sure how long they stood there holding each other, but eventually Finn made his way over to them. Though everything in Drake resisted, he let Victoria go. Turning toward the Alpha, he wrapped his arm around her shoulders. She stepped into his embrace, her long lithe body fitting against him perfectly. As he held her he knew he needed to figure things out faster regarding his life because he would not be able to restrain himself much longer. Her scent drove him to the brink of control and knowing she wanted him, to kiss and touch him, tempted him to forget what he'd told her earlier. But he couldn't. Not when she deserved more than what he had to offer.

"I'm going to increase the patrol tonight. If you'd like to stay on, I'd appreciate it."

Technically the Alpha could have ordered him to, but Drake had noticed Finn liked to ask and only make demands when necessary. It was one of the reasons he was a good Alpha.

"I'll monitor from the roof," Drake answered.

"Me too," Victoria said almost immediately.

Drake started to protest but Finn nodded. "Fine. I'll leave radios with both of you. Your shift ends at daybreak. No arguments from either of you," he added, looking pointedly at Victoria when she started to say something.

Once the Alpha had left, Victoria turned in Drake's arms. "I'm going to grab my laptop but I'll be right back. I want to do some more research while we're up here."

He nodded. "Okay." Deep down he knew he should tell her to remain in the house where she'd be more protected just in case but the most selfish part of him, the part that had been alone for so fucking long, wanted to be near her as much as he could. When she started to leave he clutched on to her hips and pulled her tight against him.

Leaning down, he ran his nose along the column of her neck and along her jaw before returning to nuzzle behind her ear. When she shuddered in his arms, her fingers trailing up his chest to his shoulders, it took restraint he didn't know he had to step back and let her go.

CHAPTER SIX

Victoria hurried down the stairs of the mansion, her laptop bag slung over her shoulder. It was almost seven o'clock in the morning, only a few hours after the late patrol shift she'd been on with Drake and she should be sleeping but was too keyed up.

When Finn had ordered them to switch out for the day shift Drake had told her he'd be taking a shower then getting some sleep. She'd jumped at the chance to sneak away from the mansion for a little bit without anyone's knowledge, even if the thought of joining him in the shower would be a lot more fun. Not that he'd actually invited her but still.

Over the past few hours she'd gotten a lot of research in on dragons but she still hadn't come up with a concrete lead on how to hunt down another living dragon. All she wanted was to *talk* to one. Just like the last four months, she'd ended up with more questions than answers. The addition of a blue and white dragon to her searches hadn't increased her feedback much. She'd found mentions of the word Moana and dragons of that description but they'd been obscure and buried deep in search engines. Nothing on any of the supernatural forums she frequented. But it was better than nothing, she supposed.

The lack of results was driving her crazy. Especially since Drake might be able to find his family.

And she knew he'd go all protective male if she told him where she was going now. Which was why she wasn't telling him or anyone in the pack.

As she reached the bottom of the stairs she ran into Rhea, one of the most beautiful women Victoria had ever known. Her father had been black and her mother Greek, giving her pretty much the most gorgeous skin tone ever, all glowing and dewy looking year round. As if she'd just come from a pampered day at the spa. Which was something Rhea would never do. She'd kick you in the teeth if you even suggested she partake in something so feminine. Her short, corkscrew curls were wild this morning, bouncing everywhere as she walked.

The female smiled and paused on the bottom stair, her bright amber eyes mirroring the warmth of her smile. "Hey, V. What are you doing up so early? I thought you'd have crashed by now."

"I'm heading to the kitchen." Which was not a lie so her packmate wouldn't scent anything off in Victoria's statement. That was the tricky thing about being around supernaturals who could smell your lies. She *was* heading to the kitchen, but not for food as she hoped Rhea would assume. She was going to the kitchen, then accessing one of the backdoors so she could sneak out and take one of the pack vehicles for her errand.

Rhea's warrior gaze flicked to Victoria's laptop bag that had a bright sticker on it that read 'She Wolf', but she just nodded. "Okay. I'm about to grab some shuteye. See ya later."

Victoria hurried away after that and didn't stop to chat with the few packmates she passed in the mansion. She was on a mission and no one was stopping her.

Unless of course Rhea narced her out to Finn or Gabriel. Even though Victoria and Rhea looked as if they were the same age, the female was as old as Finn and could be overprotective. Gah, sometimes she hated that she was one of the babies of the pack. It didn't matter that she was a full grown, mature shifter female, they all treated her so delicately sometimes. Or tried to. She understood and on her most primal level she was incredibly grateful she had such a loving pack. Not everyone was so lucky to have such a solid family. Hell, look at Drake. Still, a little independence was a necessity.

As she steered down the long driveway in one of the pack SUVs, she gritted her teeth when she spotted Solon lingering near the gate. "That little traitor," Victoria muttered, knowing Rhea had probably radioed her freaking bestie, Solon.

She rolled down her window, breathing in the chilly morning air, and slowed at the gate. She pressed the button on her gate control to open it, but didn't pull through, instead waiting for Solon to jog over to her window. She didn't have to stop for him, but she also knew that if she acted secretive, Solon would track her just to be obnoxious. So she played dumb.

"Hey, V. Where're you off to this early?" He ran a hand over his dark skull trim.

"Errands."

He lifted a dark eyebrow. "Care to elaborate?"

She mirrored him, arching her eyebrows. "Only if you care to elaborate about what happened with those three half-demon females you left Bo's club with the other night."

To her amusement, his cheeks flushed crimson. "Fucking shifter gossips." He cleared his throat. "Come on, don't hold out. What are you up to?"

It was obvious he was trying to be all casual with his question, but she didn't buy it. "I told you, errands." When he didn't respond, she sighed over-dramatically. "Someone has a birthday coming up. Don't tell me you forgot." Victoria resisted the urge to smile at Solon's anxious expression. She wasn't lying because a lot of packmates had a birthday coming up so there was no metallic scent associated with a lie rolling off her. There was practically a birthday a week they celebrated—not like their pack needed an excuse to party. But she intentionally made it sound like she was shopping for a present. And Solon was clearly buying it.

"Shit. Who?"

She raised an eyebrow. "Uh uh. I'm not your mom or your mate. You need to remember that stuff on your own."

"Damn it, Victoria. Who is it? Am I going to get reamed out for forgetting a birthday? Shit, is it Vega's birthday?"

Laughing, she rolled up the window and zoomed out the gate, pressing the button to close it as she cleared it. Cruising down the street, she glanced in the rearview mirror. No one was following her. As soon as Solon told Rhea about the conversation, the female would know exactly what Victoria had done, but by then it would be too late. Gabriel hadn't even been at the mansion this morning, off on some mission or task for Finn, so she wasn't worried about him tracking her either. No wonder Vega was feeling so smothered lately. Victoria had almost forgotten how annoying it was to have to sneak out.

Less than ten minutes later, Victoria steered into the parking lot of Bo's club. It didn't matter that it was after seven in the morning and most normal humans would be getting ready for work. Bo's club didn't cater to humans and the parking lot was packed. As she'd expected for a Saturday morning.

She'd tried calling the half-demon but he hadn't answered his cell phone or his office phone. Since he practically lived at the club it was a good bet he'd be there. Besides, she didn't know where the male actually lived. No one did. Not even Finn.

Gravel crunched under her heeled boots as she strode across the makeshift parking lot. The 'nightclub' was a nondescript warehouse that did a good job of camouflaging its true purpose. It was located near a local marina and looked like a huge storage warehouse similar to all the others in the area that housed RVs, boats and other things. Inside, however, was a different story.

When she reached the plain, white door it opened and a broad-shouldered male about the same height as her stood back to let her in. She guessed he was a ghoul because of the dark red ring around his irises. "Bo's occupied," he said in a surprisingly deep voice.

She blinked. "How'd you know I'm here to see him?" Muted music pumped into the oversized space from hidden speakers. Supernatural beings had sensitized hearing so there would be no blasting of music, thankfully.

"You're part of the Stavros pack and you're Drake's female. I don't think you're here to party by yourself."

She wasn't sure how to respond to the part about being Drake's female, but she sure as hell liked the sound of that. "How long is Bo going to be occupied?"

The male sighed. "I'll get him even though it'll get me a punch in the nuts." He nodded in the direction of one of the bars. "Grab a seat. He'll be out in a minute or so."

Doing as he said, she took the only empty seat at the nearest bar and scanned around the giant dance floor. Along the opposite wall there were roped-off booths with heavy curtains. Some closed, some drawn back. There was also a red door to the right of the booths and she knew from gossip that beyond the room, BDSM things took place. All consensual of course, otherwise

Finn would have killed Bo long ago. She'd never understood why anyone would be in to bondage, but now the thought of maybe *light* stuff with Drake could be kind of hot.

Her entire body heated up at the thought of him binding her wrists above her head as he dipped his head between her legs . . . She forced herself to shut that thought down, but she was going to go back to that little fantasy later.

She watched as the ghoul security guard disappeared behind the red door and half-smiled. So that's what Bo was 'occupied' with. Nice.

When she turned back around toward the bar she saw that the male on her left had scooted away, giving her a wide berth. She was about to sniff herself to see if she'd forgotten to put on deodorant when she recognized him from the array of faces from the fight the night before. No male was going to hit on her or mess with her after Drake's dominant display. The thought made her smile.

She avoided places like this anyway, but having an extra barrier between her and annoying males was a huge plus right now. The female bartender set a bill in front of a customer then made her way to Victoria.

She guessed the purple-eyed female was a half-demon and that those weren't contacts. Her long hair was pulled up into a tight ponytail, the shocking purple waves trailing down her back and around her shoulders.

She gave Victoria a curious look as she approached. "You're Drake's female?"

Did everyone go to those damn fights? "Who wants to know?" she snapped, wondering if this was one of the sign-toting groupies. Victoria had never been remotely jealous of anyone. She'd always figured it was part of her healer makeup, but the thought of any female going after Drake made her wolf go crazy to the point she had to rein in her beast so she wouldn't shift. That hadn't happened to her since she was a cub too young to control herself.

The half-demon grinned, revealing a toothpaste commercial smile and two sharp canines. Or maybe fangs. Maybe she was half-demon, half-vamp. "What are you drinking? On the house for the female who landed that delicious male."

"Oh, uh, orange juice." All the ragey-jealousy dissipated at the friendliness from the female.

Nodding, the bartender poured the drink and slid it over to Victoria, moving on to the next customer. Even if she wasn't being charged, Victoria left a tip and turned around to find Bo exiting the red door, a scowl on his handsome face.

Today his hair was green, matching his eyes. His button-down shirt was open revealing fingernail scratches along the ripped eight pack of his café-au-lait skin. As he reached her, he put his hands on his hips. "Am I going to get fried to a crisp for talking to you?"

Victoria was surprised that he was being open about knowing what Drake was. "No, but I'd like just a few moments of your time."

"You alone?"

"Yes."

"Fine. Come on." He started buttoning his shirt so she slid off the barstool, leaving her drink where it was.

She fell in step with him and followed him when he opened a white door that led to a quiet hallway. When the door shut behind them she couldn't hear anything from the outside club. Talk about serious insulation.

At the end of the hallway he opened the last door into what was clearly his office. Big, masculine furniture filled it but she didn't focus on any of that. "You know what Drake is," she said as she made herself at home, sitting in the chair across from the big wood desk.

"I know he's a dragon." Bo sat in his chair on the other side of the desk and leaned back. "They're very territorial, Victoria." His words almost sounded like a warning.

She snorted. "No kidding." So were wolf shifters. To the nth degree. It was biology, plain and simple. They were part beast and didn't fight their animal side. They couldn't.

"More than other shifters." His expression was serious, intent. "Just be careful if you commit. It's for life in more ways than one."

She frowned. "What does that mean?" And how the hell did Bo know so much about dragons?

Bo's head tilted to the side a fraction. "You talk to your male about that. Why are you here?"

"I'm here to talk about freaking dragons. And clearly I came to the right place." She wanted to kick herself for not coming earlier instead of using him as a last ditch effort. "Drake doesn't know..." Crap, how much could she say? "We're having a hard time finding others like Drake." That was safe enough.

He arched an eyebrow, his expression a little obnoxious. "Dragons won't be found unless they want to. Drake's fighting displays in the ring have made it obvious he's different. Most people won't even think that he's a dragon because most beings think they're extinct."

"But you've known, even before last night."

Bo nodded.

"How?"

He shook his head.

Frustrating, tight-lipped male. She didn't know why he wouldn't discuss this with her when he clearly believed she belonged to Drake. "Why haven't you told Finn you knew what Drake was?"

At the mention of the Alpha's name, the half-demon shifted in his seat, likely remembering that she was part of Finn's pack and under the protection of one of the strongest shifters on the planet. "It seemed obvious the pack wanted to keep Drake's species ID a secret so I didn't say anything. Didn't see the point."

"Have you told anyone else what he is?"

He snorted softly. "Do I look like I have a death wish?"

"That's not an answer." The deadly bite to her words took her off guard as much as they seemed to stun Bo. She was normally so laid back but the thought of anyone hurting or betraying Drake made her wolf practically feral.

"Fuck no, I haven't told anyone."

She relaxed a fraction at his words, not scenting the stench of a lie. He was hard to read though because of his demon origins. "What can you tell me about dragons?"

His shoulders lifted casually. "Not much. I pick up tidbits here and there. I know that the sacrifice of a dragon shifter will open or destroy a door to hell."

She frowned. "I thought it was just destroy." Even if a door was destroyed a new one could replace it with the right spell.

"That's a common misconception. Depends on the age of a dragon. A young sacrifice will just open it. And who the fuck can weaken a full-grown dragon to the point of sacrificing it." He rubbed a hand over the back of his neck. "You sure your male isn't going to come after you?"

She rolled her eyes. "No one knows I'm here. And I thought you were a bad-ass demon who wasn't afraid of anything."

"Half-demon, and I'm not stupid enough to think I can take on a dragon. Especially if he's got family."

Her ears perked up at that. "Do you know who Drake's family is?"

He shook his head. "No, but related dragons are connected to an extent. And before you ask, I don't know the details of how. Dragons stick to their own kind more than any other supernatural being so you can't find the details on Google. You could know one and not realize what it was."

"How do you even know this much?"

Bo paused for a moment, as if he was contemplating how much to tell her. Finally he sighed. "There's a blood-born vamp up in Tennessee who is bat shit crazy, but if you want details on dragon clans, he'll be able to tell you."

"Clans?" That was a new word. She filed it away in her small mental database of dragon facts.

He nodded. "Like a shifter pack."

"Why would a vamp know about dragons?"

Bo shrugged again. "Dunno. You'll have to ask him. But a word of advice, take backup to talk to him. Drake should do fine." He grabbed a post-it off his desk, scribbled on it, then slid it over to her. "Here's the location."

It was coordinates, not an actual address. Interesting. She memorized them before tucking the note in her laptop bag. "So what else can you tell me?"

He opened his mouth to respond, then frowned and tapped his ear. That's when she realized he had an earpiece in. It must be tuned to a specific frequency or have some magic settings because she couldn't hear anything.

When his expression darkened and his contacts began disintegrating as his eyes burned to reveal a beautiful, swirling gold, her heart rate kicked up about a hundred notches. She'd always wondered what color his eyes were but she'd never wanted to find out because he'd burned his contacts in clear anger.

"Your male is here," he growled, standing and pulling out a gun.

On instinct, she unzipped her leather jacket and pulled out the blade Drake had given her. It practically hummed with magic and she knew Bo could sense it. His eyes brightened as they landed on her blade. She didn't care if he was accepted by her pack or not, if this male thought he could attack Drake, she was going to strike him down here and now.

He kept his weapon at his side, but nodded to it. "This isn't for him. Two unknowns are here and he's facing off with them."

Panic burst inside her, bright and electric. Without responding, she turned and raced from the office. If someone thought they could hurt her mate—later she'd go back to that thought—they were about to find out what it was like to tangle with a pissed off female shifter.

CHAPTER SEVEN

10 minutes earlier

Drake was finishing his third turkey and Colby jack cheese sub—which Victoria had nicknamed turkey *diablo* because of the hot sauce he put on it—when Rhea and Solon strode into the kitchen with clear intent to see him.

Rhea glanced at Solon, then at Drake, her expression tight. She wasn't afraid of him though. That female wasn't afraid of anything.

Drake pushed his plate away and stood from his seat at the kitchen island. A low grade panic hummed through him. "What's up?" Had there been another dragon sighting? Had that male returned with more backup? He would take on an army of his kind to keep Victoria safe.

"Not much." Rhea's voice had an unnaturally high edge to it. "What are you up to?"

He looked at his plate of crumbs, then at them. What did they think he was doing? "Has there been another dragon sighting?"

They both shook their heads and he relaxed a fraction. "Then what's the problem?"

"Victoria left a little while ago."

He frowned. She'd told him she was showering and then sleeping. While he'd been showering he'd fantasized about what it would be like to bathe with her, to rub the thing she'd told him was called a loofah all over her long, lean body. He wanted to watch her nipples tighten as he teased them with his tongue. He'd seen a video of a male doing that to a female and wanted to try it with her . . . Wait. "Left? You're sure?"

Solon nodded. "Saw her leave, man. Indicated that she was getting a birthday present for someone."

"Okay." He didn't understand why they'd felt the need to tell him this or why they seemed so concerned. If Victoria was driving, they should be more concerned about those on the road with her.

Rhea cleared her throat. "Listen, I don't want you to freak out or anything but I just got a call from a vamp friend at Bo's club. Said she's there."

Drake frowned and fought the irrational urge to kill Bo. On an intellectual level he knew it was insane but after so long in Hell where nothing was his and he'd finally found someone he loved, his inner dragon was acting more and more irrational when it came to Victoria. Like when he'd seen that half-demon leaning in close to her, touching what was his. "Do you know why she's there?" To his surprise, his voice was calm and steady.

Rhea and Solon visibly relaxed so perhaps they'd expected him to freak out. Rhea ran a hand through her wild hair, making the curls bounce like springs. "No, but she's in his office."

"Alone?" No more steadiness from him. The word came out more animal than man.

"It's not like she's behind the red door or anything, man." Solon's voice was light but clear tension hummed through the male's words.

He didn't know what the red door was but it didn't sound good. "Thank you." Without continuing, he strode past them and out the swinging door. Behind him Rhea cursed, but he ignored them both and made his way to the roof.

After stripping, he rolled his clothes and shoes into a tight ball and shifted to his dragon form. Clutching the bundle in his claws, he camouflaged himself and took flight. He didn't like flying in the city in the daylight but he had no choice. Demons were not to be trusted. He knew better than most how treacherous they could be and while Bo seemed decent enough, you could never tell with them.

And Victoria was alone with him. Why the hell had she gone to see that half-demon without telling him? Fire burned the back of his throat but he forced himself under control. He had to keep that control so he wouldn't kill Bo. It would upset Victoria too much.

Minutes later he neared the club, but circled around the entire building and surrounding area, looking for other threats. When he saw none, he started to descend, but stopped when two individuals got out of a truck. He didn't want to reveal himself to anyone so he waited as the male and female made their way to the club.

The male had a hoodie over his head and as they walked, he casually leaned down next to an SUV. He stuck his hand under the fender covering the back, left wheel well then moved on as if he'd done nothing. The male moved so fast that if Drake hadn't been watching the interaction below he wouldn't have seen what he'd done.

After the two beings went inside, Drake dropped down to the earth and shifted to his human form. The gravel pricked the bottom of his bare feet but he liked the feel of it. It reminded him he was alive. Quickly changing into his clothes, he started for the door of the club but paused when he saw the SUV the male had been near was Stavros-owned. There was a distinctive sticker in the upper right hand corner of the windshield. It was small and would mean nothing to humans, but the slashing wolf paw was a warning to all supernatural beings.

Stay the fuck away from the owner of this vehicle.

As he strode across the parking lot, Victoria's scent slammed into him the closer he got to the vehicle and the rage he'd been keeping on lockdown rushed to the surface with no warning. That was the vehicle *she* had been driving. Jaw tight, he ducked under the back of the SUV and found a small, magnetized black box tucked under the fender.

He yanked it off and stared at it. Unsure what it was but unwilling to take any chance that it might be some kind of explosive, he crushed it in his fist and stalked toward the front door.

As he reached it he desperately tried to hold onto his inner dragon, but slipped off the razor wire he was walking. Fear for her ripped his control completely free. Letting out a battle cry, he released a stream of fire, burning a giant hole through the door of the club.

He'd just given away the element of surprise but he couldn't stop himself. That fucker had put something on Victoria's SUV, making him an enemy.

More fire gathered in the back of his throat as he strode through the new opening. As he entered, the up-beat music that had been playing abruptly stopped. There were supernatural beings on the dance floor and at the multiple bars. And they were all looking at him.

He didn't care.

His gaze quickly swung to the male and female from outside. They were both watching him with unreadable expressions, as if they were keeping their faces inten-tionally neutral. Both had grayish-silver eyes, like him, but the male had dark hair and the female blonde. She looked familiar, her face stirring something in his memory. Warm memories that made him feel oddly happy. Which made no sense.

He shoved the feeling back and threw the crushed device at the male's feet. Drake was vaguely aware of all the other supernatural beings quickly fleeing the club.

Some headed for a red door, probably vamps who couldn't go out in sunlight. He didn't care where they went, he just wanted them gone so he could do this without an audience.

"What the fuck is this?" Drake demanded.

The male opened his mouth to speak when a door behind the two strangers flew open and Victoria and Bo spilled out. Bo's eyes were glowing a vivid gold and Victoria had her blade in hand, looking ready to do battle. She met his gaze, uncertain before she looked at the two strangers. She was too far away for him to protect, making him edgier. He wanted to burn right through the two strangers, but reined in his dragon.

Barely.

Knowing he had to remain in control to keep Victoria safe, he found his voice. "Explain the device."

"It's not what you think," the female said, her voice softer than he'd expected. "It's a tracking device."

"Why?" he barked, unable to say more than one word. Why the fuck had they put it on Victoria's vehicle?

The male lifted his hands, palms up, in a clear peaceful gesture. "We wanted to speak to you away from the shifters and hoped the female would eventually lead us to you. We saw her leaving the shifter compound this morning by chance and followed her here. That is all."

He swallowed hard, shoving back his fire though it burned to do so. "Who are you?" The question came out guttural. When he saw Victoria move a fraction closer out of the corner of his eye, he focused on her over their shoulders. She looked fierce, like she would attack the two beings with the blade he'd given her if necessary. He shook his head sharply. Though he wanted her behind him, she'd have to move past these two strangers to get to him. He wouldn't risk them attacking her. Thankfully Victoria stilled and to his surprise, Bo moved forward a fraction, effectively placing himself in front of her, blocking her from the male and female. And he was armed with a gun.

Okay, maybe half-demons weren't so bad.

Drake snapped his gaze back to the unknown male. "Answer me."

The male watched him, his gaze flickering to a bright silver, supernova bright, as Victoria liked to call it when his eyes did the same. His throat clenched as he waited for the answer even though deep down he guessed what it would be.

"We are your siblings," the female whispered, tears spilling down her cheeks in a waterfall.

Her words grated over him like shards of glass scraping his flesh. Siblings? He didn't have family. He was alone until Victoria. Because if he'd had family, it meant they'd left him to rot in Hell. To see and suffer things no child should have to. If not for his ability to shift, he'd have gone mad long ago. Out of the corner of his eye, Finn, Gabriel, Rhea and Solon moved whisper-quiet through the burned out door.

"Family?" He let out a short, harsh laugh.

The male nodded, his expression pained. "Four months ago we felt your . . . reemergence into the world. We thought you were dead, but the whole clan experienced the same sensation when you returned. We've been looking for you ever since."

Drake laughed again, this time unable to keep the years of bitterness hidden. "Four whole months. Well thank you so fucking much. I was in Hell for fifteen hundred *years*. If you really are my family, I'm not interested." An agonizing sensation built in his chest, burning like lava until he threw his head back and screamed, releasing a stream of fire at the ceiling.

A hole ripped open, plaster and whatever else held it together crashing down between them. When he looked back at them, there was pity in their eyes. He didn't want their fucking pity. He didn't want them at all. His chest felt too tight. Hell, his body felt too tight, his dragon struggling to break free and soothe the pain. *"Get out of my mate's way!"* he roared, his animal too close to the surface, clawing to be free.

They instantly slid to the side, keeping their gazes on him, not even looking in Victoria's direction as she hurried toward him, her blade still clutched tightly in her hand. He noted the way his supposed sister's gaze widened in surprise as she became aware of the blade in Victoria's grip, but the female said nothing.

Victoria sheathed her weapon and wrapped her arms around him in a tight hug, clearly understanding he needed to be touched right now. She buried her face against his chest. "Do you want to leave?" she whispered, the question proving how much she truly understood him.

He figured he should stay and speak to his alleged family members but he wasn't in control now and he didn't want to burn down Bo's club as he let out his aggression. Instead of responding, he scooped her into his arms and strode through the gaping hole in the door into the bright sunlight. Though he wanted to shift to his dragon form and leave all of this behind, he wanted to hold Victoria more.

"Will you drive?" he rasped out, unsure why there was wetness on his cheeks.

She simply nodded and pulled a set of keys from her jacket pocket. "I'll even drive nicely." He was strung too tight to smile at her words. Then she rested her cheek against his shoulder and snuggled into his body, giving him the wordless comfort of her trust as he took them to the SUV.

Once they were in the vehicle and she'd taken over he shut down, his body numb as one of his first memories in Hell played in his mind. It was too much and since he'd escaped he'd been able to compartmentalize his thoughts. Now he had no control as the images gripped him in razor sharp talons, forcing him to remember.

Drake was twelve. He stared up from the altar in horror as he took in his new surroundings. He wasn't sure when it had happened, but he was no longer . . . on Earth. He needed to remember something, but he couldn't. All he could remember was a woman's face and dark, soulless eyes laughing maniacally as he'd screamed in agony. There was someone else he needed to remember but it hurt his soul too much. The betrayal, his new reality.

Tears leaked out of his eyes as he stared up through the broken remnants of a high ceiling at the red sky that looked as if it was covered in . . . chains or snakes. His entire body shook as he sat up. This had to be a nightmare. He wrapped his arms around himself as his surroundings came into focus. He was in a broken down throne room of what had maybe once been a castle. The walls and turrets were all crumbling, the hideous sky visible through the crushed sections of the ceiling.

Jagged pieces of glowing amber glass stuck out from the seat of a metal throne. Another shiver wracked him as he slid off the altar. Why would it be made that way? It would impale anyone who sat on it. He didn't see anyone but he felt as if he was being watched. And the high-pitched screams from somewhere close sent cold panic sliding down his spine.

When his feet touched the ground he immediately recoiled at the wetness. Looking down he saw a pool of crimson, the iron scent teasing his senses. Even above the sulfuric, rotten stench invading his nostrils, he knew that it was blood.

Covering the warm stone floors.

Another shudder rolled through him as he looked around, hoping to find clothes. His dragon clawed at him, demanding he change forms, but he wasn't sure if that was a good idea yet.

He wasn't sure about anything and he just wanted his mom and dad. They would make everything okay. More tears burned his eyes, but he blinked them back. Something primal told him he couldn't cry here.

No tears, no fear, no weakness.

Before he'd taken a step, shadows bled from the darkness beyond the throne room, gaining substance as they drew closer.

Raw fear punched through him, his fire burning in his throat as his dragon clawed at him. He needed to shift, to escape. His mind was too jumbled as he tried to get control. The shadows grew into humanoid shapes as they closed in on him. He turned in a circle, looking for an escape. There were six of them.

He backed up to the altar, slipping on the blood as he moved, but he caught himself on the stone slab and hoisted himself up, his fingers numb as he climbed onto it. He had to shift and escape.

As he stood, ready to let his dragon loose, one of the dark shadows moved quicker than he'd ever seen anything do. It was ten feet away, then suddenly it was next to the altar.

A shadow-like hand grabbed Drake's ankle and yanked hard. Thrown off balance he fell, his shoulder slamming against the altar with a harsh thud. The pain barely registered as the shadow thing wrapped long fingers around his neck.

The thing's face split open to reveal razor sharp teeth and bright yellow orbs glowed evilly where eyes were supposed to be. "You are a tasty little morsel," it hissed, its other hand moving down to grip Drake's most private area.

He jerked under the punishing hold. No one had ever touched him there. Tears burned his eyes at the violation but instead of crying he opened his mouth and screamed, burning fire in the thing's face in a long, hot stream of flames.

The shadow screeched as yellow liquid spewed everywhere and the thing dissipated. Drake shoved up and let his fear and instinct drive him. His dragon took over in a rush, his wings sprouting, his body transforming, the sharpest sense of adrenaline taking over as he took to the air.

All around him the shadow things tried to flee, but his beast wouldn't let them. Swooping down he breathed fire as they tried to scurry away, refusing to let any of them hide. Their shadowy bodies incinerated, spraying out over the blood-soaked floor like fine black dust.

The predator inside him took over, gaining a stronger foothold. He must do this to survive. No weakness. Ever. The boy inside him cried out for his mother, begging her to find him, to save him.

But she never came.

CHAPTER EIGHT

Victoria's heart broke a little as Drake sat next to her in the passenger seat, his expression stoic as he stared blindly ahead. He had a brother and sister. And they'd come for him.

It was clearly too much for him right now and she didn't blame him. Not when she could imagine what he'd been through during his imprisonment. He hadn't talked much about his time in Hell, but it was freaking *Hell*.

"How old were you when you, you know." He'd never actually come out and said the words but he must have been sacrificed to have ended up in Hell. After what Bo had told her, he would have had to have been young. Or she guessed so anyway. The idea of him being thrown into endless suffering for more than a millennium filled her with a deep, burning rage. If she found out who'd done it, she'd kill them herself.

"Twelve or thirteen, give or take. It was so long ago." His voice was monotone as he turned to look out the side window, away from her.

When he didn't add more, she didn't push. It wasn't her right to know the details, or anyone's for that matter. It was still early so instead of heading back to the mansion she made her way down Beach Boulevard, only stopping at a drive-through to grab two coffees. Drake didn't question her as she continued until they reached the Biloxi Bay Bridge. She swung a left directly after they crossed it and looped back toward the quiet beach in Ocean Springs.

In the summer the place would be busy and curbside parking impossible to find, but it was an unusually cold February morning so she wasn't surprised to see plenty of parking along the two and a half mile strip. Instead of driving down the rest of the road toward the marina, she parked right in front of the small yacht club. She figured he needed to walk off the energy she could feel rolling off him and being at the mansion surrounded by packmates wouldn't make things easy on him.

Drake looked at her in surprise, but got out when she did, grabbing both their coffees. Because he always thought of stuff like that, always tried to take care of her in even the smallest ways. She hadn't realized it when they'd first started spending time together. Obviously she'd noticed how sweet he was, but now she understood that he was acting the way a mate would. She rounded the front of the SUV and stepped over the calf-high stone barricade onto the sidewalk. "Want to walk?" she asked as he handed her one of the coffees.

He nodded, his beautiful gray eyes searching hers for a moment, before he held out an arm.

Softly smiling, she looped her arm through his and inhaled the ocean air and hot, delicious coffee as they walked parallel to the flat sand and calm Intracoastal waterway. She remained silent, letting him relax, knowing he'd talk when he was ready.

"I shouldn't have left like that," he muttered after a few minutes of walking.

She squeezed his muscled forearm. "I don't think there's a rulebook for how to behave in a situation like this."

"I'm angry at them."

"I know." She didn't blame him. Didn't think anyone could.

"Maybe I shouldn't have burned a hole in Bo's club."

"*Two* holes." It had been terrifying and impressive when he'd done it. And totally heartbreaking to see him in such clear agony. Her wolf had wanted to shred into ribbons anyone who had ever hurt him.

He let out a rusty sounding laugh. "I do feel a little bad about that."

"Want to sit?" She motioned to a bench along the walkway.

"Yeah."

"The male looked a lot like you," Victoria said as they sat, both facing the ocean. The sky was one of those clear blue days without a cloud to be seen.

"I think so too. And the female triggered something in my memory. As if she's familiar to me. Doesn't mean I flat-out believe them."

"We could do DNA testing." Worked exactly the same for supernaturals as it did for humans.

He grunted and was silent for a long moment as they stared out at the water. Finally, he spoke. "The first time I saw someone tortured in Hell I cried out for my mother. I don't even know if I have one. Or had one. But that memory sticks out more than anything else. I called for her over and over and she never came. No one did. I don't . . . know why I'm telling you. Or why I'm even thinking of it now." His words stunned her, his voice so remote it shredded her.

Victoria's throat was tight as she set her coffee behind her on the bench table. Without asking if it was okay, she stood then sat in his lap, wrapping her arm around the back of his neck as she embraced him. She was pretty sure there weren't any words she could say now to take away his pain but she could hold him. She just wished she had some magic healing power to take away all his emotional pain.

Thankfully he returned her embrace, burying his face in her hair and inhaling deeply. "Victoria."

The way he said that one word, like a prayer, made her grip him tighter. No matter what happened with his family or anything else, she was glad he had no problem leaning on her. Because she would never let him down.

Conall eyed the newcomers carefully, not making any aggressive moves. He didn't need his weapons. Not when he could breathe fire. But he knew who these shifters were and fire wasn't going to stop them.

Finn Stavros, powerful shifter leader of the Stavros pack. Gabriel, his Guardian, and two warriors with him. The female warrior made him do a double-take as the strangest vibrating sensation welled in his chest, but he kept his focus on the Alpha. He wasn't going to be attacked because of stupidity.

The Alpha's icy blue stare cut through Conall for a moment before Stavros looked at Bo Broussard, the owner of the club. A half-demon Stavros allowed to operate in his territory. It was interesting how many supernatural beings lived in harmony in this location. The Alpha was also mated to a blood-born vampire. Which was very interesting. It gave him hope they'd be able to negotiate together without violence.

"May we use your club to discuss a few things in private?" Stavros asked Broussard. Even though the shifter phrased it as a question it was clear to everyone the Alpha wasn't asking.

Broussard sighed as if this was an everyday hassle and nodded. "Yeah. Grab anything you want from the bar too," he said as he waved a hand at the ceiling.

Conall raised his eyebrows as the hole in the ceiling mended itself and the dusty mess on the floor vanished. When he glanced at Stavros it was clear the Alpha had never seen the half-demon do something like that. After he gave the gaping hole in the front door the same treatment, Broussard headed for a red door. When he reached it, he turned and looked at them. "Unless this place is on fire, I would appreciate it if no one disturbs me." Without another word, he disappeared through the door, closing it softly behind him.

The four others pinned Conall and Keelin—who was being unusually quiet—with their stares.

Stavros stepped forward and nodded at the wall of empty booths. "Talk with us?" Again, not exactly a question.

Conall nodded. "Of course."

Conall and Keelin sat in the rounded booth while the Alpha sat across from them. The three others stood nearby, giving them space. Against his will, Conall found his gaze drawn to the female with the wild hair and beautiful light mocha skin once more.

Her amber eyes were bright, her wolf gleaming in them as if she considered him an enemy. It shouldn't have bothered him, but for some reason it did. He would analyze it and that annoying vibrating inside him later.

Frowning, he looked at Stavros. "We apologize for entering your territory without asking. Circumstances prevented it."

"Why were you flying over my compound early this morning?" The question was casual as the Alpha threw an arm back against his side of the booth. But there was no denying the edge to his words, not when his wolf glittered in his eyes.

Conall's frown deepened and he glanced at his sister. They hadn't gone anywhere near the Alpha's compound in dragon form. "Neither I nor my sister have flown over your compound. Ever."

The male's eyes narrowed a fraction, but Conall wasn't lying and wouldn't put off the acidic scent associated with an untruth. "Then who was it?"

"I don't know." But if there was another dragon in the territory, that concerned him greatly. No one knew why his brother had been locked in Hell or who had done it. Of course no one knew he'd been locked there in the first place until months ago. "What did this dragon look like?"

"Cobalt blue body, white-gold wings." A succinct response.

Conall liked that the Alpha didn't make small talk. In order to gain this male's trust to a certain degree he needed to be forthright. Which meant revealing more about his kind than he cared to do, but it was necessary to bring his brother home. "That sounds like a Moana dragon. They live near the water, but make their homes on land. My clan is not at war with them. Was the dragon hostile?"

Stavros shook his head.

"They're the least violent of all of our kind," Keelin said, her voice shaky and he could guess why. She was still reeling from their brother's anger toward them. "They wouldn't attack without a reason. It's possible they heard about a dragon living here with a shifter pack and were simply curious."

Keelin had been so excited and hopeful to find their brother and likely hadn't expected the reception they'd just had. Not that he blamed his brother. And he knew without a doubt after seeing the male that they were related. Even if they didn't look so similar, he felt the connection in his bones. Once he discovered who'd put his brother in Hell, he was going to avenge him and make the guilty party suffer for an eternity.

"Why did it take you so long to come for your brother?" The way Stavros said the word *brother* made it sound as if he didn't believe they were actually related.

Conall reined in his anger, but Keelin shifted against the seat, her agitation clear. "We couldn't exactly take out an ad online," she snapped. The mini outburst was unlike her. Normally she was the most diplomatic of everyone in their clan.

"I thought you *felt* him." There was a slight edge of sarcasm in his voice.

"We did, when he reemerged into the world. But we're not telepathically connected on a continuous basis." Conall's throat tightened as he thought of how long his brother had been locked away. How none of them had known, had just been living their lives. Well, that wasn't exactly true. Their parents had gone into a deep sleep hundreds of years ago, their mother still mourning the loss of her oldest son and unable to take the grief. Conall wondered if she knew he was back. He'd never gone into a Protective Hibernation before so he wasn't sure how connected sleeping dragons were to the rest of their clan. Though he doubted she or his father knew about Drake's re-emergence. They would have returned by now.

"What do you want with him now?" Stavros demanded.

He blinked at the question. "To bring him home where he belongs. We are his family, his clan." And he was next in line to rule since their father was in a Protective Hibernation and had stepped down. Conall was the current leader of their clan but would give the position to his brother. It was rightfully his.

"You didn't do a very good job of protecting him before," the one named Gabriel said, his voice dry.

Before Conall could respond, Keelin jumped up, shoving the round table in the half-moon shaped booth out of their way so that nothing separated them and the Alpha. But her ire was directed at Gabriel as her eyes burned like liquid silver. "I was five and my brother was ten! He was our protector, our big brother. Then he was just gone one day. We didn't know or we would have razed this entire fucking planet to the ground to find him." The bitter words from his peaceful sister rattled him.

Even if they were true.

Conall tensed as the male stared at his sister with an unreadable expression. Conall remained still, waiting to strike, but Gabriel gave one short nod and said, "I apologize."

Still humming with anger, Keelin didn't respond as she sat back down. She'd come out of a deep sleep a year ago and was still adjusting to this world. Sometimes he wondered if she'd been too sheltered. But that sure as hell wasn't the issue he needed to worry about now.

"What's your clan name? And what's Drake's real name?" The Alpha had barely moved from his position, even when Keelin had freaked out. As he spoke again, every line in his body was pulled taut.

"I'll not tell you my clan name before I've spoken to my brother again." As for Drake's name, that was an odd question. "His name *is* Drake. Dragos after our father, but we called him Drake for short."

The Alpha's mouth curved up the tiniest fraction but it was the beautiful female who laughed. "Holy shit. Looks like Vega was pretty spot on."

Conall frowned at the Alpha. "What does she mean?" he asked, refusing to look at the female. She was too much of a distraction.

Stavros's stare was intense. "When Drake came out of Hell he didn't know his name or much about his history. I didn't realize it at the time though. Vega, my daughter, covered for him and told us his name was Drake."

The sharpest sense of sadness invaded Conall. His brother hadn't remembered his own name? Oh yes, whoever had put his brother in Hell was going to pay.

He was going to strip away everything the guilty party cared for and make sure they suffered as Drake had.

CHAPTER NINE

Victoria was careful driving back to the mansion, even putting the SUV on cruise control when she could so her lead foot wouldn't get out of control. Drake didn't seem to notice though.

After he'd told her about that horrible memory, he'd been even quieter than normal. They'd sat watching the water for a while before taking a long walk down the beach strip then cutting through one of the historic neighborhoods and walking around the small downtown area of shops. He hadn't talked much, not about anything important anyway. Certainly not about his supposed siblings.

But she was pretty sure he wanted to. Just as she was certain they were related to him. The other male, whose name she still needed to find out, looked too damn similar to Drake for there not to be a familial link.

As they pulled up to a red light, she tapped her finger against the steering wheel.

"What's wrong?" Drake asked, turning away from looking out the passenger side window.

"When I went to Bo's he told me about a blood-born vampire in Tennessee who might know more about dragons. He said the male was bat shit crazy—his words, not mine—but might be able to help with information on dragons. He also said to take backup, meaning you."

"That's why you went to see him?"

She nodded. "I didn't tell anyone because the pack still tries to coddle me sometimes. I just wanted to do what I needed to do, then come back to the mansion. Without an escort." Even though she was a grown woman who'd used her healing gift on most of them at one time or another, they treated her like a seventeen year old cub sometimes. It was because she was in her twenties where most of them were decades older. In some cases older than that. Just because she understood their reasoning didn't mean it wasn't annoying. She loved that Drake had never treated her that way. "I knew Bo would be more willing to talk if it was just me."

Drake's eyes flicked to silver, as if a switch had been flipped. "Thank you."

As a feeling of warmth spread through her at those two simple words, a horn blasted behind them, making her jump in her seat. As she pressed on the gas, she decided to just say what she needed to say. "So what are you going to do? About your alleged siblings?"

"I don't know. I want to go see the vampire in Tennessee."

"But you now have two dragons who could probably answer all your questions." She understood he was feeling betrayed and probably a whole host of other emotions, but Victoria was good at reading people and the agony she'd seen on those dragon's faces had been real.

He shrugged, the action stiff. "They could lie. I want to speak to an impartial being."

Drake had that tone of voice that told her arguing would be pointless. And the truth was, she didn't want to argue with him. Not about this. His life, his decision; she just wanted to support him. "Okay. I'm going with you. When do you want to leave?" She didn't care how soon. The pack would learn to live without her. They finally had a lead on dragons—other than the ones right in their city—and she wanted to jump on it.

His answer was immediate. "As soon as possible."

"Today?"

He nodded. "How long do you think it will take us to reach the place?"

She'd looked up the coordinates on her phone when they'd stopped at a café downtown to grab more coffee and it wasn't too bad of a drive. "It's eleven now and it'll likely take us an hour to pack and say goodbye to every-one." Meaning convince her Alpha and Gabriel to let them do this without an entourage. Drake wouldn't want that and she didn't either. It was time to spread her wings a bit more. "So if we leave around noon and fac-toring in gas stops, I'd say we can make it by ten, ten thirty."

Which would give them a lot more alone time. Something she was craving, especially since she knew he wanted her as much as she wanted him. It would also give them enough time to catch some Zs before hunting down the vampire early in the morning. If this vamp was blood-born he was naturally powerful so going early would make more sense. They wanted to catch him when he couldn't go outside. Of course it was possible he could, but day walkers were incredibly rare.

"You're sure you don't mind?" His voice was hesitant, his posture stiff.

She didn't like it. "Drake, this thing between us, it's not casual." Obviously. She still couldn't put into words exactly how she felt. Not out loud anyway. She was terrified that if she did, she'd lose him. After being abandoned by her aunt and uncle when she was ten, she didn't like to take anything for granted, least of all this thing with Drake. "Would you let me go off by myself?"

"No. But you have a pack, a family." Again with the hesitancy.

"*We're* family." The words were out faster than she had a chance to analyze them. But they were true. Considering the way her own blood relatives had deserted her, she figured she got to choose her family.

Still stiff, he nodded once, his eyes brightening to that supernova as he turned to look out the window again. It was clear he'd withdrawn into that shell he'd encased himself in when they'd first met all those months ago. Under other circumstances it might have annoyed or even worried her, but she understood that it was his coping mechanism.

As they pulled up to the mansion, she rolled her shoulders once. Time to get her game face on and make it clear to both her Alpha and Gabriel that she didn't need a babysitter to help Drake out. And whether they liked it or not, she was going.

High in the air above the Stavros shifter pack's rolling estate, he watched as Dragos and the wolf shifter female got into an SUV. They'd been out all morning and he'd been watching.

Watching and waiting.

They'd returned about an hour ago and were leaving again. It was too risky to try attacking the male now. He needed to get Dragos when he was vulnerable and away from this new pack. What the fuck was a wolf pack doing taking in a dragon anyway?

He couldn't risk taking on the wrath of that pack either. Not when the Alpha was mated to a blood-born vampire with powerful ties to her old coven. Rumor had it that her former coven and new pack had formed an alliance. He also knew that shifters and vamps had recently signed so-called peace treaties.

But pieces of paper could easily be discarded. Unlike mate ties.

No, he had to bide his time unless he wanted his clan to go to war with shifters and vamps. Which he definitely did not. He'd kept his secret for almost fifteen hundred years and he wasn't going to fuck things up now.

Sacrificing Drake as a young dragon had been easy enough. He'd just had to use the stupid male's weak, trusting nature against him. Unfortunately Drake was intelligent and might figure out he'd been behind the betrayal.

It didn't matter that the witch who'd helped him was now dead, Drake might eventually put the pieces together. That witch had spelled Drake with temporary memory loss right before they'd killed him, but that had been a long time ago. He had to make sure his past deeds never came back to haunt him. Which meant he'd have to find a scapegoat.

As the SUV left the estate an hour later, he followed, watching as it made its way to the highway and headed north. He wasn't sure why Drake wasn't flying. He'd seen the male fly since he'd escaped Hell so clearly the male could. Driving seemed like a waste of time.

High in the atmosphere, he started to drop down to gain more speed when a flash of silver caught his eye below. It was only for a moment but he knew that Conall and Keelin must be below, following their brother. They would be camouflaged too, but occasionally it slipped during long flights.

Knowing that they were tailing Drake too wasn't a surprise, but he forced himself to let his dragon take more control as he flew. He couldn't risk letting his camouflage drop for even a moment. They could not be allowed to see him.

In a fight he wasn't certain he could take them both on. Keelin wasn't a warrior but Conall was and if they thought anyone wanted to hurt their long-lost brother, especially him, they'd attack. He had no good reason to be here now.

Yes, he had to be very careful if he wanted to live.

Finn rubbed a hand over the back of his neck as he sat on the end of a weight lifting bench. For the most part the pack used their private gym to spar with each other and let out aggression but they had some modern workout equipment. Lyra stood next to him, arms crossed over her chest as they listened to his packmates' concerns about Victoria leaving. Meaning he got to listen to a fucking bitchfest that he'd 'let' her go.

As if anyone let that female do anything.

"I like Drake a lot, but I don't know if it was wise to let her go." Ophelia, one of his older packmates—and their doctor—was coming from a maternal place more than anything.

"Last time I checked, Finn is Alpha and Victoria is a grown-ass woman." Lyra's voice was dry and nonthreatening, but it made Ophelia straighten in indignation.

"I am aware of that," the petite doctor bit out.

"Are you?" Lyra asked.

Grinning, Finn leaned back and let his mate take control. He'd been going back and forth with his pack for the last twenty minutes about the situation. The pack wasn't a democracy and for the most part, no one ever questioned his decisions. But when it came to Victoria, it seemed everyone had a damn opinion. He and his inner wolf understood his pack wasn't questioning his dominance which was why he'd let the bitching commence. Even if it was making him insane. He had better shit to do right now. Namely, he could be naked and buried balls deep in his mate's tight body.

"Of course I am! I'm not questioning Finn, just—"

"No, are you aware that Victoria is a woman? All grown up and capable of making her own decisions. I've seen the way you guys treat her." Lyra looked around at the group of ten packmates, letting her gaze fall on Gabriel last. "She puts up with it because she loves you. And it's just a guess, but I think she feels grateful you all took her in when she was so young and that's why she doesn't push back too hard. It's not fair to use that gratitude against her. Even if you're not doing it intentionally."

Everyone grew silent, even Ophelia. Finally the doctor broke the silence. "Shit."

Finn didn't think he'd ever heard her curse and bit back a smile as he stood. When he did, everyone murmured goodbyes and started dispersing.

Except Rhea and Gabriel. He raised his eyebrows at them. Rhea cleared her throat almost nervously, the action out of character for the female. "I know that Victoria is grown up but that doesn't negate the fact that two unknown dragons are definitely tailing Drake and Victoria to Tennessee."

Finn didn't know if they were for certain, but there was a damn good chance of it. They weren't letting their brother out of their sight. Which was why he'd already set a plan into motion. But Rhea didn't know that yet.

Rhea continued. "I think it might be prudent to send a small group of warriors after them."

He nearly snorted at her too-polite tone. "Why don't you ask Gabriel what he thinks about that?" Finn asked, throwing an arm around Lyra's shoulders and pulling her close. His mate tucked right into him where she belonged and his body sighed in contentment.

Gabriel gave Rhea an obnoxious smile when she turned to him. "Finn's already ordered us to follow. Me and you. We head out in ten."

She punched him in the arm. "Why didn't you tell me, jackass?"

Gabriel just shrugged. "It's fun to see you get riled up."

Rolling her eyes she turned back to Finn and Lyra. "Victoria know we're coming?"

"No, but she won't be surprised. Keep your distance if you can. If not . . . Lyra's right. Treat her like the adult shifter she is." His mate's words had hit too close to home. He'd never even thought that Victoria put up with their overprotectiveness because she felt grateful. He didn't like that thought at all. She was an integral part of their pack and they all respected the hell out of her.

Now he worried they'd started to do the same thing to Vega. Of course Vega was a teenager and still needed protecting. And hell, he was never going to stop protecting his daughter. But maybe he could loosen up a bit.

As Gabriel and Rhea left, Gabriel paused in the doorway and flipped the small lock into place, grinning as he shut the door behind him.

"I thought they'd never leave," Lyra muttered before jumping him. Literally. Wrapping her legs around his waist, she tackled him to the ground as her mouth devoured his.

Finn quickly flipped her onto her back and rolled his hips against hers. She'd been back in his life for four months after years of being separated and he couldn't get enough of her.

Didn't think that would ever be possible. And he would never waste an opportunity to show her that.

CHAPTER TEN

"This is it," Victoria said, seemingly proud of herself as they pulled up to a two-story cabin outside of Pigeon Forge, Tennessee, in the heart of the Smoky Mountains.

"Only took us how many tries?" Drake couldn't keep the teasing note out of his voice. They'd gone up the wrong mountain at one point and had to backtrack despite having a GPS in the SUV. He'd told her it was the wrong mountain, but she'd been so insistent. Not like being stuck in the vehicle with her was a hardship though.

"Being a know-it-all is not an attractive quality." She stuck her nose in the air before jumping from the vehicle.

Smiling, he followed suit and got out, inhaling the crisp air. The scent of the mountains reminded him so much of Victoria that he started to get another fucking hard-on. Which was ridiculous. Unless he wanted to be perpetually hard around her, which he sort of was anyway, he needed to get himself under control. He ordered his dick down, something he'd been struggling with most of the day. They'd only stopped a couple times for

gas and grabbed food to go so it'd been just him and Victoria alone all day.

Which was normally perfect. There was nowhere
else he wanted to be than with her.

Except he couldn't act on his damn desires. The only
thing that would help, other than masturbation, was
taking to the air and expelling all this pent up energy.
Then he'd be able to take control once again.

"I hope the forecast is right and it snows," he said as
he reached the back doors and opened them.

"Really?"

"Yeah. I like it when it snows." Even if he hadn't seen
it since he'd escaped Hell. Something rammed at his
memory bank with more insistency than his previous
hazy memories. Maybe something important.

"What is it?" Victoria placed her hand over his when
he stood motionless in front of the doors.

He turned to look at her, placing his other hand over
hers, drinking in her strength. When everything felt out
of control, she was the only thing that made him feel
grounded. "I have this memory. It's of me when I was
young, about ten, with another boy who was just a little
older. Dark red hair, green eyes. We were playing in the
snow. It was thick. Layers and layers and we took turns
playing a stupid, dangerous game." He hated that his
mind was a jumbled mess, but he was positive this was
real.

Victoria just watched him, patiently, not pushing.
Something he loved about her. He wanted to tell her he

did *love* her. The carving on the blade he'd given her should have made it clear but he wanted to say the words. Needed her to know. But not yet. Not until he was worthy. She deserved a male who she could be proud of. Not one with a screwed up mind and no way to support them. Maybe once he knew more about where he came from or more about his kind, it would make a difference. And he needed to tell her exactly what type of male he'd been in Hell. The things he'd done. He didn't want to, but she needed to know who he was if she was ever to accept all of him. The thought of telling her *everything*, however, was too much.

He cleared his throat which had gone strangely tight. "One of us would stand in the snow and the other would fly above and make circles around the other with our fire. It was definitely stupid."

"Why?"

"Young dragons aren't as in control of themselves as adults and our natural shields aren't as strong until we're older." Apparently he knew that too. He made a mental note of it. "I guess we thought we were indestructible."

"It's a good memory though, right? You're smiling."

He nodded. It was very good. That much he was certain of. He and the boy had been friends. Best friends. There was something else there though. Something he couldn't pinpoint. It played at the edges of his mind, jumping out of reach when he tried too hard to grab onto it.

"Was it with your brother?"

He chose not to comment on the fact that they weren't totally sure Conall—Finn had told him and Victoria his siblings' names—was indeed his brother. "No. I don't think so. The boy's eyes were a bright green and his dragon coloring was different than mine. Dragons in the same clan have similar coloring. Not exactly the same, but enough that you know what clan they belong to." He was certain of it.

"You're remembering even more." Victoria beamed at him, her smile stealing his breath to such an extent he almost dipped his head and captured her mouth.

His gaze landed on her soft, kissable lips, devoid of any lipstick. She never wore it, just a gloss that made her lips shiny and taunted him. His control around her was slipping too much. Stepping back, he let his hand fall from the door. Maybe touching her wasn't the best idea. "We should get all our stuff inside." He'd wanted to go see the blood-born vamp tonight but she'd been insistent they wait until morning, so wait they would. She was right. They needed rest and to be on their game when they went to speak to the vampire.

A small frown played across her mouth but she nodded. "Okay." When she opened the doors, he reached in and grabbed their bags. Like usual she protested that she could carry her own stuff, but, like usual, he ignored her.

Just as the woman from the rental agency had told them, a key was waiting under the mat. Not prime security, but who the hell was going to break into this lone cabin halfway up a mountain?

Once inside, they found three bedrooms upstairs, all with huge bathrooms. The place had a rustic feel to it, but everything inside was top quality and all the appliances were new. Finn had said he'd take care of getting them a place and while Drake didn't know much about cost, he could tell that renting this place wouldn't be cheap. And he hated depending on someone else for shelter.

"How much is it to rent this place?" he asked as they reached the big bedroom at the end of the upstairs hallway. The master bedroom, Victoria had told him it was called.

"I don't know." She stepped inside and glanced around. "You take this one. It's got a king-sized bed." He started to protest but she pivoted and hurried from the room, not meeting his gaze as she passed him. "I need to run. My wolf is getting edgy. I'll be back in half an hour. Put my bags wherever." Her words came out like rapid gunfire as she practically sprinted from the room.

Drake started to go after her, but stopped at her scent. There was something heightened about it, something that made his dragon claw at the surface and if he went after her, they'd end up naked. In some ways not going after her was harder than anything he'd endured in Hell.

Still in wolf form, Victoria loped up to the front door of the cabin, gravel from the driveway crunching under her paws. Snow was definitely in the air. The man who'd been working at the last gas station they'd stopped at, at the foot of the mountain, had told them they might get a few inches of snow tonight and that it would mostly melt by noon tomorrow. Apparently it had been an odd winter.

Not that she cared about the damn weather. After being in that SUV with dark and delicious Drake she was going out of her freaking mind with lust. That wasn't like her. Even these past few months when she'd been hiding her feelings for him, she'd never had a problem with keeping all her emotions locked down.

Now that she knew how he felt about her, however? Her wolf had been let off that metaphorical leash and didn't understand why she couldn't have Drake, in her bed.

Right freaking now.

Growling to herself, she shifted forms on the dimly lit porch, skin replacing fur as the rush of the change overtook her. It was a momentary discomfort that gave way to pleasure. Once she stood, she stalked to the west edge of the long, wraparound porch on the first level and glared into the darkness of the woods, not caring that she was naked.

"I can smell you, Rhea." Victoria had scented the female on her run through the woods earlier, but the tricky female had stayed out of sight. She was pretty sure the warrior wasn't alone. Finn had probably sent Solon too. Or maybe even Gabriel. Whoever else was with her, Victoria couldn't scent. When Rhea didn't respond, Victoria turned on her heel and headed for the front door, snagging the clothes she'd left folded. "If you get cold, there's an extra bedroom," she tossed over her shoulder as she stalked through the front door and locked it. If the female wanted in, she could ring the damn doorbell.

Upstairs she could just faintly hear water running. The shower. Drake was in there, naked. How hot would it be if she jumped in there with him? Or how embarrassing would it be when he rejected her? That was a slap of icy water right in her face, pushing her sexual hunger back down a fraction. The male was so frustrating, even when he wasn't trying to be.

Frowning, she went to the refrigerator and yanked the door open. Her frown deepened at the sight of a bottle of champagne and a plate of chocolate-covered strawberries. There was a small white note that said 'Enjoy your stay'. Huh. Finn must have bought a special package or something. She would have to thank him later.

Grabbing the bottle, two flutes and the plate, she left her clothes on the counter and headed to the living room area, naked. Just through the French doors there was a huge deck with a whirlpool hot tub off the south side of the house, with a direct lookout over the mountain. She was sure in the daytime it was a beautiful view. Right now, she didn't care about the view.

She was going to crack through Drake's wall tonight. If her naked body wasn't enough to do it, she was screwed. After turning on the whirlpool, she dipped her toes in the water and sighed in relief. The real estate woman hadn't been kidding about getting this place ready. The water was warm and felt amazing. Quickly, she twisted her long hair into a knot at her nape so it wouldn't get soaked.

Sitting on one of the built in seats, she popped the champagne, poured two glasses, submerged deeper into the water and waited. Luckily she didn't have to wait too long.

She swore she felt him before she even heard Drake opening one of the doors behind her. That earthy scent rolled over her as she turned in her seat and crossed her hands under her chin to look up at him. He wore dark jeans that highlighted his muscular thighs, making the juncture between her own legs flood with heat. She just hoped the water covered her scent of desire. Or maybe she didn't.

"How was your run?" His voice sent a shiver through her, but he didn't seem to notice. He also didn't seem to notice her state of undress yet; he was too focused on her face.

"Good. Why don't you join me? Finn must have bought us a package or something because we had champagne and strawberries in the fridge. I managed to control myself from eating all of them." At least her voice wasn't shaky. She'd never been so bold before and was nervous about how he'd react to her being naked.

His lips quirked up when he saw the chocolate-covered strawberries. "It's a miracle you didn't lick off..." His gaze burned bright as it strayed toward the water. He was towering above her and could no doubt see that she wasn't dressed. He cleared his throat as his gaze snapped back to hers.

His eyebrows drew together as he watched her, almost in question, but he didn't say anything. Just stripped off his sweater, revealing all those delicious muscles she wanted to rub her face, tongue, breasts and fingers over. She wanted to cover every inch of him in her scent. It was totally primal and even though she'd always been in touch with her wolf side, she felt as if more of it was coming out now. Clawing away at the surface, wanting to take what was hers. This new side of herself was a little terrifying.

His expression changed subtly, his desire shining clearly in his eyes. A burst of hope leaped inside her. Maybe this would work after all. When he started working the button of his jeans free, her mouth actually watered. Like she was Pavlov's dog and he was the dinner bell. As he started to push them down his hips she turned away, champagne glass in hand. Her cheeks were flushed and it had nothing to do with the warm water.

She couldn't be ogling him like he was a steak dinner. She needed to be smooth about this so he wouldn't bolt and so far, she was failing. Despite her desire to play it cool, she turned when he slid into the water. Disappointment punched through her when she saw he was wearing boxer briefs. Well, that and more lust. She could see the outline of his very hard length under the black cotton. That sight punched through most of her disappointment.

Meeting his supernova gaze, she suddenly felt awkward. So much for a flawless seduction. Now things just felt weird. Hoping to keep things somewhat normal, she reached behind her for his glass and plucked it from the deck. "This champagne's really good."

As he sank into the water across from her, he took it from her hand, his gaze dipping to her barely covered chest. Sure, the bubbles were fizzy and swirling, but her cleavage was clear.

"Thanks," he rasped out.

Deciding to take a chance, she moved to his side of the hot tub and sat directly next to him. He went completely stiff, his back going ramrod straight, watching her almost warily. But the heat was still there, more than simmering now. The liquid silver of his eyes was mesmerizing, making her lightheaded. "What are you thinking right now?" she whispered, amazed she could talk at all.

"I want to know what color your nipples are." His eyes widened after he'd spoken, as if he was as surprised as she was by the bold statement.

Her wolf pranced around in victory.

Setting the glass behind them, she stood up, her nipples pebbling tight, the reaction a combination to the cool rush of night air and the heat from his gaze as they zeroed in on her pale, pink nipples. She felt exposed yet powerful standing in front of him like this. And so, so needy.

His big body shuddered, his eyes going heavy-lidded as he set his own glass down. He leaned forward, his head dipping as if he wanted to taste her and it took all her restraint not to just shove her breasts at him. Because that would be a little crazy.

Right?

Her nipples tingled, the heat between her thighs growing out of control as she stood there and he just watched. Hungrily.

"Touch me?" It was supposed to come out as a seductive demand, but instead came out as a shaky question. She wanted his hands on her. Everywhere.

This time when he reached for her with his big hand, he didn't stop until he cupped her left breast. They both shuddered this time. Her heart pounding erratically, she kept her gaze on him, watching in fascination as color infused his cheeks. Not from embarrassment.

He was ridiculously turned on. His breathing was harsh, uneven, and he looked as if he was about to pounce on her. *Yes, please.*

She didn't care that they were going from zero to *this* in one night because the truth was, this wasn't a big jump. They'd been building to it from the moment they'd met. From the moment he'd burned all those vamps attacking her pack in that cemetery and gone all growly to anyone who looked at her wrong. He'd cemented everything when he'd given her the blade showing a wolf and dragon intertwined.

Oh, so slowly, he rubbed a thumb over her nipple, teasing it, staring at it almost in awe. "You're so beautiful," he murmured, his gaze zeroed in on her breast. Then he lightly pinched her nipple, as if testing her reaction.

She couldn't stop the groan that escaped. Didn't want to. She wanted him to know exactly what he did to her.

Moving slowly, she closed the rest of the very short distance between them, the warm water swirling around her hips as she came to stand right in front of him. He looked almost nervous so she was going to make sure he knew all this was okay in her book.

When she clutched onto his shoulders, he looked at her face, but still held her breast almost reverently. He was so gentle for such a big male. Digging her fingers into his muscles, she spread her legs and straddled him, her knees sliding against the smooth bench, her inner thighs rubbing against him as her bare mound moved over his unfortunately covered erection.

He jerked against her, swallowing convulsively. "We shouldn't."

"Why not?"

He seemed confused for a moment, as if he couldn't remember what his silly reason was so she took advantage and kissed him. He didn't need to be worthy or ready for her. That was such a ridiculous concept. She wanted him just as he was and made sure he knew it.

She went slow enough that he could stop her if he wanted. When her lips touched his, soft and sweet, it was like coming home. It was the only way to describe the warmth that spread through her, starting where their mouths touched.

Gently, she bit his bottom lip, tugging it playfully with her teeth, shivers racing through her when he rolled his hips against her. His other hand snagged around her waist, pulling her close as his tongue teased insistently against hers.

As they learned the taste of each other, he continued strumming her nipple slowly, as if he had all the time in the world and nowhere to go. Which was good because that was exactly how she felt. She arched into his hold, letting her other breast rub against his chest, the friction making her crazy in the best way possible.

She couldn't even feel the cold air anymore; she was so surrounded by his heat and—Drake suddenly jerked back and pushed her off his lap, keeping his hands

gripped tight around her hips before he shoved her behind him.

That was when she realized two things simultaneously. One, they and the hot tub were freaking *glowing*,
like a bright lighthouse beacon.

And two, they weren't alone.

CHAPTER ELEVEN

Drake stared at his two siblings who were watching him with grim expressions. DNA test or not, he was almost certain they were related as he looked at them now. And he was pretty sure the reason the female looked so familiar was because she was a replica of their mother. That thought was clear in his mind, like one of the bright neon signs on the wall at Howler's. This female looked like his mother. Which meant he'd had one.

His first instinct was to demand to know why they were here but he, Victoria and the hot tub were putting off an impossibly bright light and it was coming from him. As he looked around at the water, his anger at being interrupted fizzled, along with his lust. The light immediately dimmed. Behind him, Victoria peeked her head around him, but didn't move. Probably because she was naked.

"Why are you here?" he asked quietly.

"We need to talk but perhaps you both would like to put on some clothes?" His sister glanced away as she spoke, looking out over the moon and starlit mountains.

His brother did the same, turning around to give them privacy.

Drake reached around and squeezed Victoria's hip. He didn't want to take his eyes off the other two. Even if his instinct told him they weren't enemies, he wasn't taking any chances with Victoria's safety.

She paused and he could tell she didn't want to leave but finally she said, "I'll be right back."

He inwardly smiled but didn't move a muscle until she was inside. Once the door shut behind her, he moved from the hot tub and tugged his clothes on. "Talk."

At that one word they both turned around to face him.

"You're serious with the shifter." Conall wasn't asking as he watched Drake intently.

The shifter? "Her name is Victoria." He didn't keep the edge from his voice as he walked around the hot tub, closing the distance between them. Motioning to the line of cushioned, oversized, wooden chairs, he lifted his eyebrows. Unless they planned to attack, they could all sit and act somewhat civil. Even if that was an illusion for all of them.

"I know. I . . . We haven't been introduced properly and I didn't know if I should call her by her first name." Conall actually flushed, seeming embarrassed as he and Keelin moved to the chairs.

The sight eased something tight in Drake's chest. "You can call her Victoria."

Conall cleared his throat again. "I'm sure you know by now but I'm Conall and this is Keelin." He motioned to his sister who was watching him silently, her gray eyes moist. Crap, was she crying?

At the sound of the French door opening he turned to find Victoria stepping out. She'd pulled her hair out of the twist thing and it fell in soft waves around her shoulders and over her breasts. Breasts he'd gotten to see and touch. Soon he'd be doing a whole lot more. He should hold off and wait until he had more to offer, but after having a taste of her—it wasn't happening. He only had so much control. Just like the male he'd been in Hell, he certainly wasn't a gentleman. His need to claim Victoria was damn near overwhelming, overriding everything else.

She wore dark jeans and a blue cashmere sweater much too big because it was his. She'd given him the sweater for Christmas—the first time he'd ever celebrated—and he loved that she'd put it on now. Now his scent would cover her even more.

Smiling in that soothing way of hers, she directed her warmth at the others as she approached. "We haven't been properly introduced. I'm Victoria."

After introductions were made, they all sat. Drake didn't know what to say and thankfully Victoria broke the ice. "Why don't you tell us why you're here, other than to see your brother?"

"You believe we're siblings?" Keelin asked, her voice as soft as it had been at Bo's club. The hope there made him feel guilty for the way he'd reacted before.

He shot Victoria a quick look for support before focusing on Keelin. "I would like to do a DNA test, but yes."

Relief bled into her gray eyes as she smiled. "We followed you from Biloxi because we're not letting you out of our sight. Whether you want our help or not, you're getting it. You're our blood and even if you don't remember us, we remember you. You were the best big brother, protective and loving and..." Keelin's voice broke but she didn't break his gaze.

Something warm spread through his chest, his throat growing tight, but he wasn't certain how to respond to the kind words. He was getting used to it from Victoria, but this female was still a stranger. "Do you look like our—your—mother?" It felt too strange to say our when for so long he feared he'd either been abandoned by his parents or never had them at all. As if he was this thing who'd just been spawned and left to rot in Hell.

She nodded, her long blonde ponytail falling over her shoulder. "People say we're carbon copies."

"Is she..." He couldn't say it.

"Both our parents are alive but they're in a Protective Hibernation." This time Conall answered.

He wasn't exactly sure what that was, but he could guess. "Protective Hibernation?"

Conall answered. "They found a place to go to ground—a cave most likely—and barricaded themselves in. No one knows the exact location, but it's on our clan's land. We're sort of like bears in that sense, but we hibernate for a lot longer."

That sounded familiar. If Drake remembered right, dragons came out of Protective Hibernation only when they were ready and could remain in hiding for decades, even longer. "How long have they been in it?"

"Hundreds of years."

Yes, that definitely sounded familiar. He didn't respond.

"I was in one too, for a long time. I only came out a year ago. This new world is fascinating. Are you finding it the same?" Keelin said.

Drake's gaze swung back to Keelin. "Anything would be better than Hell."

When her eyes went wide, as if she didn't know what to say, guilt immediately speared through him. He hadn't meant to make her feel awkward.

"Is a Protective Hibernation something all dragons do?" Victoria asked, smoothly taking over.

He reached out, taking her hand in his, his inner dragon calming when she linked their fingers.

Keelin shook her head. "No. My mother insisted I go into one to keep me safe." Bitterness laced her words.

Drake wondered if it had anything to do with him being taken but didn't ask.

Conall cleared his throat. "We need to talk about what's happening between you two. When you were in the hot tub, you were sending out a beacon to pretty much all supernatural beings, letting anyone within distance see your light."

"What *was* that?" He hadn't even known he was producing the light until he'd sensed a shift in the atmosphere and saw his siblings standing on the deck.

"When dragons mate we put off an energy. It manifests in different ways, but the Petronilla clan, your clan, gives off light."

Petronilla clan. Yes, he knew that name. "Mate?" He wanted Victoria for his mate, but he hadn't planned to take her tonight.

Conall nodded. "Even humans, if there were any around here tonight, could have seen. It's why we're careful when we mate."

"When you say mate, do you mean have sex or do you mean actually take a mate?" Victoria asked.

Conall looked at her, his gaze shuttered. "Take a mate. Once a dragon picks a mate, we tend to put off that glow whenever we're with our chosen in a sexual way until the mating is complete."

Victoria's fingers tightened in Drake's, but she didn't look at him as she continued. "Are there any specific uh, rituals or, I guess traditions when dragons mate?" Her cheeks had flushed pink and Drake loved that she was asking.

He wanted to know too, but he'd figured nature would take care of itself and they'd figure things out. He might not have ever been with a woman but the Internet was very informative and he knew what he wanted to do to Victoria, how much pleasure he could bring her. If he didn't get it right the first time, he would keep trying until he did. And not stop.

"Not specifically, but dragons bite each other when they seal their bond. And..." He glanced at his sister then back, his expression dark when he looked back at Drake and Victoria. "When dragons mate, it's for life."

Drake frowned, unsure why this was a bad thing. It was his understanding that shifters and vampires were the same. Unlike some humans who left each other, wolf shifters mated for life so it made sense that dragons did the same. "Why is this concerning?"

"If one mate dies, so does the other." Conall flicked a glance between the two of them.

Victoria's fingers tightened in his again, but she didn't respond.

Luckily Conall continued. "It's why our kind are so protective of our secrets and why clans tend to live together. There's strength in numbers and mates are intensely protective. And possessive. No matter what happens with you and Drake we hope you will keep our secrets," he said, directing the last part to Victoria.

The statement made something dark inside Drake twist, but Victoria simply nodded, seemingly nonplussed.

"No matter what happens?" he growled.

Conall's gaze swung back to his, his expression carefully neutral. "I simply meant if she wasn't . . . willing to go through with the mate bond. It's a big risk to take for both parties knowing that if one dies, so does the other."

If something happened to Victoria, Drake wouldn't want to live anyway. He might not have much experience in this world, but he knew that much. Hell would be nothing compared to a world without Victoria in it. When he looked at her, he couldn't get a read on her expression. She smiled at him, but it didn't reach her eyes. Maybe she didn't feel the same. The sharpest sense of pain slid through his chest. He'd assumed...

Turning back to his brother, he let Victoria's hand go. It was too hard to touch her. An acidic scent rolled off her and when he looked at her, her emerald green eyes flashed with hurt. More guilt speared him, but he didn't reach for her again. He couldn't touch her and think straight.

"There's more." Keelin's soft voice interrupted his thoughts. "We have about two hundred and fifty members in our clan and you are what is considered royalty for our people."

Drake frowned, not sure he understood. "How so?"

"Our father is the clan leader and while he's in Protective Hibernation I've taken over as leader. But the honor is yours," Conall said. "And as soon as you're ready I will relinquish all the responsibilities to you."

That tightness began to overwhelm him again, the need to shift and fly a desperate hum inside him. Royalty? "I don't want it."

Conall's eyebrows crashed together. "But it's your right as the oldest."

He clenched his jaw tight. He barely knew anything about this world, he certainly couldn't take on the responsibility of a dragon clan he knew nothing about. "No." The word came out more savage than he'd intended.

Keelin delicately cleared her throat. "If you decide not to take over that's okay but everyone wants to see you again. We would also like you to live with us for as long you'd like. Preferably permanently."

A home to live in? Forever? His throat tightened and he risked a glance at Victoria. She smiled softly, clearly pleased for him. He should be happy too. Part of him was. He had a family who wanted him, but he still had so many questions. Like how had he ended up in Hell? Because someone had to have sacrificed him. And what if Victoria didn't want to live with his clan? He didn't even know where they were located. He still wanted her as his mate, but couldn't read her emotions right now.

Rubbing the back of his neck, he shelved some of his questions. It was after midnight, and after being in the SUV all day he was edgy. Not to mention he hadn't gotten to finish what he'd started with Victoria in the hot tub and he had a feeling they wouldn't be finishing tonight. There was more to the mate bond than he'd imagined.

"Where are you two staying?" Victoria asked when Drake didn't respond to his sister.

"Um, we haven't . . . we're . . ." Keelin stumbled over her words.

"Staying with us. There are two extra rooms here." Victoria looked at him questioningly so he just nodded. His instinct told him to trust Conall and Keelin and so far his gut hadn't let him down.

"We're parked nearby so we'll just get our vehicle and things," Conall said.

"Were you just planning to keep following us?" Drake asked suddenly.

Conall nodded. "We're not letting you out of our sight again. Not literally of course, but someone had to have sacrificed you to Hell." His brother's jaw tightened, his eyes going pure silver. "And that's not going to happen again. We're going to find who did it and destroy them."

Savage, true words.

The conviction in his brother's voice caused the strangest sensation in Drake's chest. He wanted to reach out and drag his brother into a hug but wasn't sure if he should. So he remained where he was. Throat tight, he nodded because he didn't trust his voice. He wanted vengeance too, he just had no idea how to find it. Not until more of his memories returned.

As his brother and sister stood, he and Victoria followed suit, walking them to the front of the house where they disappeared down the driveway. Getting so many answers tonight had been unexpected.

Right now the only thing he cared about was knowing where he stood with Victoria. He knew he should have more concerns, but she was it for him. If she didn't want to mate with him after hearing all of that, he needed to know now.

CHAPTER TWELVE

Victoria sat on the end of the king-sized bed in the master bedroom while Drake retrieved her things from the other room. He'd been insistent on moving her bags into his room and she'd needed a few moments alone so she was taking advantage of the silence.

She was glad Drake hadn't minded her asking his siblings to stay with them. He'd seemed extremely pleased she'd be sharing a room with him, but the way he'd dropped her hand so abruptly during the conversation about mating had her reeling. He'd seemed almost angry with her earlier and she wasn't sure why.

When he stepped into the room with her bag and toiletry case, she jumped up. Then she felt foolish for being so nervous. "Thank you for getting those."

He just grunted and placed them next to an oversized distressed-style dresser before shutting the door. Instead of looking at her, he started pacing in front of the door like a caged beast. She'd never seen him like this and wasn't sure what to make of it.

It wouldn't be long until his siblings were back and she wanted to talk. "Drake."

He stopped, pivoting toward her, his jaw clenched tight. "Do you want to mate with me?"

Her eyes widened, her heart rate increasing. "Right now?"

"I just mean ever. Do you want to be my mate?"

And here it was. The conversation she wasn't ready to have, especially after what his brother had revealed about mates being so bonded that they literally couldn't live without one another. She was naturally strong as a shifter, but she was infinitely weaker than Drake. It was simple biology. She would be a weak link for him. A huge weak link for a male who'd never gotten the chance to experience life. Chances were much higher that she would die first, and it would be a death sentence for him. But she couldn't lie. He'd scent it if she did. "I do."

Instant relief flooded his face. He shoved his hands through his dark hair, the shaky action showing off the muscles of his arms as they flexed. She tried not to notice how sexy it was, but couldn't help it. "But? And don't lie. You pulled back out there. I *felt* it." His voice shook with anger and it registered that she'd hurt his feelings when she hadn't meant to.

She took a step in his direction, wanting to touch him, knowing they both needed it right now. The need to comfort him was high and not because she was a healer. He didn't move away from her, but he also didn't step forward so she stopped, feeling as if a giant chasm yawned between them when it was really only a few feet. "I wasn't pulling back. Drake, there's so much you haven't done yet. So much you haven't seen or experienced."

"What does that have to do with mating?" he demanded, his expression fierce.

"Everything. What if you're settling for me because I'm all you've known in the short time you've been out of Hell?"

His head jerked up like she'd slapped him. "Just because I was in Hell doesn't mean I'm stupid. I might not understand a lot of things, but my dragon claimed you before I'd ever *seen* you. I scented you in that cemetery, I was crazed to get to you before I'd seen your face. Once I got to know you . . . I don't need any other fucking experience with women if that's what you mean. Why would I when I have you? You're mine."

Those two words warmed her from the inside out, but she still couldn't believe it. Just couldn't. He wasn't thinking clearly, and he was just being stubborn. She needed him to stop and consider the consequences of what he was saying. "What if we mate and I'm killed? I'm weaker than you and whoever put you in Hell might be out there. What if they want to get to you through me?" Her voice shook as she thought about all the years he'd lost already. If his life was cut short because of her...

His expression softening, Drake crossed the few feet between them, cupping the side of her face in his big hand as his other hand settled on her hip. His eyes blazed bright silver as he stared down at her. "I love you, Victoria. That is the one truth I know." He said it with total conviction and the words slammed into her heart with enough intensity she felt it to her core.

Her eyes burned with tears, spilling hot over her cheeks. She didn't bother wiping them away, instead reaching for him, her hands settling on his chest. "You can't," she whispered.

He didn't pull away. "Why are you fighting this?" His voice was low, rumbling and confused.

She didn't blame him for being confused. Too many emotions swirled inside her, out of control and she couldn't get a handle on herself. Her inner wolf was clawing at her, telling her to shut the hell up and just jump this male, take what was hers. "I'm afraid."

His frown deepened as he swiped her stray tears away with his thumb. "Of what?"

"Losing you." After everything he'd been through, she felt like a freaking coward right then, but fear could be an overwhelming, tricky bitch. She was drowning in it. Her only real family had abandoned her as a cub and she'd come to learn that you chose your family but still . . . the thought of losing Drake was too much.

His expression softened even more with understanding. "I could be taken from you anyway. Luckily I'm hard to kill."

Throat tight, she forced her vocal cords to work. "I love you so much it scares me, Drake. I just don't ever want you to regret me. To settle." Because that was the real crux of the matter. The mating thing was the icing on the cake of her fears, feeding them and fucking with her head. Making her balk at taking the next step in their relationship. Because after that big step, there was no going back.

"I know you don't like being treated like a child by your pack and I don't like being treated as if I don't know my own mind. You're mine, Victoria. If you don't want to mate with me, I will accept it." His silver gaze said he'd still fight for the right to be with her.

That was all she needed to know. "I want to."

Triumph and relief glittered in his eyes as he crushed his mouth to hers. No more sweet, gentle kisses, but a dominant taking from the possessive male she'd come to love more than she ever imagined possible.

Fear still lurked in the back of her mind, lingering and clawing for purchase but she shoved it back, savoring the kiss of this male. This male who was an absolute miracle in her life. After fifteen hundred years in Hell he shouldn't be so sane, so loving. But he was.

His tongue teased against hers, wickedly demanding as his hand slid up under her sweater, his palm spanning her back and pulling her flush against him. She arched into him, only stopping when he stilled.

Lifting his head back, he cocked it to the side. He let out a growl of frustration, his dragon flickering in his eyes. "They're back."

Damn. She'd been so lost in his taste she hadn't heard anything else. And, yep, they were glowing again. She glanced at the open windows over her shoulder. One wall was all windows and a sliding glass ceiling-to-floor length door. Sheer buttercream colored curtains were pushed back and something told her they wouldn't do much to block the light Drake was putting off.

Not that it mattered anyway. Looking back at him, she said, "When we take the next step, I'd like to be alone." Because she really didn't want his brother and sister listening to her and Drake.

He nodded. "You'll still stay with me tonight." A demand.

When he rolled his hips, rubbing his erection against her lower abdomen, her eyes grew heavy-lidded for a moment. "We should go greet them and show them to their rooms." But now she wished she'd never invited them to stay. She wanted to finish what she'd started with Drake. Her body ached for his, for the release she knew he could give her.

He growled in response, but followed her when she stepped out of his embrace and headed for the door.

Even though she was disappointed they'd been interrupted, part of her was a little relieved. She wanted him more than anything and knew she wanted to mate with him, but she still needed to wrap her mind around the fact that they'd soon be linked. Her relief had nothing to do with the fact that she was still waiting for the other shoe to drop, she told herself.

Nothing at all.

High in the night sky above the cabin Dragos had settled down at for the evening, he scanned the surrounding area looking for the dragons who should be arriving any moment. Of course they'd likely camouflage themselves until the last minute.

He didn't care for the Veles clan, but they'd had a long-standing distaste of the Petronilla dragons. When he'd anonymously called their clan leader and told him that the supposedly deceased Dragos was indeed alive and where to find him, he'd been certain the dragon would send someone immediately. Now he wanted to know what was taking so long for them to move into action.

Dragos had been putting off that blinding mating light earlier. Stupid to do it outside. The royal male might not have known what happened during mating though. It wasn't something explained to children and he'd been dropped into Hell long before he reached his maturity so he wouldn't have known about it.

Luckily he could work the male's mating hunger to his advantage. If Dragos mated with that wolf shifter and she was killed, her pack would come after the Veles clan. Which meant the Marius vampire coven would back the Alpha's new mate Lyra in attacking the Veles's.

Dragons were strong but if the full force of a shifter pack and vampire coven descended on the Veles clan, the clan would take a serious hit. Possibly even be obliterated. That would be a definite if the shifters and vamps worked in tandem with the Petronilla clan. Some of those Marius vampires could fly, giving them an almost equal advantage with dragons.

The vamps and shifters would have to find the Veles clan first, but he would help them. Anonymously of course. The Veles clan had prime territory he wouldn't mind taking over. But that would be a bonus. He just wanted Dragos dead.

Dragos's parents deserved the male's death. When they came out of their Protective Hibernation, it would be the sweetest thing to see the agony on their faces that they'd lost their son again. If he could kill Keelin before they woke up, it would be even better.

She was weaker than Conall, an easier target, especially since she was so trusting. Her kindness would give him an advantage. She'd been in Protective Hibernation so long he hadn't been able to strike at her. If he'd known where she'd gone to ground he would have tried, but dragons were exceptionally secretive about their Hibernation. For good reason. The year since she'd been out her brother had kept a close eye on her.

An SUV pulled into the driveway, parking next to Drake's. When Conall and Keelin exited, his ire grew. He'd thought they'd left for good. If they were staying in the cabin this could create a problem. He wanted them both dead, but he wanted to be the one to kill them, especially Conall. Obnoxious bastard. Unfortunately the male had proved tricky to destroy so far.

He needed to act quickly though. If their parents woke from Protective Hibernation soon he'd lose his chance. They were so damn overprotective. Too much so.

Something from the woods caught his eye. A flash of movement. Fast. Too fast to be human. Probably a wolf or bear or whatever the hell was in this forest, but he wanted to get a closer look.

Swooping down, he kept his camouflage on as he descended. As he glided, a wild rush of air directly above him told him the Veles dragon—or dragons—had arrived. Looked as if his job here was done. He hoped the Veles dragons finished off Drake, but if not, he'd do it himself.

Veering left, he went lower, but turned away from the cabin. He didn't need to see the destruction. No matter who won, he'd hear about it later.

Victoria put the champagne back in the refrigerator and closed the door. Though she was exhausted, she was nervous about sleeping in the same bed with Drake. Which was stupid. She had nothing to be nervous about.

Other than the fact that she didn't know if she trusted her control where he was concerned.

The kitchen and huge living room were connected, with exposed wood beams across the high ceilings making the space seem even larger. As she stepped into the living room, Keelin appeared at the bottom of the stairs, her long hair damp.

She smiled almost nervously at Victoria as she covered the distance between them, her steps almost tentative. "I thought I heard someone down here."

"Just me." She half-smiled, feeling nervous too. "There's not much in the fridge. Just some champagne." Because she'd polished off those strawberries.

"I'm okay, but thank you. Are you going to bed?"

"Ah, yeah, unless you need something?"

"No." But the female shifted from foot to foot, clearly wanting to say something. Wearing a long-sleeved, silky, black pajama set with white trim and a matching black and white robe, the female looked put together even now.

"You sure?" She wasn't going to force the issue but if Keelin was anxious, Victoria hoped she would open up. This was Drake's family after all.

Keelin opened her mouth to respond but glass from the nearby window shattered in an explosion, shards flying everywhere as something bright and gleaming hurtled into the room.

Without thinking, Victoria threw herself at Keelin, tackling the petite female. Pain detonated in her right shoulder as they hit the floor and she rolled them behind the leather couch.

As she cried out from the onslaught of whatever had hit her, her wolf took over instantaneously, the shock of her shift brutal and jarring as her bones shifted and realigned, fur replacing skin.

Keelin let out a scream of rage as she jumped to her feet, breathing fire in her human form at something beyond the couch.

Victoria tried to jump up, to help, but her legs refused to work, her paws barely sliding against the hardwood floor. As darkness swept her under, the strange lethargic feeling spreading out from her shoulder to the rest of her body, the most horrifying screeching sound filled the air.

It reverberated through the house, shaking the windows as blackness completely claimed her.

CHAPTER THIRTEEN

At the sound of glass breaking and an ear-splitting scream downstairs, a vise tightened around Drake's heart, squeezing all the breath from him as fear nearly paralyzed him.

Victoria.

Without pause he raced for the door but a ball of fire ripped through the wall of windows, blasting the glass inward.

His dragon took over without his conscious thought. He couldn't let whoever was outside in. He had to keep his mate safe. Breathing fire to combat another attack, he raced toward the gaping hole, his body starting to shift as he ran. He managed to control the complete transformation until he burst out into the cold night air. Letting his animal loose, he snapped his wings out and dove over the back deck, rolling midair and diving straight for the thicket of trees below as a shot of flames erupted from his left.

A steady burst of panic rippled through him. He had to get back to Victoria.

Before he slammed into the tops of the trees he shifted directions, forcing his body into a glide. He gained momentum and shot toward the skies. Though it felt

167

like an eternity, he estimated less than thirty seconds had passed as he whipped back around toward the cabin.

That previous burst of panic was now a full blown attack on his nervous system as he raced toward the cabin. The predator in him catalogued the carnage as he flew. The bottom window had been blasted out, just as the window in the master bedroom had been. Keelin fought with a male, both in human form, in the living room. A dragon he was certain was Conall was locked in a freefall high above the forest with a smaller shimmering yellowish-orange dragon. A third dragon of similar coloring was diving toward the open window where Keelin was.

Where was Victoria?

Fear raked against his insides, the unknown making him insane. Find and save Victoria. That was all the predator inside him was capable of focusing on.

On a burst of rage and the need to protect, Drake shot through the air faster than he'd ever flown. The biting wind rushed over him but he barely felt it as he made like an arrow toward the offending shifter diving for the cabin.

The animal turned toward him the moment before impact. There was nowhere to go.

Opening his jaw wide, Drake slammed into the other dragon, clamping his teeth down on the animal's neck as he released fire once again, burning and biting right through the animal's neck. As he rolled them over, his wing slammed against the house, taking off pieces of the roof as they tumbled to the back deck. The dragon screamed, the sound scraping over Drake's senses until he ripped the head free, tossing it to the forest below before his body slammed against the wooden surface of the deck.

The other dragon's body tumbled off the deck, ripping the railing free as it fell to the forest below. Not caring where the body landed, he shifted to his human form, the rush of the change invigorating him right before he raced into the living room to protect the females. Unable to avoid the glass, he stepped into the carnage, his heart pounding out of control as he searched for Victoria. He was vaguely aware of the glass slicing into his feet but it barely registered.

Keelin was on the ground, her clothes in tatters as Gabriel crouched next to her, a blade in one hand as he reached for Drake's sister with his other. *Where the hell had the Guardian come from?* The front door had been kicked down so maybe he'd entered while Drake was fighting the other dragon. A headless male corpse lay a few feet away, blood everywhere, no doubt slaughtered by Gabriel. "Where's—"

Rhea popped up from behind the couch, her expression grim.

"It's Victoria," the female said, those two words piercing him deeper than any blade or demon's claws could ever manage.

No. No, no, *no.*

Unable to speak, he launched himself in that direction, more terrified than he'd ever been in Hell. Everything else funneled out around him as he found Victoria lying on the ground in wolf form, her clothes shredded around her unmoving body.

She was breathing, but she was too still. He sat next to her, gently stroking her head, but was too afraid to move her until he knew what had happened. She didn't make a sound. "What happened?" he rasped out, his voice scratchy, as if he hadn't used it in weeks.

He was vaguely aware of Conall entering the room, but didn't take his focus off Victoria.

"Those were Veles dragons. They hate us, but they haven't attacked like this in hundreds of years," Conall said.

"One of them poisoned Victoria. She shoved me out of the way and got hit with that bastard's dart." Keelin's voice broke on the last word.

Drake looked up, never taking his hand from Victoria's head. "What kind of poison?"

Conall's dragon was in his eyes as he looked at him, his rage clear. "It's unique to their clan, taken from their teeth."

"Like the poisonous dart frog?" Rhea asked, also crouching next to Victoria.

"Similar. Veles dragons remove their back teeth and grind them into a powder before mixing it into a liquid form. It's incredibly deadly and must be treated soon."

"How?" That was all that mattered to Drake. Because as soon as Victoria was well, he was going to destroy anyone who'd had a hand in her poisoning.

"Within twelve hours. She might have more time because she was protected with your dragon's essence, but that's..." He looked around at the others, as if thinking he'd said too much, but continued. Drake had no clue what his brother was talking about, but caught up fast when Conall continued. "That just protects her from dragon fire to an extent. It's not a long-term thing in battle, but I'll explain that to you later. We need to get her to our clan healer. She can remove the poison from Victoria's system."

"Where do your people live?" Gabriel asked, his expression tense, the fear he felt for Victoria's safety palpable.

"Northern Montana. We could fly there in enough time, but it would be impossible to maintain our camouflage the entire time and the ride might not be safe for Victoria."

"What's the nearest airport to your land?" Gabriel snapped as he pulled out his phone.

As Gabriel and Conall talked, Drake had never felt so fucking helpless in his life. He didn't know how to help Victoria. Could literally do nothing for her. He was *useless.* "Tell me what to do." He said it to them all, desperate to *do* something.

"Hold her, pull her into your lap. Touch is healing," Keelin said quietly, standing near the edge of the couch, her body trembling as she wrapped her arms around herself.

Not needing to be told twice, he lifted Victoria's body and pulled her close. In wolf form, she was all black, her fur the same color as her dark hair. She was beautiful but so very still. His throat clenched tight, adrenaline pumping through him overtime. He wanted to let his dragon free, to burn everything in his wake to the ground. The primal violent urge snapped him out of his thoughts. Victoria was all that mattered. Not vengeance. He couldn't lose her.

"Why did they attack?" he demanded, not caring which of his siblings answered.

Gabriel had gone outside and was on his phone, hopefully getting a flight. Something Drake should be doing for her. God, he hated this helplessness, that he didn't know how to do such simple things like make a flight reservation. He wrapped himself around her, trying to protect her, reach her with his embrace and his love. *Hold on, sweetheart. Please hold on.*

Conall answered. "All dragons are naturally wary of other clans but we do enough inter-clan matings that we keep the peace for the most part. When you disappeared, however, our mother was convinced their clan had something to do with it. She struck hard and viciously, taking out many of their warrior males. Our clans battled back and forth for about a decade until we had to call a truce or risk dying out. They have clearly not forgotten our blood feud."

"How did they find Drake though?" Rhea asked.

"That's a good question." Conall looked murderous as he glanced at the dead male. When he looked over at Keelin, the scent of something burning lingered in the air, as if his brother was reining in his fire. "Did he hurt you?" he asked their sister, a note Drake had never heard before in his voice.

That was when Drake realized the way her clothes had been ripped. The pajama top she held together in front of her chest had been ripped down the front and her pants were gone. Nausea swelled inside him. He'd seen enough in Hell that he understood this. He cradled Victoria closer. "Keelin, did he..." He couldn't finish. Everything had happened so fast, he'd never imagined she'd been sexually assaulted.

She shook her head, looking back and forth between Drake and Conall. "No. Gabriel and Rhea saved me." Tears spilled down her cheeks and for the first time since he'd met her he realized how fragile she was, her smaller stature aside. "I'm sorry I didn't protect her," she whispered.

Before he could respond, Gabriel strode back into the room, his boots crunching over the glass. "Got a private plane that'll take us about an hour out from your place. A direct flight. Can your clan meet us with a ride?" When Conall nodded, Gabriel continued. "Lyra's called her former coven and they're sending some vamps to clean this up. I don't hear any sirens but that doesn't mean some humans didn't see that little light show."

"We need to burn the bodies before we leave," Conall said. "They'll disintegrate if burned with dragon fire."

Gabriel nodded once. "Then I'll let you take care of that. Rhea and I will start packing up everything." His gaze landed on Drake, his expression tight. "You just hold onto Victoria. She's going to be okay."

Throat tight, all Drake could do was nod and hold his future mate closer. He thought he'd been prepared for anything, but not *this*. Never this. It didn't matter how many creatures he'd fought and killed in Hell or how many injuries he'd sustained. He'd never known true pain until now. Gently stroking her head, he held her closer but was careful not to squeeze too tight. Around him everyone was moving, cleaning up, removing the dead body and bringing all their bags downstairs, but he was barely aware of anything, even as he carried Victoria to the SUV.

All he cared about was saving her.

CHAPTER FOURTEEN

Conall glanced back at the shut door of the private cabin. Once they'd boarded the private plane, Drake had taken Victoria to the bedroom and shut everyone out. They might not be mated yet, but his brother was certainly feeling the mating hunger.

Conall hated that this shit had happened on his watch. He was supposed to bring Drake back, to protect his brother. Everyone had failed Drake before. He wouldn't do it again. It didn't matter that he'd been ten when Drake had gone missing. They were brothers. He should have known his brother wasn't gone for good.

Facing forward in the plush leather seat, he found Gabriel watching him curiously. "What?" he asked the Guardian. Conall didn't know much about wolf shifters and their pack dynamics. They didn't keep their species as secretive as dragons, but shifters and vamps still locked things down pretty tight, the inter-species communication limited for the most part. Though he did know things must be changing since the Stavros Alpha had mated a vampire and they had a child together. *That* itself was hard to believe.

"You're worried about your brother," Gabriel said.

"Of course I am. I'm surprised you are." Because that male wasn't just concerned for Victoria, he cared about Drake too. Conall had seen the worry in his eyes on the drive to the private airport.

Gabriel's dark eyebrows rose.

"I saw you fight in the ring," he clarified.

The male just grunted. "Just stupid male bullshit. I needed to make sure he was serious about Victoria."

Drake definitely was. That mating light he'd been putting off had been intense. Like the sun, for lack of a better analogy.

"Have your kind been healed from this poison?" Gabriel asked so quietly Conall almost didn't hear him.

Conall nodded. "Been a while, but yeah. Our healer will have to extract it from her body." And it would likely be painful but he didn't think Victoria would mind if it saved her life. His gaze flicked up to the front of the plane where Rhea and Keelin sat talking quietly. His sister was normally wary of outsiders, but she seemed to have taken to Rhea quickly. Which was good.

He wasn't sure why he even cared, but he did. That female made his heart pound out of control and they'd barely said two full sentences to each other.

"She's single," Gabriel said before standing and heading to the bathroom in the back.

Conall scrubbed a hand over his face. Shit. He was too damn obvious if this stranger noticed his interest in Rhea. It didn't make sense either. His heart had been claimed by another female long ago. Until she'd left him to mate with another. Conall hadn't thought he'd ever get over her. Hundreds of years later and no female had interested him for more than sex. Even that had gotten old long ago. His fist did well enough. That and fighting. So it didn't make sense that a wolf shifter was drawing out this strange humming sensation in his chest.

Whenever she was near, his body flared to life. And now was the worst time in the world for him to be noticing a female. Drake deserved his full attention.

Glancing back at the closed door as if he could somehow see past the barrier, his hands balled into fists. Whoever had hurt Drake's female would pay with their life.

When he sensed Keelin heading his way, he turned back around. His sister seemed better than she had at the cabin, but still shaken. She'd always been sheltered, even up until she'd gone into Protective Hibernation. So much of this was hard on her and he wished she'd listened to him and stayed back at their compound.

"This is a beautiful plane," Keelin said as she sat in the seat Gabriel had vacated. She always made small talk when she felt out of sorts.

Conall nodded, his gaze straying to the front of the plane. "Yeah." The pilot was human too, but he hadn't batted an eye as Drake had carried a wolf onto the plane. And Conall was fairly certain their flight hadn't been registered anywhere. The private airport they were flying into had been closed down about a year ago. He hadn't questioned Gabriel though because he didn't give a shit if they broke a thousand human laws. He nearly snorted at the thought of humans and their stupid laws with their broken legal systems all over the world. Shifters and vamps might be more brutal in the way they executed justice but their crime rates were very low.

"So . . . Fia texted me." Her words were like the equivalent of a nuclear bomb going off.

His head snapped around until he faced his sister. "When?"

"Before we got on the plane."

He didn't respond, not wanting to ask why the female had contacted Keelin. Fia, the female he'd been betrothed to mate, had left him for a royal member of the Devlin clan. Keelin had only discovered it once she'd come out of her Protective Hibernation but she'd remained friends with Fia. Conall had never said one way or another if he minded even though he hated the thought of his sister still in contact with Fia.

"She asked about Drake," Keelin continued when Conall remained silent. "Said she'd heard from some clan members that he was back and wanted to know if she could come for a visit."

A shot of pure surprise jolted through him. Fia hadn't been to their land for hundreds of years. "Alone?"

Keelin's eyes filled with an emotion that looked a lot like pity. "You know her mate would never let her go anywhere without him."

"What did you say?" he bit out.

"Nothing. I didn't have time to respond and I never would have invited her without your approval. I know she hurt you." Oh yeah, that was definitely pity.

His jaw tightened.

Keelin continued. "It might be a good show of peace-keeping to invite their royal members for a visit, especially after the Veles attack. We'll need all the support we can get if this isn't an isolated incident." His sister was one of the physically weakest dragons of their clan, but she made up for it with her wisdom. Something their mother had chosen to ignore for so long.

He hated that she was right. And he would sacrifice his pride to gain allies. Anything to keep Drake safe. He would never fail his brother again. "You're right. I'll let you handle inviting them." At that, he stood and headed for the mini-bar. A couple shots of vodka would barely affect him with his metabolism, but the burn would be welcome.

Drake curled his body around Victoria's wolf, holding her close. He'd sequestered them from the rest of the plane, not wanting to see anyone else. He hated that she'd been wounded, might even . . . No. He couldn't think that way. But deep down he wondered if this was his punishment for all the bloodshed he'd caused in Hell. For the way he'd savored killing.

He might have been innocent when he'd gone to Hell, but he hadn't come out that way. Victoria was sweet and everything right with the world. Everything he didn't deserve.

Victoria's poisoning was his punishment. He knew it.

When he closed his eyes all he saw was bloodshed and fire. The memory from his time in Hell was overwhelming, taking over his mind even as he tried to banish it. He didn't want to think of his time in the realm of the damned, not when he was holding onto the female he loved.

The memory sucked him under no matter how hard he tried to fight it.

Wings spread wide as he stood in the middle of the blood-filled arena reminiscent of the Roman Coliseum from Earth, he screeched loudly, breathing fire on one of the last of his thirty opponents. Thirty? Pathetic. His dragon would have laughed if possible.

The stands around him shook with cheers and screams of anger.

Finally, his last two opponents approached from the crimson-tinged sky that never changed its shade, an Akkadian demon riding a mythical Adze. He'd never seen the two creatures work together, but they wanted him in chains so they must have come to an agreement. The Adze could occasionally shift to other forms, mainly humanoid, but in its true form it looked like a giant dragonfly as it did now.

Screaming, it opened its mouth to reveal razor sharp teeth—which it used to suck its victims dry of blood—as the Akkadian let out a battle cry.

Instead of taking to the air, Drake shifted to his human form, his strength rippling through him as he underwent the change.

The black and red Adze's wings flapped too fast for most eyes to see, like a hummingbird from Earth, as it flew at Drake.

The Adze's teeth were filled with venom, dangerous and deadly even to Drake, and he knew he'd have a better chance of defeating it in his smaller form. Being bigger wasn't always the best. And right now he didn't want to just incinerate it. He wanted to pull it apart with his bare hands. Wanted to bathe in its fucking blood.

There weren't many rules in this coliseum. Anything went during the fights and the dirtier the better. The only rule was that no one interfered with those battling. The rule was often broken, it was Hell after all, but those who broke it ended up in chains and dragged deep down into the bowels of a place Drake didn't even want to imagine. Because if he lost, he'd be taken there too. If they could hold him and he wasn't certain they could. He didn't plan to lose and find out what kind of tortures could be meted out on him.

Racing for one of the dead demons he'd killed minutes before, he snatched up a giant bone with a spear attached to it. He wasn't sure what type of bone it was, but from the thickness and the fact that his fire hadn't incinerated it earlier he guessed it was from an avian-type creature. Maybe wyvern. There weren't many in Hell, but he'd fought them and they were difficult to kill because they were so similar to dragons.

Without pause, he turned and threw the bone-spear, aiming for where the rider was heading, not where he was now. Timing was everything.

The spear met its mark moments later, hurtling into the Akkadian demon's throat with all Drake's force. Thick, sulfuric-scented blood arched out in a macabre splatter as the demon flew back through the air, its back slamming into the sharp bones of another dead creature on the hard-packed dirt floor. Drake hadn't expected that, but he'd take it.

One more to go. With the Akkadian demon down for the count Drake turned toward the Adze hovering about twenty feet away, watching and waiting.

Drake wasn't going to make the first move. Not with this one. The cheers of the crowd grew deafening around them, but he tuned everything out.

He didn't care about the creatures in the stands. He only cared about his next kill. After spending hundreds of years in self-induced solitary confinement, creating pain made him feel alive again. He'd lost his childhood, could barely remember that weak boy he'd once been. This was the only thing that let him feel something.

Finally the creature moved, flying down toward Drake's left, its mouth open wide, ready to strike. But Drake had seen this type of creature attack before and knew what to do. Using a nearby broken pillar as a springboard, he jumped on it and propelled himself through the air.

The Adze couldn't turn fast enough with its chosen trajectory. Drake let his talons free even while in human form and sliced through both wings as he leaped over the creature.

An ear-piercing scream of pain rent through the air as the Adze began its fall to the blood-soaked ground below.

It knew its time was near. Drake was going to rip the rest of its body apart, piece by piece, adding another river of crimson to this god forsaken arena.

His eyes snapped open and he managed to shove the memory back down where it belonged. For now. Guilt and horror suffused his veins even if he understood that survival and vengeance—and probably a touch of madness—had driven him in captivity. He swallowed hard and tightened his grip on Victoria without squeezing too hard. The last thing in the world he could ever do was hurt her.

Now he just needed her to be safe. To live. He'd pay penance a thousand times over, even return to Hell if she would just *live*.

CHAPTER FIFTEEN

Drake stared out the window of the dark-tinted SUV limousine, but kept his grip secure around Victoria's still form draped over his lap. The vehicle was huge enough to accommodate the six of them and the three other shifters who'd arrived at the airport an hour ago. One was driving but the other two dragons from the Petronilla clan were in the back with them.

They'd given him some curious stares but he ignored them. Ignored everyone except Victoria. Her breathing remained steady and she'd actually moved a couple times, but she hadn't opened her eyes. The few sounds she'd made had been a soft whining, as if she was in pain.

Which shredded him.

"How much longer?" he asked, his words cutting through the otherwise quiet interior. They hadn't even turned on the radio.

"Twenty minutes out," Conall said quietly.

His brother sat right next to him, a silent support. Drake hadn't thought he'd care one way or another about getting to know his siblings, but right now it was a relief to have others in his corner. As if their support could somehow help Victoria.

He hated that she'd been dragged into this. His sweet, loving healer had been poisoned trying to protect his sister. He buried his face against the top of her head, not caring what anyone thought of him. Her scent even in wolf form, was reassuring. She was still here, alive.

And he'd be damned if that changed. Victoria wasn't going anywhere.

Lifting his head to stare out the long window across from him he frowned at the sight of a neon sign proclaiming the Petronilla Ski Resort was eight miles away.

"Your clan owns a ski resort?" Rhea asked.

Keelin nodded. "Yes. We also own thousands of acres surrounding it that the clan uses for flying in privacy. Our homes are all separated from the resort so you won't have to worry about privacy. If you need to shift, you'll have plenty of room to run."

Drake hadn't even thought to ask what the clan did for money or anything. He'd been more focused on Victoria, even before her attack. Still was. He also wondered if his parents were in Hibernation near the clan's homes. Or if they sensed he was back. For that matter... "How is it that I speak English?" he blurted, the question odd enough for the situation, especially with no segue to it. He'd wondered about it when he escaped Hell. When Vega had spoken to him in English in that prison cell, he'd spoken it right back as if he'd known it his whole life.

Everyone turned to stare at him, no doubt wondering if he'd lost his fucking mind. Which he might well do if Victoria didn't survive. *Fuck.* He couldn't even go there. He needed to stay positive.

Keelin met his gaze. "Each dragon clan has unique . . . gifts. We're not sure why but I think it has something to do with the fact that since the beginning of time we've basically been what humans would consider an endangered species. So we have gifts to make up for it. It's a miracle we still live and to an extent, thrive. The Petronilla clan can communicate in any language, with anyone on the planet. Well, as far as we know. It's been very useful for business with the ski lodge and our other endeavors."

Drake just nodded, digesting the information. It explained a lot. Like how he'd known that ritual chant to close the Hell Gate in New Orleans. He still didn't know the language he'd been speaking or how he knew it, but it was as much a part of him as breathing. Later he'd ask Keelin more when they didn't have an audience. He needed to remember to censor himself and not just blurt out random things that entered his mind.

The three warriors with them might be part of the Petronilla clan, but to him they were strangers. Which basically equaled enemy. Almost everyone was an enemy until he discovered who'd put him in Hell and how those Veles dragons had known where he and Victoria were. He wondered if it had anything to do with the mating light he'd been putting off. At the thought that he'd been the cause of Victoria's poisoning, that invisible dagger embedded itself deeper in his chest, twisting and shredding his heart. He'd give anything to take away her pain. To see her open those beautiful eyes.

As they passed a big wood and metal sign on the side of the icy road that said Petronilla Ski Resort, Keelin spoke, as if sensing his unspoken question. "The turn off for our village is five miles from here and we have visible and invisible security. Once in the village we'll all be protected. And our healer will take care of Victoria." She spoke with a quiet authority. For some reason her words soothed Drake.

He nodded, swallowing hard. "Thank you."

True to Keelin's word, five miles later the driver steered their SUV limo through two high, open gates. As soon as they were through, the gates started to close. There was a small area of shops as they quietly cruised down the main street. Large homes dotted up the side of the snow-covered mountainside. From what he could see, most of the lights were on, making the place look like something out of a postcard Victoria had shown him of a place she wanted to visit in Switzerland.

"We're almost there," he murmured to her, hoping she could hear him. It was likely his imagination but he could almost swear she burrowed closer to him.

A mile down the road they pulled into the driveway of a large two-story Swiss chalet log-style home. The only reason he even knew the style was because it was one of Victoria's favorites.

God, Victoria. *Don't leave me*, he silently begged, cradling her closer. He couldn't live in a world without her.

Tiny shards of silver were raking across Victoria's insides, trying to claw their way out of her body. At least that was what it felt like. What the hell was going on?

Through a haze of agony she saw Drake sitting beside her, his expression a mask of concern. She wanted to reach out and tell him everything would be okay but couldn't move. Crap, she was in wolf form.

On a . . . massage table it looked like. That was weird. Couldn't be right. If she was getting a massage, it sucked. She was definitely getting a refund—

A howl ripped from her throat as another surge of pain pulled at her insides.

An unfamiliar female moved next to Drake. Tall, model gorgeous. What the hell? She was saying something, but Victoria couldn't make out the words. Her ears were ringing and agony sliced at her everywhere, as if her body was being turned inside out.

Oh God, make it stop. Someone please make it stop.

Suddenly the pain stopped for one brief moment. She sucked in a breath and it started up again, the slicing and cutting an agony she'd never imagined.

The woman had her hands on Victoria's middle, right around her ribs. She could feel the warmth and that was the only part of her that didn't hurt. Much.

Because even breathing hurt at this point.

The woman looked at Drake and said something. He nodded and gently ran a hand over Victoria's head. She leaned into his touch, the feel of him immediately soothing despite the pain.

Until another slam of those damn knives raked through her. Releasing another howl, she jumped to all fours and turned on the table, snapping her jaw at the woman.

Surprise clear on her face, the female jumped back as Victoria collapsed on the soft surface. Her stomach cramped, her body bowing wildly as her human side took over with no warning, the shift from animal to human faster and more painful than she'd ever experienced.

"Victoria." Drake went to touch her but the female stilled him, placing a gentle hand on his forearm.

"Give her a moment to adjust," the woman murmured.

Adjust? Victoria wanted Drake to hold her close. Right now she needed all the comfort she could get. And she really didn't like the sight of that woman touching what was hers. She rolled onto her side, not caring that she was naked. "Get your fucking hand off him," she growled, her wolf in her voice.

To her surprise the woman grinned and faded into the background as Drake reached out and cupped her face. Unexpected tears streamed down her cheeks but she couldn't seem to stop them.

"Hold me." She didn't care that she sounded like she was begging. She felt as if her body had been through a blender and she was so damn confused. The only thing that could make it right was Drake.

Without pause, he scooped her up in his arms, slipping his arm under her legs and one under her back as she curled into him. His scent immediately soothed her. He murmured soothing sounds and she was sure she heard words like *baby*, *sweetheart* and *I love you*. Each word soothed the already fading pain as a sensation of lethargy took over, her limbs going almost numb as she curled tighter against him. She couldn't remember what had happened, but she wanted to tell Drake that she was okay. That everything was going to be okay. But she couldn't force her vocal cords to work as blessed sleep took over.

"Drake's female is going to be okay." Greer, their clan healer, stepped from the room where they'd taken Victoria.

Conall relaxed. The sounds of agony coming from Drake's female had made everyone waiting flinch each time she howled. Now that all was silent, it was as if everyone let out a collective breath.

"He wants to be alone with her," Greer continued.

No surprise there. If Conall had a female he'd want to take care of her and keep the rest of the fucking world out. Unfortunately everyone in the clan wanted to see Drake now. Of course it wasn't happening, but dragons were damn nosy and in a few hours there would be more visitors than just the half dozen waiting in the foyer.

"Thank you, Greer," he said. "Lennox, can you get rid of everyone? Tell them we'll contact everyone when Drake is ready." Which he knew wouldn't work completely, but at least it would clear out the guest house for the rest of the day. The sun had already risen, so half of the clan would be headed to the ski lodge for work. At least he wouldn't have to worry about everyone.

Lennox nodded, his dark gaze flicking over to Rhea where she stood leaning against a wall next to Gabriel. He looked at the female with clear interest. Wearing boots, cargo pants, and a fitted leather jacket over a snug black T-shirt, she looked sexy and fierce. So unlike Fia's serene, almost fragile beauty. But he liked the difference. Probably more than was wise. He didn't want anyone else noticing. At least Rhea didn't pay Lennox any attention.

"Now," he snapped out, earning a surprised glance from Lennox, who immediately jumped into action.

That humming sensation was back in Conall's chest as he nodded at Gabriel and Rhea. Damn it, what the hell was that? "I'll show you to your rooms. If they're not to your liking we'll find you something else."

To his surprise, Rhea snorted and pushed off the wall with Gabriel. "Just give us a warm bed and we'll be happy."

Conall paused, something dark inside him clawing at the surface, that humming growing more intense. "You'll be sharing a bed?" Why did that thought sting?

She blinked. "Hell no. I just meant Gabriel and I are easy to please. Give us warm, *separate*, beds."

"Could you have said no faster?" Gabriel muttered, his voice teasing.

Rhea's amber eyes glinted with mischief. "Sorry to hurt your ego, big strong Guardian."

Gabriel rolled his eyes and looked at Conall. "Who will be keeping guard of Drake and Victoria?"

"I will as soon as I show you to your rooms."

Satisfied with that, the Guardian nodded and the two followed Conall up the wide, open staircase to the second level. First he showed Gabriel to his room, then Rhea to hers. He'd chosen a room with minimal luxury, teak furniture. A king-sized platform bed was against one wall, the comforter soft plums and grays—and the fact that he was paying attention to the fucking colors and room style told him he needed to get the hell away from this female.

"This is beautiful, thanks." She was staring out the expansive wall of windows that overlooked the mountains, the snow-capped peaks glinting under the sun rising in the cloudless sky. The light outlined her silhouette, highlighting her trim curves. She was powerful, this female. Powerful and deadly.

He didn't know why, but on her he found that extraordinarily sexy.

"The blackout drapes are remote controlled."

Nodding, she turned back to face him. "Great. I'll probably snag a few hours of sleep then check on Drake. You sure you're good to guard him? I'm actually not that tired if you want company."

His first instinct was to say yes, but he ruthlessly shoved it down. If he spent more time with her, he would get to know her. And he did *not* want that. "No, but thank you for the offer. You and Gabriel are guests."

She snorted softly again in that way that made him smile. "We might be guests but Drake and Victoria are still our people."

An invisible vise squeezed around his chest at her words. His brother might have been in Hell but he'd clearly been well cared for since his escape. The knowledge was the only thing that eased the knife in Conall's chest. It was clear the female didn't care that Drake was a different species. Maybe it shouldn't surprise him, but it had been decades since he'd interacted with other shifters or vamps and in his experience other supernaturals only looked out for their own kind. "I appreciate all you've done for my brother."

She shrugged, as if it was no big deal. "Drake's cool. Plus he saved my Alpha's daughter."

Conall nodded, feeling strangely tongue-tied as he stood in the doorway watching the lithe, strong female linger by the window, watching him expectantly. That was when he realized he was staring too hard. He cleared his throat. "You have my and Keelin's cell numbers. Please text or call if you need anything." As he shut the door he cursed himself for speaking so formally to her.

He'd sounded like an idiot. He couldn't remember the last time he'd had any interest in the opposite sex. Even his few bed partners after Fia had left him had been more of a chore than anything else. He'd searched out females for relief, but had ended up feeling nothing during, and even less afterward. Okay, maybe not nothing. But he'd felt even more hollow.

Now he found himself wondering what Rhea looked like naked, how she would taste against his tongue as he brought her to orgasm. Would she be quiet or talk dirty? His cock hardened at the thought of her shouting his name as she came against his face and he cursed himself again. She would be leaving soon enough and he wasn't going to bed a female Drake was friends with.

Not when he had nothing to offer her long-term. And a female like Rhea deserved more than a male like him could give her. He might not have known her long, but she was funny, a little sarcastic, and had jumped right into the fray when they'd been attacked at the cabin. Yes, she was definitely a female who deserved more.

Besides, she didn't even seem interested. There had been no lingering looks or any indication she might want something physical with him. Which was just as well—even if it did sting his ego.

CHAPTER SIXTEEN

The warmth surrounding Victoria was all encompassing and without opening her eyes she knew Drake was holding her. His earthy scent surrounded her, permeating every inch of her. She loved his scent, wanted to bury her face against his chest and soak him in.

She tried to open her eyes but found she couldn't. Instead of freaking out, she sighed and listened to Drake murmuring sweet things to her. The words all ran together, but the meaning was clear enough.

She wasn't sure where they were or why she couldn't open her eyes though, which was frustrating. She wondered if this was how Drake had felt when he'd escaped Hell. He'd been so quiet and reserved the first month, barely saying two words to anyone but her or Vega.

He still didn't talk much, but in the beginning he'd been even more silent. Yeah, he had that strong and silent thing down to an art. A memory of the first time she'd taken him shopping at the mall sliced through her mind.

He'd been so fascinated by all the stores of their small mall. To him it had been huge, everything a little overwhelming. During that trip was the first time she'd realized she wanted to kiss him.

When they'd passed a jewelry store he'd seen a beautiful necklace and told her that one day he'd buy her something like that. As if she needed jewelry. His words had been so innocent and sweet. She hadn't understood then, but now she realized how much he must have struggled with not being in control of his life, not being able to purchase things without asking someone for funds, being dependent on others for everything.

Something she'd taken for granted because the pack took care of each other. She hated that he'd been dealing with that.

Why hadn't she realized until now? Her body finally listened to reason as her eyes snapped open and she looked up. She stared into Drake's intense silver gaze as he held her against his chest. They were in a big bed, with him sitting up against a tufted headboard—definitely not the bed at the cabin—and he was shirtless. She ran a hand over his hard chest, the skin to skin contact grounding her. Looking down she saw she was in someone else's pajamas. Pink and white striped cotton. Not her style but she'd go back to that later.

"You're awake." Relief punctuated those two words. He clicked on a bedside lamp, the soft light illuminating him and throwing shadows against his face.

"What happened?" She had a vague memory of being at the cabin and—crap, they'd been under attack. "Is Keelin okay? Are *you* okay?" she asked before he could respond to her first question.

He nodded, staring at her as if he never wanted to stop. "Everyone's fine, including Gabriel and Rhea, who'd followed us. Dragons from another clan attacked the cabin. While saving Keelin, you were hit with a poison dart. We brought you to my clan's land in Montana and their healer extracted the poison from you. You've been asleep for almost twenty-four hours." His voice was raspy, as if he'd been awake the whole time.

Her eyes widened as she slowly straightened in his arms, looking around the opulent, huge freaking room. It was as big as her Alpha's back at their compound. "Have you gotten any rest?" she asked, looking back at him. Reaching up with a shaky hand, she cupped his cheek, her palm scraping against the sexy stubble.

"I haven't left your side." He still watched her as if worried she'd disappear.

"I'm not going anywhere," she whispered, hoping her words eased the fear lurking in his silver gaze.

He was silent for a long moment, as if he was trying to find his voice. "I thought I'd lost you."

"But you didn't. Luckily I'm hard to kill too." Her words mirrored his earlier ones. But deep down she worried that she was an even bigger threat to him. What if they'd been mated and she'd been poisoned? Would he have been weakened? Almost died? She swallowed, fighting that fear.

To her relief he gave her a ghost of a smile. Not much but she'd take it. "I'm…" Her words were cut off by a loud rumble as her stomach growled.

He frowned and leaned over to the nightstand table, grabbing his phone. After making two calls, one for food and one to a female named Greer, he hung up. "Food will be here soon."

"Thank you. You can let me up." Because she was suddenly aware that nature was calling and she really wanted to brush her teeth.

He shook his head, the stubborn set of his jaw making her smile.

"Well, I need to take care of some business so..."

Confusion marred his expression for a moment before he nodded and released his grasp around her. She swung her legs off the bed and didn't protest when he helped her to her feet. Her legs were shaky, but she was okay to walk on her own. She couldn't believe she was in Montana and couldn't remember a thing about the flight. Or she assumed they'd flown. Questions started to bombard her but she ignored them for now. When they reached the bathroom, she put up a hand when it was clear he intended to come in with her. "I don't need any help in there, promise."

Drake's expression said he wanted to argue, but he just nodded and leaned against the wall next to the door. "I'll be right here."

After freshening up, including washing her face and brushing her teeth, she felt a hundred times better. The bathroom was nearly as big as the bedroom; all shiny black marble and gold trim everywhere. It was the kind of room that screamed money. The skylight above her let her know it was daytime. Maybe morning.

When she stepped back into the bedroom she found Drake talking to a stunning woman who had to be six feet tall. Her hair was a unique copper color that highlighted the woman's bright green eyes. Wearing skintight, white pants, a white, fuzzy sweater with sparkles of gold in the threading and white, furry boots, she looked like she was ready to hit the slopes and look damn good doing it. Must be Greer. Victoria fought the insane twinge of jealousy that punched through her at seeing Drake talking to the female. Jeez, they were just talking.

The woman smiled warmly at Victoria, smoothing a hand down her pants almost nervously. And that was when Victoria remembered she'd nearly bitten the woman.

"I, uh, think I might owe you an apology. Did I imagine trying to bite you earlier?" she asked as Drake moved to her side, hovering as if he was afraid she'd fall over. She really hoped that hadn't been real. Mostly she just remembered an excruciating agony, as if her body was splitting apart at the seams.

Laughing, the sound like music, the woman's smile widened. "You didn't imagine it but no apologies are necessary. You were in a lot of pain and I had to use my healing gift to draw out the poison. Unfortunately, drawing it out is very painful. Something about the way it morphs to our blood cells makes it difficult for me to withdraw it. But it's done and you look wonderful."

Victoria nearly snorted, but knew the woman was being kind. She'd just seen herself in the mirror and she looked as if she'd been run over by a truck. Twice. Nothing a shower and some food wouldn't cure though. "Thank you for what you did and I'm sorry for snapping at you about touching Drake." That memory was vivid in her mind too, making her flush in embarrassment at the angry way she'd growled at the woman.

Drake was silent next to her, but he wrapped a supportive arm around her shoulders as he kissed the top of her head.

The female just smiled. "Don't worry about it. No one would blame you for being protective of your mate. Once you've had time to rest I'd love to talk to you more. I've never met another healer before. We're a bit insulated from other supernaturals."

Victoria leaned into Drake, using him for support as a wave of exhaustion swept through her. "I'd really like that too." When her stomach rumbled the woman smiled and headed back for the door.

"I'll be back to check on you soon. I'm Greer, by the way."

Victoria nodded and before the door had shut, Drake was leading her over to the bed. "I'll bring the food to you." A soft order and one she wasn't inclined to argue with. As she leaned against the headboard, stretching out her legs, she watched as he rolled the silver cart over to the bed. When he lifted the dome-covered plate, she grinned to see a giant hamburger topped with carmelized onions, sautéed mushrooms and two thick slices of melted Swiss cheese. And French fries on the side. One of her favorite meals. "How'd they know what to make?"

"I told the chef earlier to be ready when you awoke." He still watched her nervously.

Before she reached for the tray she stood again and pulled him into a big hug, wrapping her arms tight around his waist. "I can see the fear on your face. I'm not going anywhere. Why don't you take a shower while I eat?" Because she could see he needed the rest.

"I'm fine," he murmured against the top of her head.

Leaning back she looked at him before standing on her toes. She brushed a kiss over his mouth, surprised when he didn't deepen it. But maybe she shouldn't be. It was clear he was worried about her and probably didn't want to hurt her. "Go. Shower. I'm going to devour this and then we'll talk." Then she wanted to take a shower too. And change out of these pajamas. *And* see Gabriel and Rhea. She needed to see with her own eyes that her packmates were okay too.

He paused. "You're positive?"

After a few more minutes of convincing him she'd be fine, she did just as she'd said and devoured the contents of the entire plate. For how she felt she probably could have put away another hamburger, but the food was making her tired again. She rolled the cart over to the door and slid back into the bed. The thing was huge, bigger than a king-size. Maybe California king. She wondered if dragons were naturally taller or bigger than other shifters. Keelin didn't seem to be, but Greer certainly was. And why the hell was she worried about their freaking height right now.

She had more important things to worry about. Like who had attacked them. Closing her eyes, she smiled to herself when she heard the shower shut off. Not long after, the bathroom door opened. Cracking open an eye, she saw steam billow out as Drake stepped from the bathroom wearing only a towel.

"Lose the towel and get in bed with me," she murmured. His eyes widened but she just grinned and rolled onto her side, putting her back to him. "I won't peek." Even though she wanted to. "I just want you to hold me."

The light clicked off but with the natural light streaming in from the bathroom's skylight, there was enough illumination in the bedroom. A moment later, the bed depressed as he got in behind her. When his big arm wrapped around her waist and pulled her close, she willingly curved into him, laying her arm over his. The soft hair of his arm tickled hers, grounding her, reminding her that she was safe here. His earthy scent surrounded her, his hard chest a solid presence against her back. "Tell me more about what happened," she murmured, sleep pulling at her again. Should she be this tired?

"We'll talk later. Rest." His voice was gentle even though his words came out like an order.

"Then tell me more about your time in Hell." The words came out of nowhere and when he stiffened behind her, she wondered if she'd crossed a line. But she had to know more. After realizing how hard it must have been for him to assimilate—to still do so—it was time to push him about opening up. Especially if they were going to take the next step as mates. Something she knew without a doubt she wanted.

"What do you want to know?" he finally asked.

"You never talk about it." Not that she blamed him. "I just . . . want to know you more. I want to know everything about you, Drake."

Drake struggled to answer her, his throat growing tight. He knew a lot of time had passed since her question and he could swear he sensed her disappointment that he wasn't answering. It was the only reason he forced his vocal cords to work—even if he didn't want to. "When I was relatively young, about two hundred, I think, I made a friend of sorts. Time is of no use in Hell so it's just an estimate." He could hear the bitterness in his voice, but couldn't hide it. Didn't want to. "He was a vampire and . . . charming, I think is the word you would use. He told me he'd been sent to Hell in the same manner as me, sacrificed. Up until that point I hadn't had much contact with others. I stayed in my dragon form as much as possible because it was safer."

He'd stayed in his dragon form as a defense, living two hundred years in loneliness to that point. Clearing his throat, he continued, the words torn from him almost against his will. But he wanted her to know more about him, just as he wanted to know everything about her. Even the bad parts. "The real torture was the silence and nothingness. Not the fire and brimstone that so many think it is—though there are parts of Hell just like that, worse than you can imagine—but the abject nothingness is…" He didn't know how to continue down that line of thought, wasn't even sure why he'd brought it up.

"The stench there is horrific. Like sulfur and rotten eggs, but so much worse. Sometimes I swear I can still smell it on me," he muttered, his grip around her tightening.

She squeezed the arm he had around her, in silent support, the simple action more soothing than she likely realized.

Now that Drake had started, he wasn't stopping. "But he showed me a section of Hell that wasn't as bad. And that term is relative to the place. We would go there and talk. Mainly he talked. I'd been so sheltered before I was sacrificed so I drank in the conversation. I don't know how long we were friends but I think it was a couple years. And I don't know if he'd always intended to betray me or not, but he eventually sold me out to a hoard of level eight demons."

She shifted against the sheets, her delectable body moving against him. "Level eight?"

He paused. "There are different levels, up to thirteen. I don't know what the correct translation would be, but it's the best way I can describe them."

"What happened?" The question came out as a hoarse whisper.

"Hell is a vast place, almost the same size as Earth, and when he was going to be tortured for some infraction against these demons, he told them about me and where to find me. They thought they could take me because of their sheer number." His voice was dark, deadly. "They were wrong. Once I finished with them I flew my so-called friend to their territory and dropped him off. I never saw him again. I never saw anyone for years after that. I carved out a territory and made it clear what would happen to anyone who crossed me. After obliterating those level eights, word spread and I was left alone for a while. My . . . fire, or any dragon fire in Hell becomes a permanent thing on the prey's body. Like phantom pain. Even though they're not burning anymore, the pain still lives with them. They're in constant agony because of how deeply I burned them."

And he wasn't sorry he'd done it. For all the horror they'd inflicted on others, they deserved everything they got from him. Part of him wanted to tell Victoria that he'd enjoyed hurting them, but he held the confession back for now. Later he'd tell her. Maybe. God, he was so unworthy of her, so dirty. She didn't need to know that side of him.

"I'm so sorry, Drake." Her soft voice angered him.

"I don't want your pity," he snarled. Never from her.

Turning in his arms, she slid her arm around him and clutched on to his back, holding him close. His muscles flexed under her fingertips as he leaned into her touch. "I don't pity you. Not at all. But I do love you and that means I get to care."

Shock slammed into him just as hard as it had the first time she'd said the words. Love. He loved her too, but it still stunned him that she felt the same. Instead of responding, he pulled her closer against him, needing her more than he needed air.

He slipped out of the guest house kitchen, the side door closing quietly behind him. It was as if he'd never been there. He used his gift of camouflage since the house was being protected fairly well. Everyone had slightly let down their guard now that Dragos and his female were in the Petronilla village. Because no one knew that one of their own had betrayed the male to rot in Hell. Or that he'd been the one to contact the Veles clan.

Why couldn't Dragos have just stayed where he was? His life would be so much simpler now. He'd already accepted that he'd never take over the Petronilla clan. It had taken over a thousand years, but he'd finally had to live with the truth. He would never be clan leader. Not with all his power gone.

That fucking witch who'd helped him sacrifice the stupid boy had betrayed him once he'd gained unstoppable power. She'd set up a failsafe spell if he ever tried to kill her after the deed they'd committed together. So he hadn't tried to kill her. He'd hired someone else to do it. Unfortunately the spell she'd woven included intent on his part. It hadn't mattered that he hadn't been the one to drive that dagger into her chest. It had been done on his orders.

After she was killed all his newfound power had been drained, all his work for naught, the sacrifice, everything he'd worked so hard for. To make it even worse she'd made sure he was marked so no other witches would work with him. Since her kind kept their grimoires and knowledge of the dark arts secret, every time he'd attempted to regain his power doing spells on his own, more had been siphoned off. He was still strong, but not the warrior he'd once been.

Glancing around the side of the house over the blanket of snow, he cursed that his footprints would be visible. But there was no hiding that. He might be able to camouflage himself, but that didn't extend to covering his tracks in the physical sense.

Leaving this way was a small risk. Soon a new snowfall would cover the tracks anyway. While he could have used the front door or even asked Keelin to escort him to the house, he hadn't wanted to seem over eager. Everyone had been told that Dragos and his female were resting and wouldn't be receiving visitors until tomorrow at least.

The shifter female had been poisoned by one of those Veles dragons. Unfortunately she hadn't died. Then maybe Dragos would have died too. He wasn't certain if the male had actually mated with her yet though. Without meeting her and scenting the two of them together he couldn't tell. And he wouldn't ask anyone.

No, he had to play this right and if anyone remembered him asking too many questions it could work against him later. He was very good at remaining unnoticed and he planned to keep it that way.

But the chef in the kitchen had been speaking to Greer—both unaware of his presence—as if the wolf shifter and Drake were mated so he had a plan to take them both out at the same time. Poison was simple and unlike those Veles dragons, he wouldn't fail. This time, Greer wouldn't be able to heal them. He'd target the shifter female with something much stronger than the Veles poison. Something that would affect her kind specifically. Liquid silver. If she died, Dragos would die too. Getting it shouldn't be too hard either.

Nice and neat, exactly the way he liked it. Unless of course they weren't mated yet, but that was a bridge he'd cross later if necessary.

Even if they weren't, her death would make Dragos suffer. Since all his family deserved any pain he gave them, the shifter's death would still accomplish inflicting agony. They should feel exactly how he'd felt when he'd lost everything, when those he loved most were taken from him. Feeling his rage heighten inside him, he shoved it back down. When he got too emotional, his dragon tried to take more control and he couldn't allow that to happen. Couldn't allow his animal to go feral.

Once he made it to the sidewalk, he kept his stride even and quiet as he hurried down the street. Only when he was far enough away from the guest house did he let his camouflage fall. Turning down a side street, he headed toward Main Street. He planned to pick up pastries from their local bakery so he had a reason to have been away from his own home when he returned.

Always cover your bases. Something he never failed to do.

CHAPTER SEVENTEEN

This is beyond stupid. Bran Devlin wouldn't even look at his brother as they cruised down the highway toward the Petronilla village. Instead he stared out the darkly tinted window of the SUV they'd rented—annoyed they didn't have a bullet resistant vehicle—scanning the snow-capped mountainous landscape. They were roughly twenty miles out when they shouldn't be here at all. *It makes us look weak.* As leader of the Devlin clan that was something he couldn't afford. Something his normally astute and deadly brother would understand. Bran might hate that he'd been forced into ruling the clan after his parents' deaths, but he took full responsibility for his people. Coming here like this wasn't a smart tactical move.

Fia wants to see Dragos. They were childhood friends. A sigh broke into Bran's thoughts, his brother Gavin not bothering to hide his frustration at having this conversation again.

We should have waited a week or so to arrive. Not shown up the same fucking evening the male's mate had come out of a Veles dragon poisoning. How could his brother or even Fia think this was intelligent reasoning? It was poor form. But his brother could never deny his

213

mate Fia anything. The female was his brother's only weakness. But normally his brother could rein in Fia's sometimes frivolous requests.

You didn't have to come. A bite to Gavin's words.

Turning to look at him, his jaw tight, Bran glared at his brother through his one good eye. *And let you walk into this viper's nest alone?* That was perhaps harsh considering the Devlin and Petronilla clans were peaceful with each other. But his brother had basically stolen Fia from Conall, the current leader of the clan. It didn't matter that it was years ago; males tended not to forget those things. Bran's attendance for this gathering had nothing to do with his clan leader duties and everything to do with being a big brother protecting his younger sibling.

Is that what this is really about? Gavin asked.

What else would it be about? Your fucking mate says jump and you ask how high. So here I am because of that female. Harsh, untrue words. Ones that would earn him a fist across the face. And one he wouldn't block.

Gavin was silent for a long moment, his green eyes flickering from dragon to human as he watched. *You have partial eyesight. You have no reason to be ashamed or to avoid interaction with others.* Soft, unexpected words. *Even if you seem to hate our kind.*

Jaw tight, Bran turned to look out the window again. He wished his brother had just smashed his nose in rather than say all that. Gavin was ten years younger than him and usually the more passive of the two. Unless any ill mention was made of Fia. So Bran had been expecting, no *craving,* the physical violence over the words he'd just thrown at his brother. Not . . . softness.

I don't hate our kind. And he wasn't ashamed, he just didn't like the pitying stares, especially from females. As a whole, the dragon species were incredibly beautiful. Except for him. He was a lone fucking freak among his people who'd been born with a birth defect. Not that it had ever slowed him down. He missed his former job with a secret black ops group the US government ran in tandem with other countries to keep the world from finding out about supernaturals. Because humans simply could not handle that shit. They could barely handle the fact that their neighbors might believe in a different god or be attracted to someone of the same sex. If they found out they weren't at the top of the food chain? Fucking war.

"Are you two talking telepathically?" Fia asked from the front passenger seat, her voice holding a lyrical quality. "It suddenly got tense in here."

Bran didn't respond as Gavin leaned forward and murmured quietly to his mate. He ignored the sweet way they spoke to each other, wishing his brother could communicate telepathically with his mate so he wouldn't have to listen to them. But it was a Devlin gift, passed on only to those with Devlin blood. In the same way the Petronilla clan could understand any language, the Devlin's were able to communicate in this way. It definitely had its uses.

"You're going to love Keelin. I haven't seen her in hundreds of years but every time we talk on the phone it's like no time has passed. And I can't believe Drake is back...." Fia's voice was excited, but Bran tuned her out as she continued chattering on.

He wasn't sure if she was talking to her mate, him, or the other warriors in the SUV, but he didn't respond. He didn't care about meeting some female or her back-from-Hell brother. He just wanted to get this shit over with and return home. He had enough business to deal with, without this impromptu trip.

Especially when he knew his brother was holding something back from him. He'd sensed it before they'd left their territory, but Gavin had feigned ignorance when Bran pushed him. He just hoped it was personal bullshit and had nothing to do with the Petronilla clan.

Drake walked down the sidewalk, ignoring the curious stares from the few people out jogging or walking pets. Dragons who had dogs? That was certainly an oddity. Victoria would probably find it amusing. When a female with a fluffy, white dog that looked rabid stopped on the opposite sidewalk as if she might cross the street, he increased his stride and didn't make eye contact. He didn't want to get caught up in conversation with anyone now. Or ever really.

He didn't know these shifters. Everyone was an enemy until he knew what had really happened to him.

He probably should have just driven or had someone drive him but he'd wanted to stretch his legs. And he didn't want to fly until he had miles and miles of open space and freedom. He and Victoria had spent the whole day in bed, with her sleeping most of the time and him just holding her. He wanted to do more than hold her, but she'd been so exhausted and he'd known it wasn't the right time.

She'd woken up about an hour ago and was now visiting with Rhea and Gabriel. Since the Guardian had sworn he wouldn't leave Victoria alone, Drake felt free to leave her for a few minutes.

This was a conversation he needed to have in person.

When he reached his brother's home, he found the high, iron gate around the property unlocked. Pushing it inward, he let it fall back into place before striding down the long, stone walkway to the two-story home that was much larger than the normal sized homes he'd seen in Biloxi. Not quite a mansion but it was very large, especially for just one person. He'd noticed that about all the houses in the village.

The front door wasn't locked when he tested it, but he rang the bell anyway even though Conall had said he could come in whenever he wanted. Moments later a tall female with inky black hair secured in a bun and an apron tied around her waist opened the door, her expression annoyed until her gaze landed on Drake. She smiled warmly, her grayish-green eyes sparkling. "Dragos, you never have to ring the bell."

He cleared his throat. "Drake is fine. Is my brother here?" He didn't recognize the female and wondered if she knew him. He hated not recognizing people when he was certain he should. It made it that much more difficult to figure out who he could trust. The female seemed startled by his abruptness and he inwardly cursed his rudeness. Fucking social niceties. "Ah, he said I could come by whenever I wanted."

Motioning for him to come inside, she stepped back. "Of course you can. I . . . Conall said you didn't remember much but I guess I hoped he was exaggerating. Do you truly not remember me?"

Inexplicable guilt threaded through his veins and he wasn't sure why. "No."

Her eyes welled with tears, but she quickly blinked them away. Taking him by surprise, she grasped his hands in hers, her grip strong. "That's okay. We'll get to know one another again. I'm your Aunt Alma. Your mother's sister. I was there for your birth. I was the third person to hold you, after your parents. You were a giant, wrinkly thing."

Aunt? She looked to be about thirty-five, maybe forty. Something deep inside him warmed at her touch and he found himself half-smiling. A faint memory tickled the recesses of his brain. "Did I steal a roast or some form of meat from your house, or maybe barn, once? You scolded me, then made me cookies." The first part of the memory was fuzzy but he remembered the cookies. That didn't seem like an effective method of punishment.

A sharp peal of laughter escaped as she nodded. "It wasn't a roast, you devoured an entire cow from one of my pastures. You were seven and your dragon side was growing and you plucked a cow right out of our pasture. I never told your mom either. Not that I think Arya would have punished you either."

"And you made me cookies."

Her eyes crinkled at the corners, the delight on her face bright. "I did."

That warmth spread through his chest again. Feeling compelled, he stepped forward as if to hug her, but then worried that might be strange. She took away his choice then, covering the short distance between them and pulled him into a tight embrace.

Her strong arms wrapped around him and it was so familiar, so . . . welcoming, he wasn't sure what to do with the emotions welling up inside him. So he patted her back awkwardly. "Hopefully my memories will return soon," he murmured.

She squeezed him hard once before stepping back, her eyes wet again. "They will. And I hear you've brought a mate with you."

He nodded, unsure what she thought of his soon-to-be mate being a wolf shifter. Not that he cared what anyone thought, but he wanted to be prepared for his clan's reactions. It would help in determining his future interaction with them. Because if Victoria felt unwelcome, he'd leave.

"Good. I can't wait to meet her. And I can't wait until you two start making babies."

Drake blinked at her words, not sure if there was a response to that. The thought of having children with Victoria pleased and terrified him. Kids right now? He didn't know enough about the world yet to contemplate being able to care for a helpless, tiny being. As he tried to think of something to say, the front door opened behind him.

Instinctively he tensed, turning toward the door. Two familiar scents teased his nostrils, but he couldn't place them. When two males stepped inside, both their eyes widened in surprise.

"Boys, so glad you're here." Alma moved past Drake and motioned for the other two males to enter.

They did so almost hesitantly. "We didn't realize you'd be here, Dragos," the one with dark hair said.

Cody. Drake remembered the male's name with startling clarity, though he wasn't sure of his relationship with either male or how they were related. For some reason, the sight of Cody raked against Drake's senses. Or perhaps his dragon simply felt annoyed. Drake kept his expression neutral so his emotions wouldn't show.

He tried to remain civil, keep his voice polite and remember social niceties. Even if he didn't trust anyone.

He didn't bother attempting to smile, knowing it would come off more as a baring of teeth. His dragon wasn't feeling nice right now being confronted by two relative strangers. "I didn't know I would be here either, Cody."

The male's dark eyebrows raised. "You remember." He glanced at Alma before looking back at Drake. "We were told you had lost your memory."

Drake lifted one shoulder casually, not ready to reveal more about himself than necessary. "I remember your name." He looked next at the other male, a handsome male with blond hair close to Drake's height. A mix of emotions filled him as he made eye contact with him. Nevin. "And you are Nevin?" He phrased it as a question as he spoke even though he was certain he was right.

The other male smiled and nodded. "Yes, we're cousins. Both of us, actually." He motioned to Cody.

When Drake focused on the other male again that wary feeling was back.

"Drake, you and Cody got into trouble as children and Nevin often got you out of it," Alma said, the joy on her face evident in her words.

If his aunt liked the male perhaps he wasn't all bad. Another memory resurfaced with vivid intensity, searing his brain.

Drake swooped down at a dangerous angle, heading straight for the sharp plane of the cliff wall. Adrenaline surged through him, the rush of wind over his body exhilarating as he grew closer, closer ... At the last second he turned up sharply, his underbelly grazing the rocky incline as he shot up to the sky.

When he breached the top of the cliff, green grass and thick trees spanned out for miles and miles, as far as he could see. He couldn't even see his clan's castle from here. There weren't many humans this far north which was why they lived here.

As he started to dive back downward, a blast of heat licked underneath him as his cousin Cody flew under him.

Drake banked left to avoid getting burned by the flames. He was young and still developing his natural protection. As he flew in the opposite direction another dragon appeared from up over the cliff.

Nevin. His other cousin. If Drake had been in human form he would have smiled.

Nevin's giant wingspan glittered under the bright sun as he flew high over Cody. Turning his giant body at what seemed to be an impossible angle, he angled himself over Cody and swatted him with his wing, sending Cody into a spiral toward the earth.

Now Drake wanted to laugh. Cody had been mean to him all day and Drake didn't understand why. His father said he'd talk to him about it later, but Drake didn't think there could be a very good reason other than Cody was a jerk.

They were family. They weren't supposed to try to hurt each other.

Drake blinked as the memory dissolved as quickly as it had arrived. He narrowed his gaze at Nevin. "You were protective of me as a child."

The male gave a small smile. "Yes."

And you were a dick, he thought as he looked at Cody, but didn't say the words aloud.

"We just stopped by to speak to Conall, but it can wait if he's busy," Nevin said.

Alma nodded, speaking before Drake could. "He is busy but I'm sure he'll be available later." She gave the two males brief kisses before practically shooing them out. Shutting the door, she turned back to Drake and smiled softly. "I know you didn't come here to get bombarded and there will be plenty of time to meet the rest of the clan later. In the meantime you can tell me about this mate of yours and we can revisit the topic of babies."

"Aunt Alma." Conall's slightly chastising voice made them both turn toward the stairs. Drake had heard faint footsteps earlier and figured he'd be down soon. His brother's expression was softer than Drake had ever seen it as he approached them.

His aunt set her hands on her hips as she turned toward Conall. "Don't Aunt Alma me. You and Keelin are taking your sweet time settling down, though at least Keelin has an excuse, being forced into Protective Hibernation for so long. One of you needs to add more children to the clan."

Anger slid through him at the thought of his sister being forced to do anything and he wanted an explanation. "Forced?" The question came out louder, harsher than Drake had intended.

His aunt's lips pressed together and Conall's expression tightened as he nodded. "More or less by our mother. It's a long story and one I'll tell you another time."

"I'll be in the kitchen if you need me." The tall female hurried away before Conall or Drake could respond.

"She lives with you?" Drake asked when she was gone.

Conall shook his head. "No, she just likes to drop by unannounced and cook for me."

"Is that normal behavior?" Drake was still trying to figure out what counted as normal in this new world and that didn't seem typical.

Conall snorted. "It is for her. She'll do it for you too . . . That is, if you decide to stay." He seemed suddenly uncomfortable and Drake wasn't certain why. His expression wasn't clear enough for Drake to read his facial cues. "Is everything all right with Victoria?"

Drake nodded. "Yes. I wanted to speak with you in private."

Conall locked his front door then tilted his head toward a room off to the left of the foyer. "If the door's locked no one will disturb us."

Drake followed his brother into a room with slim but high windows reaching the ceiling. Maybe eighteen feet. "Are these homes built differently?"

Conall nodded and sat on an uncomfortable-looking tufted settee. At least that's what Victoria had told him the thing was called. There was more than one of them at the mansion in Biloxi too.

Drake sat across from him on a high-backed uncomfortable chair in a rich, plum color.

"Sorry about the furniture," Conall muttered, as if he'd read his mind. "I let Keelin decorate when she came out of her Hibernation and this shit is uncomfortable."

His brother's words immediately eased the tension in Drake's shoulders. It was still surreal to have siblings and the deepest part of him wanted a relationship with them. Feelings and sensations more than actual memories were trickling in about his siblings. Conall and Keelin had looked up to him. He knew that much.

"Was Keelin truly forced into Protective Hibernation?" The sharpest sense of protectiveness swept through him. He might not ever want the responsibility of clan leader, but no one was going to make his sister do something she didn't want to.

"Not forced so much as guilted into it. When our parents decided to go into Hibernation, our mother convinced Keelin to do it also. After she lost you, she was terrified of losing another child and she used that against Keelin. Not in a malicious way. Our mother is . . . strong willed. And unfortunately Keelin bent. I tried to convince her to remain with me and our clan, but in the end it was her decision to make."

Too many emotions started to pummel Drake. He hated that his sister had felt the need to go into a deep sleep out of guilt and that his parents had suffered so much. "Were our parents harder on you after I disappeared?" When Victoria had been sleeping today, safe in his arms, Drake had had far too much time with his thoughts.

Conall watched him for a long moment, as if weighing his words. "More protective."

The two word answer made Drake wonder if his brother didn't want to discuss his—their—parents. So he decided to change the subject and talk about the original reason he'd come. "I'm here for an awkward reason," he blurted, immediately cringing at his words.

Conall didn't seem fazed though. "Is this about mating?"

"No." He might not have ever been with a woman but he had no questions about what to do. Even though he'd seen only violent couplings or orgies in Hell, he read enough since his escape and trusted his instincts where that was concerned. He would bring Victoria so much pleasure she'd never want to leave him.

"Thank god," Conall muttered, his lips curving up a fraction. "What's going on then?"

"I don't have any occupational experience." In other words, no fucking job skills. Something he wanted to rectify soon.

"Oh." Conall blinked, as if Drake had truly surprised him. "I've already set up a bank account in your name. There's five hundred thousand in it to start, but anything you want, is yours. Everyone in the clan has their own jobs and are free to pick any profession they want to pursue. The majority of the clan currently works in hospitality because of the ski lodge, but in a couple decades we'll likely move on and start over somewhere else. We'll keep the land though and come back to it eventually. And we all have separate accounts, but we also have a joint account so if anyone needs more than they currently have for whatever reason, it's theirs."

"I don't want handouts." The very thought raked against every part of Drake's being.

"This is *not* a handout. You were in Hell for how fucking long? This is your clan, your family. Anything you need will be taken care of. You will have any education you want. *If* you want. You'll have any sort of training you want for any field. Or if you want to sit around and do absolutely nothing for the next decade, no one will judge you."

Except he would judge himself. He also realized that he'd insulted his brother when Conall had been nothing but generous. "Thank you for everything. I didn't want you to think I was trying to just take from you."

Conall's lips pulled into a thin line. "It's not taking. We're *family*."

The concept was still foreign, but he nodded. "Okay. Thank you." He would still get an education and training in . . . something, but for now, he could live with the situation. Five hundred thousand seemed excessive, but he wasn't sure and didn't want to ask and risk insulting his brother again. "If I would like to purchase something for Victoria today, how would I do that?"

Standing, Conall pointed upward. "Come on up to my office. I've got credit cards and other paperwork I'd planned to wait on, but I'll give everything to you now. If you have something specific in mind for Victoria, I can help you now. We have a lot of shops in town or there's always the Internet."

Drake nodded. He hadn't purchased much since he'd escaped Hell because he'd been too ashamed to ask Finn for funds, even though the Alpha had freely offered them. But it didn't feel shameful to accept help from his brother. It felt more like he was accepting a gift from someone who truly loved him. Not from someone who felt as if they owed him.

As they headed up the stairs, an unbidden richly drawn image seared into his mind. Like a snapshot. He paused at the top of the stairs and his brother did too.

"What's wrong?" Conall asked, his body tensing in alert for danger.

"When we were children, did you and Keelin used to sneak into my room late at night?" The scene was too vivid in his mind for it to be imagined.

Conall blinked, his jaw tightening before he answered. "Yes. You used to tell us stories when we couldn't sleep. Keelin was too young to understand much but she wanted to join in. Our parents knew because more often than not, they carried us back to our own beds in the morning, but..." He swallowed hard and Drake's own chest grew tight. "When we lost you it was like losing a limb."

His brother's words punched through him like a battering ram. As his brother started to look away, Drake gave into his instinct and pulled Conall into a hug, wrapping his arms around him and not caring if his brother rejected him.

Conall didn't though. "I've missed you so much," he rasped out, his voice strangled.

Drake had too. Even if he hadn't remembered much until now, he'd missed his family on the most fundamental level.

CHAPTER EIGHTEEN

Drake absently patted his pants pocket as he stepped inside the front door of the guest house, making sure the gift he'd bought for Victoria was still there. He'd only planned to buy flowers for her because they made her smile, but he'd seen something else and had decided to get it also.

When he stepped inside he found Keelin sitting on the bottom stair, looking at her cell phone. She smiled when she saw him, standing and shoving her phone into her jacket pocket. "I was hoping you'd arrive soon."

"I was shopping." Her eyebrows rose, so he continued. "With Conall."

Keelin snorted, the sound seeming out of character for his petite sister. *Sister.* He still hadn't gotten used to the word. "I wish I'd been there to see that."

"I wish you'd been with us too." The words were out before he realized he'd meant to say them.

She blinked in surprise, all humor leaving her face. "Really?"

He nodded. "I was rude the first time we met and I wish I could go back and change that first meeting. I hope we can get to know one another better." They'd been so young when he'd been taken and sacrificed. Obviously there was nothing they could have done and it was clear they hadn't known or they would have attempted to find him. That knowledge soothed the edges of the resentment burning inside him that whoever had betrayed him was still out there.

She beamed at him, her smile blinding as she threw herself at him, wrapping him in an unexpected hug. Her head came to the middle of his chest as she squeezed him tight. "You don't know how much I needed to hear that. I can't wait to get to know you better too." Taking a step back, she still smiled at him. "This new world has been tricky to navigate since I came out of Hibernation so I can imagine it's worse for you."

"No one will ever force you into Hibernation again." Not even their parents. He knew what it was to have his will taken away from him and he'd never allow it to happen to anyone he cared about.

Her smile brightened again as she said, "Thank you."

In that moment a burst of anger erupted inside him at whoever had stolen so many years from him. So many years he'd lost with his family. He pushed the feelings back down, not wanting them to intrude on his time with his sister.

Keelin's cell phone buzzed and after she glanced at it, she looked up at him. "Victoria is out with Gabriel and Rhea and they want me to bring you now."

"Out? Where?" He hadn't thought she'd leave the house, which was why he'd gone. He didn't care that his thoughts were irrational. Victoria was capable of defending herself and was with two trained warriors. On his clan's land. Still, his inner dragon clawed at him with fierce determination to get to her.

"Not far," Keelin said, intentionally vague, he was certain. "Why don't you get a coat and we'll meet them?"

"I'm fine." Cargo pants and a long-sleeved black T-shirt were good enough. He wasn't wasting the time to grab a jacket. He had a higher body temperature, the same as all dragons he'd assumed. But he noticed Keelin was wearing a thick jacket with fur trim over black ski pants. "Does the cold affect you the same as humans?"

She paused for a moment, then shook her head. "No. We tend to dress similar to humans so we don't draw unnecessary attention to ourselves. Besides, I look great in this jacket."

Something warm inside him unfurled at the light note in her voice. The Stavros pack had welcomed him and been kind to him, but he hadn't felt accepted in the same way he was starting to with his siblings. "How far is Victoria?" Because a raw energy had started to hum through him at the thought of being separated from her any longer.

"Not far. Come on."

She didn't have to tell him twice. The possessive need to get to Victoria was more than just a simmer beneath the surface now. His shifter side was demanding he make his claim.

Victoria waved at Drake and Keelin as they made their way toward her up the big snow-covered hill. Rhea and Gabriel stood quietly nearby. After being cooped up in that guest house all day, well two days really, she and her wolf had been ready to get out and run. Later tonight she'd run in wolf form but for now, being outside inhaling the crisp winter air, was therapeutic. Twilight had already fallen and the sky was slowly lighting up with a brilliant blanket of stars.

And she'd decided that her male needed some fun in his life. Especially after what had happened in Tennessee. Keelin had told Victoria that Drake hadn't slept the entire time she'd been asleep after the poison had been extracted from her body. And she was fairly certain he hadn't slept today when she'd dozed again either. She was going to make sure he got some sleep tonight, but until then, she was going to make sure he relaxed. He deserved it.

His expression grim, he trudged up the snowy embankment looking as if he was going to a funeral. When he and Keelin reached the top, his frown deepened.

"Why are you outside?" he barked.

Everyone froze for a second, Rhea and Gabriel looking away before giving them space as if they didn't want to be part of this. Victoria poked Drake in the chest. "Well it's good to see you too."

His face flushed, but the darkness in his gaze remained. "Shouldn't you be in bed." Not a question.

Rolling her eyes, she grabbed his T-shirt and tugged him down to her. Luckily he didn't withdraw, even if he still looked like the grim reaper. She brushed her lips over his, needing to taste him, to reassure herself of his presence, even if the kiss was relatively chaste. He let out a soft groan, his big body melting against hers as he pulled her close.

"Get a fucking room," Gabriel muttered.

Oh, they were going to very soon. Letting her boots fall flat against the crunchy snow, she reluctantly withdrew from Drake, though she didn't move out of the protective cage of his body. Not that he seemed inclined to let her go. "Did everything go okay with your brother?" He hadn't told her what he planned to talk to Conall about and he'd seemed unsure of himself.

Not so now. Drake nodded. "Yes. Are you sure—"

"Don't mother me," she said softly, for his ears only. She might have almost died, but she was still here and she didn't like being smothered. Something he knew. And especially not from him. She got enough of that craziness from her pack and she loved that Drake treated her like an equal.

He opened his mouth once as if to argue, but nodded. "Okay. I bought you a present today."

Excitement jumped inside her. "What is it?"

A half-grin played across his sensuous lips. She wanted to lean up and lick him. "I'll give it to you later. First tell me why we're out here."

"Keelin said when you were young you loved playing in the snow and even though they didn't have toboggans back then, you guys made makeshift sleds. I thought you might like to get out and relax." She nodded at a row of five plastic, sleek looking sleds big enough for two people. Gabriel, Rhea and Keelin were all choosing theirs about ten yards away.

The top of the hill was lined with trees and now Drake noticed there was a small, wooden shed in between two of them. Lennox, one of the warriors, come out carrying a blue and black toboggan where they must be stored. Drake had been so focused on getting to Victoria he hadn't been paying attention to anything else, including his surroundings.

Dangerous, the predator inside warned. He'd stayed alive a long time because of his predator instinct. He wouldn't let himself be distracted like that again. He *couldn't.*

Being on guard around Victoria was a priority. His throat was tight as he looked back down at his mate, his sweet healer. "Thank you." Because she was right. The thought of going sledding with her, of doing something normal like this, filled him with a sensation that was so foreign he wasn't sure he remembered the word for it.

It felt a lot like pure, unadulterated happiness.

Memories of playing with a small, blonde haired little girl, obviously Keelin, and a boy who looked like Drake, obviously Conall, hummed through him. Sometimes the girl would shift to her dragon form. She'd been so small as a dragon, her form adorable. But there was also a memory of playing in the snow with a redheaded boy. It had to be real.

Victoria smiled and softly kissed him again, the feel of her lips making the memory dissipate. His entire body tightened, her crisp scent drawing him in, teasing him. When she pulled back he stopped a groan from escaping. "I want to give you your present now."

Her green eyes lit up. "Are you sure it's a publicly appropriate gift?"

He blinked, unsure what she meant for all of two seconds before her meaning set in. The thought of laying her out on his big bed, having her naked beneath him as he claimed her was a potent image in his mind. One he forced himself to shelve. For now.

He reached in to his pocket and pulled out a small rectangular-shaped, red box. It wasn't overly expensive, but when he'd seen it at the jeweler's store in the village he'd known it was meant for her. The owner had told him that a human artist from the nearby town made custom pieces and sold them through jewelers in the area. Apparently this piece had been delivered two days ago and according to the owner wouldn't have lasted long in his store. Drake believed him.

Practically jumping up and down, Victoria snagged it from his hands. When she opened it up, she went still. For a moment she stopped breathing and he worried he'd chosen wrong.

"It's platinum," he blurted. Maybe she thought it was silver.

"It's beautiful," she whispered, pulling out the necklace by the delicate chain. Two platinum wings with fine green emeralds placed along the feathers glinted under the rising moonlight and stars. And they weren't angel wings, the style much more similar to dragon wings. Which made him wonder at the human designer who'd made them.

When Victoria's gaze met his, a sheen of wetness greeted him, making his throat tighten until she threw her arms around his neck and buried her face against it. "Thank you. It's perfect."

"You're perfect," he murmured.

Giving him a watery laugh, she turned around. "I'm glad you think so. Will you put this on me?"

The delicate chain and clasp was awkward in his hands, but he managed to get it on.

Her face was lit with raw joy as she tucked it under her green sweater and said, "So nothing happens to it while we're sledding." Then she grabbed his hand and tugged him toward where the others were talking and laughing.

His gift was another symbol for how badly he wanted to claim her. The desire to mark her was a living, growing thing in him and one he wasn't sure he could control any longer.

Conall waited at the foot of the hill for Drake and Victoria to slide down on their toboggans. When he'd received a text from his aunt that Drake was out sledding he hadn't believed it. Mainly because he hadn't thought his brother would let Victoria outside.

Not that Victoria seemed like the type of female to let any male walk all over her. Which was good. Dragons were notoriously overprotective and a strong female mate was a necessity. Even if they hadn't technically mated yet, it was coming soon. Drake's scent was all over her and vice versa, but mated shifters put off a distinctive scent, letting other supernaturals know they were taken.

"Are you joining us?" Victoria asked as they reached the bottom of the hill. Drake put his feet out to slow them down, his arms wrapped protectively around the wolf shifter even when they were doing something as simple as sledding.

"No, but I need to speak to Drake about a visitor he has." Conall's gaze flicked over to Rhea and Gabriel racing each other down the slope, the fierce female grabbing the male's rein to disrupt his balance and slow him down so she could win. He started to smile then caught himself as he focused on Victoria and Drake.

He didn't need to think about the sexy female in any capacity. A small part of him wished there had been a clear sexual relationship between Rhea and Gabriel. It would have put her directly in the off limits category. But his inner dragon clawed at that thought, not wanting anyone to touch the strong female. No one but him.

"Victoria can hear anything you have to say."

Conall nodded and motioned back toward the bottom of the hill which led to the road where his SUV waited. As they reached the curb, far enough away from everyone that they wouldn't overhear, he shoved his hands in his pockets and leaned against the passenger side. "A female from another clan is here to see you." His gaze snapped to Victoria when she started growling low in her throat.

She blinked and flushed red, as if realizing what she was doing. "Sorry, I don't know what's wrong with me."

Drake just looked smug, pulling her close. "Growl all you want. The sound is . . . appealing."

She flushed even darker, then nudged Drake before focusing on Conall. "Please continue. No more growling, I promise."

"I should have started with, a childhood *friend* is here to see you," he said to his brother. "One of our clan members mated a member of the Devlin clan's royalty and when she heard you were back, insisted on coming right away. They weren't supposed to be here for another two days, but came early. I'd planned to speak to you about it tomorrow." There, he sounded almost normal talking about his former betrothed, even if her early arrival annoyed him.

"Why are you talking strange?" Drake asked.

And Victoria was frowning at him too. "Do you not like this female?" she asked softly, all caring and concern that made him want to squirm under her intense gaze.

"Fia is a lovely female."

Victoria snorted. "Come on. What's wrong?"

How did they see right through him? "She is my former betrothed."

"You were *engaged* to this female?" Victoria asked while Drake simply watched him with an unreadable expression.

Conall nodded.

"Oh." Victoria just bit her bottom lip then looked at Drake, as if waiting for him to say something.

His brother frowned. "We were all friends?"

Conall nodded. The three of them had been close, learning to fly and cause mischief together. All the clan's children had been close.

Drake grunted. "I don't remember her and I don't care to meet some female who hurt my brother."

It took a lot to surprise Conall and in that moment, something inside his chest cracked. He'd missed Drake more than he'd allowed himself to admit. His brother was the one who'd taught him how to sled, how to fly figure eights and how to sneak treats from Aunt Alma's kitchen without getting caught. When he'd disappeared, or died as they'd all assumed, it had ripped out a chunk of Conall's heart. He'd tried to hide his mourning so as not to upset his mother even more, but he'd never gotten over his brother's disappearance. "It's not like that."

"Hmm," Victoria murmured, as if she didn't believe him.

"It's *not.*" Why did she make him feel like a child explaining himself? "Things ended but she's still a kind female." That was what had made things so hard. "We were promised to each other since we were young. After you . . . disappeared, our parents made an alliance in an effort to keep the clan strong. As we grew older, I developed feelings for her. She did not return them. Things ended and our families are still cordial. It is not an epic story."

Drake was quiet so long Conall wondered if he'd ever speak. Finally his brother shook his head, as if he'd made a decision. "I'm enjoying this time with my mate. Tomorrow I'll make a decision whether to see her."

"Drake—"

His brother's expression was set. "We will sit down and discuss everything about her current clan. Before any outsiders meet my mate, I will know *everything* about them."

Conall held back a smile and nodded. That sounded like the brother he'd known as a child. The male wanted to look at every angle of any situation. It was a smart, tactical move as well, and showed natural leadership.

Something he appreciated. Especially if Drake decided to take over ruling the clan. "I will meet them at the gate and tell them."

"I'll go with you," Rhea said, appearing as if from nowhere, the stealth of the female beyond impressive. No one ever surprised him.

Her subtle vanilla and jasmine scent teased him. Not that he should be noticing her scent at all. But when she was around, he lost focus, everything else fading into the background. "That's not necessary."

"If another clan of dragons wants to be in Victoria and Drake's presence, I'm meeting them." There was no room for discussion in her firm voice.

Which was, to quote the younger generation, fucking hot. That damn humming sensation in his chest was back as he looked into her amber eyes. Instead of responding, he simply nodded at her and headed to the driver's side of the SUV. She climbed into the passenger side.

When he pulled away from the curb, he asked, "How much did you overhear?"

"All of it. So you were betrothed, huh?"

He found it interesting that she used the same word, not engaged, like Victoria had. "Yes. How old are you?"

She laughed, the throaty sound rolling over him, wrapping him up in her innate earthiness. "That's a jump in conversation."

"You used the term betrothed." Which told him she was from a different generation.

"Oh, right. I'm almost a hundred and fifty. And . . . I was betrothed a long time ago too. I imagine it's hard to meet up with an ex."

He frowned at the thought of her betrothed to someone else. "What happened?" Because he couldn't imagine any male leaving this vibrant, strong female. She would have been the one who'd left, he had no doubt.

"He died." There was an extreme amount of buried agony in those two words, even if her tone was flat.

Shit. "I'm sorry." Ineffectual words, but what else was there to say?

She just nodded and they fell into a comfortable silence as he drove through their quiet village to the main entrance gate. He hadn't thought he'd want anyone to accompany him to see Fia for the first time in hundreds of years, but he was glad to have Rhea beside him.

Having this female with him soothed something inside him he didn't understand. Even if it was as if Rhea was encased in ice. Her facial expressions, even her scent, was damn hard to read. And didn't that make him want to get to know her even more. Thoughts of her writhing beneath him, or riding him, as they both found release vividly played in his mind. Something in his consciousness told him there would be a lot more than sex between them.

He buried the thought deep.

CHAPTER NINETEEN

Bran stood in front of the SUV, leaning casually against the vehicle as Conall Petronilla and an unknown female with blades strapped across her chest exited the main gate. He was certain the female had left her jacket unzipped intentionally. After a quick inhale of scents, he realized she was a wolf shifter. Interesting. Back in black ops he'd worked with his fair share of all species, and wolves were fucking brutal. They tended to kill and ask questions later.

Out of respect for the other clan leader, Bran pushed up from the vehicle and nodded at Conall, who was a similar height to him. He closed the distance between them. "Thank you for meeting me here. I know we're early and I apologize."

Conall's stony expression never changed. It wasn't hostile, but it wasn't warm and friendly either. "Entrance is denied tonight. Drake's mate is still resting and his full priority is her."

"Understood. We'll find lodging and wait for you to contact us. Again, I apologize for the intrusion." He wasn't going to do the 'I told you so' thing to his brother but hell, how had Gavin and Fia not seen this coming.

"I've already contacted the ski lodge and they have a cabin reserved for you. I didn't know how large your party was so if you need more lodging, let the concierge know and they'll accommodate you."

It took a lot to surprise Bran, but the show of respect—when his clan didn't deserve it for their rude behavior of showing up so damn early—was impressive. "Thank you."

"Wow, dragons are so civil." The female spoke for the first time, drawing both their attention to her. She glanced at Conall and shrugged, amusement clear on her face. "Wolves tend to attack people who show up on their doorstep and maybe ask questions later."

"What pack are you from?" Bran asked even though he was certain he knew. This clearly wasn't Dragos's mate, but she must be part of that female's pack. The information Keelin Petronilla had given Fia was scarce.

"Stavros."

He nodded. Just as he'd thought. The rumor was that Dragos had been living with the Stavros pack. He'd heard of Finn Stavros and the male was powerful. Even more so now that he was mated to a blood-born vamp. "I'm Bran Devlin."

"Rhea." No last name and no attempt to make polite talk or shake his hand. Just an icy glare that said if he made one wrong move, those blades were coming out.

Conall let out a low warning growl, drawing Bran's attention back to the male who hadn't moved a muscle. Just stood there with his eyes glowing pure silver. And it had everything to do with the curly-haired female. Interesting.

Bran took a step back, not out of fear, but to show the other male he respected his not-so-subtle claim. "You have my cell number."

Conall nodded and motioned for Rhea to move in behind him. She raised an eyebrow, as if to laugh that anyone wanted to protect her, but she moved for the gate first. As they started to open the gate—and Conall knew there were any number of warriors stationed in the air as backup—the passenger door to the SUV flew open.

Bran cringed and reined in a curse.

Fia and Gavin got out, Fia's expression confused, her ivory skin glowing in the pale moonlight. "What's happening? Why aren't you opening the gates for us?" she asked Conall, who kept that stony mask in place.

Bran let loose the anger he usually kept in check, his fire burning the back of his throat as he shot his brother a dark look. Gavin gave him an apologetic look, but didn't say anything to correct his mate. Per usual.

"Fia," he snapped. "Get back in the vehicle."

"Is this about our history, Conall?" she asked the other leader, completely ignoring Bran, her voice bewildered.

To everyone's surprise, the wolf shifter female stepped forward. "This has nothing to do with you. Drake doesn't want to see anyone but his mate right now. Something I'm certain you can understand as a mated female." Her voice was kind, but firm.

"I do understand. We were just so close as children, like siblings, and when he re-emerged into the world I felt it too. I didn't realize it was him until Keelin confirmed it and..." Her voice was watery and she seemed close to tears. Real tears too because that was one thing Bran respected about Fia. She didn't cry for show.

"Drake doesn't remember you, Fia. He doesn't remember most of his former life. Tonight is not a good time, but I'll be in contact with your clan leader tomorrow." Conall's voice was just a fraction softer than when he'd spoken to Bran. But not by much. Whatever his feelings had been for Fia at one time, it seemed clear they were over.

"Get in the SUV," Bran ordered, an edge to his voice. He didn't give her any of the softness Rhea or Conall had.

Eyes wide, she did just that, Gavin close behind her, but not before throwing Bran a hard look.

"Being clan leader sucks sometimes," Conall said, the informal speech surprising Bran as he stepped back to the gate, keeping his body protectively in front of the female.

A grin tugged at Bran's lips, but he locked it down. "Yeah it does," he muttered. And to think some dragons actually wanted all the responsibility of a clan, he thought, shaking his head as he walked back to the SUV.

"That was very sweet what you did," Victoria said almost absently, her back to Drake as she eyed the interior of the refrigerator. The guest house was now empty except for Gabriel and Rhea who were upstairs.

Drake knew his brother had ordered guards around the house too, which was fine with Drake. But he didn't want anyone else inside. Not when he craved privacy with Victoria.

"What was sweet?" His gaze trailed to the formfitting jeans hugging her backside. They'd returned to the house not long ago and he was having a hard time concentrating on anything other than thoughts of getting her naked. After sledding or tobogganing or whatever it was called, with her cradled in front of him as he held her close, he wanted no more barriers between them. He wanted skin to skin.

Craved it on the deepest level.

But he worried it might be too soon. She seemed like her old self, but she'd only bounced back earlier this evening from the poisoning.

"The way you subtly stood up for your brother. Gah, I'm so hungry." She shut the refrigerator door with a growl and headed for the pantry, practically stomping in her bare feet.

"It wasn't *sweet*. We're not letting unknowns into this territory until I know more about them." He was not a sweet male. Something she needed to understand. He should explain to her exactly how violent he could be, the things he'd done in Hell, but he didn't want to. Not yet. Right now all he was concerned with was keeping her safe. Because no one was getting near his soon-to-be mate. As he eyed the sway of her hips, hungry possessiveness swept up inside him, threatening to suck him under.

Frowning at the strange energy humming off her, he followed her into the oversized pantry. He was amazed by all the food lining the shelves for a second before his focus was on Victoria again.

Hands on her hips she eyed the shelves, scanning the various foodstuffs. When she moved right past a box of chocolate bars, he realized she wasn't even looking because his female never ignored chocolate. "Victoria, what's wrong?" When she turned to look at him, her eyebrows were drawn tight together and she wrapped her arms around herself. He didn't like the way she seemed to be closing him out. "Tell me." A soft demand.

Her arms immediately dropped and her gaze landed on his lips. When she licked her own, moistening them, his cock hardened even more, to an almost painful point. *Aaaand*, he started glowing.

The interior of the pantry lit up in an electric pale gold glow, highlighting Victoria's flushed cheeks and soft skin. Her crisp mountain scent intensified, filling the enclosed space until all he could think about was tasting her. All of her. The desire pounding in his veins was an erratic beat, making him insane with need.

Ever since he'd heard that conversation between Vega and Victoria about some male having his face between his female's legs, he wanted to experience the same thing. To bring Victoria the ultimate pleasure with no fucking interruptions.

Because if anyone dared come in here right now, he'd burn them to a crisp.

"Take off your sweater." He'd meant to form it as a question but it came out as a subtle demand. He needed to see her again. All of her. What they'd started in that hot tub had lit something inside him and that fire was never going out. It was an incendiary thing.

Her wolf flickered in her gaze as she reached for the hem of her sweater. Slowly. Not because she was nervous, he quickly realized. She was teasing him.

His cock pushed insistently against his pants, hard and aching.

Way too slowly she tugged the sweater over her head to reveal a scrap of black lace barely covering her full breasts, her light pink nipples tight buds that begged for his tongue to lavish over. But not yet. He needed to see all of her.

"Pants," he demanded, the one word wrenching from his throat with difficulty. Right now he didn't trust himself not to tear her clothes off. Later, he would take his time, slowly baring each inch of her to his hungry gaze.

Her hands shook as she unbuttoned then slowly slid her jeans off until she stood in just her bra and matching lacy black panties with a little green bow in the middle. She also had on the necklace he'd given to her. Seeing it hang between her breasts while her bare feet were curling against the hardwood floor, the image she painted was so erotic it was hard to draw in a breath.

Listening to all his primal instincts, he covered the distance between them, his hands latching onto her hips in a dominating grip as he moved her back against the shelves.

Her eyes went pure wolf as she arched into him, her hand reaching between them to stroke his hard length through his jeans. His throat tightened, a raspy, animalistic sound tearing from him before he pulled his hips back. He'd stroked himself to release plenty of times since he'd gotten out of Hell, always thinking of Victoria while he did, and just the thought of her touch was enough to set him off.

Fuck.

She couldn't touch him now. Not if he wanted to think straight. Hell, he could barely concentrate just seeing her long, lean body and inhaling that addictive scent of hers. "Hands on the shelf behind you," he ordered.

When she let out a throaty chuckle, he was relieved she wasn't angry he wasn't letting her touch him, or that he was ordering her around. This dominance welling up inside him gripped him hard and he didn't even try to hide it.

Leaning down, he ran his nose along her jaw line, inhaling her sweet scent, but not kissing. Not yet. He trailed down the delicate column of her neck, barely flicking out his tongue as he slowly moved down her chest and in between her soft, luscious breasts. He withdrew one hand from her hips and let a single claw free to slice through the middle of her bra.

He'd buy her another, a whole store's worth of lingerie. She let out a soft gasp as the silky pieces fell open to reveal her breasts. For the span of a heartbeat he stared at them, his mouth watering, but he held onto the last bit of his restraint.

Barely.

As he went down on his knees that addicting scent of hers intensified as he crouched lower to skim down her taut abdomen, barely grazing his nose and lips along her soft skin on a single-minded mission. Later he'd come back and rake his tongue and teeth over every single inch of her body, taking his time, but he was walking a razor thin wire now, the need in him pushing and demanding. With her scent only intensifying it.

Demanding he taste her.

She spread her legs wider, her breathing harsh as she revealed how damp her panties were. The scent of her need was almost enough to knock him on his ass. When he looked up at her, her long, black hair tumbled over one breast, the hard nipple peeking out through the thick strands and her full lips were parted a fraction as she watched him. "What are you going to do?" She had to realize his intentions, but maybe she needed words.

He'd read about modern sex and watched some videos and sometimes humans liked to say what they were going to do before they did it. The idea of saying those words to Victoria now made him so damn hot.

"Taste you." He tried but couldn't force any more words out.

A little shudder raked through her, her eyes going even more heavy-lidded as she watched him. Keeping his gaze on her face, he used the claw to slice through the thin band of material on either side of her hips. When it fell to the floor with a whisper of sound, he ran his palm down one leg until he reached her ankle.

Lifting it, he guided her foot up and over his shoulder, opening her fully to him. The sight of her so open to him like this made him completely freeze for a moment. Her soft pink folds glistened with her wetness, her scent making every primal part of him flare to life.

When her hands landed on his shoulders, her fingers curled into him. She was strung just as tight as he was, wanted him just as badly as he wanted her. With the exception of the male she'd mentioned to Vega, Drake wasn't sure if Victoria had been with other males before. He immediately discarded that thought. If she had, he was going to make her forget all of them.

He couldn't tear his gaze from the perfect triangle of dark hair covering her mound. Nothing he'd read or seen had prepared him for this. Going with his instinct he leaned forward and flicked his tongue over the hard, little bud peeking out from her folds.

The moment he made contact her fingers dug into him and she let out a soft, mewling sound that punched right though him. He wanted to hear it again. But louder. Her sweet taste coated his tongue, making everything inside him pull taut.

With his thumbs, he slowly parted her folds, enjoying how slick she was against him, how soft she was and knowing he was the one who'd elicited that response. Using control he didn't know he had, he licked her again, this time moving lower and dipping inside her so he could taste more. Her taste was beyond addicting.

Her hips jerked and another moan tore free from her, this one louder, harsher. He repeated what he'd done before, dipping inside her before stroking upward and centering on her clitoris. From what he knew, this was one of the most obvious erogenous zones for women and he planned to tease it until Victoria found her pleasure.

Stroking and teasing, increasing the pressure the louder Victoria moaned, he used her clear and loud responses to guide him. Each time she shuddered, her whole body moving from a stroke, he understood the exact pressure she needed. He finally found a rhythm as he focused on that tight, pulsing bundle of nerves. He wanted to slide a finger inside her, but wasn't sure she was ready and didn't want to ruin things by asking.

Not when her hips were rolling against his face and her taste coated his tongue, her body quivering until finally she clutched onto his shoulders, her nails digging into him until she pierced through his shirt and skin. He liked that she was marking him, especially as she shouted his name in a purely possessive way.

"Drake." Over and over, she said it until her grip loosened, her leg going lax over his shoulder.

Though he could drown in her taste, he pulled his head back, the sharpest sense of triumph humming through him as he looked up at her. Her eyes glittered a bright emerald, her expression sated and beautiful. He'd done that.

Perhaps he had more to give her than he'd originally thought.

When her leg fell from his shoulder completely, he went to stand, to pull her close to him, but she sank to her knees in front of him, wrapping her arms around his neck and pressing her breasts to his chest. He wanted to burn his shirt off right then, to get rid of all form of barriers between them.

"That was amazing." She looked a little dazed, her eyes still heavy-lidded as they watched each other.

Leaning forward, he brushed his mouth over hers, dipping his tongue between her lips and wondering if she liked the way she tasted. She hummed in enjoyment, giving him his answer.

As their lips danced, she reached between their bodies and worked the button on his pants free before tugging the zipper down. He wanted to claim her more than he wanted anything, more than he'd wanted free from Hell, but he didn't want to do it in the pantry. She deserved a bed, a—

When she wrapped her long fingers around his hard length, he forgot to breathe. His abdominal muscles tightened along with his balls, everything in him going still at the feel of her touching him like this. No female had ever touched him so intimately. To have Victoria's soft hands on him, his mate, it was almost too much to believe.

She pulled her head back, her eyes gleaming. "Let me please you too." Her voice was husky, her erotic scent even stronger. She wanted this; it turned her on to do this.

Which got him even hotter. Unable to form a response he just stared at her, trying to keep his eyes open as she began stroking him in long, even pulls.

Looking down between their bodies, he watched as her hand moved along his hard length, up and down, stroking him until he wanted to explode in her grip.

"Harder," he rasped out. The pleasure was a molten ball deep in his abdomen, growing hotter with every second.

Instantly her grip tightened and her strokes increased in tempo as his breathing jacked out of control. He needed... *Fuck.*

He buried his face in her neck, breathing her in, letting his canines descend and rake against her neck then shoulder. Wolf shifters marked their mates, but he wasn't sure if this was normal for a dragon shifter.

She moaned in pleasure, the sound setting off his most primitive nature. Instinct drove him to pierce her skin, his teeth sinking into her shoulder, just beneath the surface. He wanted to go deeper but feared hurting her, not so far mindless with pleasure that he couldn't hold back. She shuddered, her grip becoming harder and faster and he lost it, releasing himself in her hand and over her belly. His climax seemed to go on forever, just the feel of her touching him making him want to mark her everywhere.

As he came down from his high, his cock was still half-hard in her now loose grip and something told him he'd be hard again soon. When he withdrew his canines from her tender skin, she let out a soft gasp and remorse immediately filled him. Holding her hips lightly, he gently nuzzled the wound, licking it even as it was already healing.

He looked down at her. "I'm sor—"

She smiled softly, almost shyly. "Don't be. That was amazing." She looked between their bodies, and, stunning him, she rubbed her hand over the remnants of his release, rubbing it into her stomach.

That sweep of raw possessiveness surged through him again at the sight, the glow from within him turning supernova in the small room.

"I like your scent on me," she whispered, the tone of her voice almost hesitant, as if she was asking whether what she was doing was okay.

"I like marking you that way." His voice was hoarse, as if he hadn't used it for an eternity.

His cock started to harden again so he kissed her, drawing her tight against him as he ran a hand down her spine and clasped her hip tightly, his declaration clear. She was his. Not tonight but very soon he would be making her his in every way possible.

CHAPTER TWENTY

Drake finished scanning the file on Bran Devlin and set it aside next to the stack of others on the over-sized desk in Conall's library. Something about being in the library and the files he was reading triggered something deep inside him. Victoria was sitting across from him in the library but for a moment everything around him shifted as another sharp memory slammed into him, transporting him to when he was just a boy.

Drake stood outside his father's study and stared at the door. He knew his father was in there because his mother had told Drake to come see him. But he didn't want to.

He started to leave when his dad's voice boomed out, "I can scent you. Come in."

Swallowing hard, he opened the door and stepped inside. Tapestries hung on the stone walls and the big fireplace blazed with a low fire. Not that his dad needed the warmth. The hundred plus candles on the chandelier created a soft glow around the room. Normally he wouldn't even pay attention to this stuff but it was better than looking at his dad. Because Drake knew he was going to be in trouble and didn't want to see his dad's disappointment.

"You just going to stand there in the doorway?" his dad asked without looking up from the map he was poring over on one of the desks. His parents created their own maps from

their aerial flights. Eventually humans would catch up with them but he didn't think it would be anytime soon.

The door shut behind him with a heavy boom. Instead of going to the desk, Drake silently headed for the fireplace and sat on the fuzzy, bear rug. Seconds later his dad sat next to him. Drake hadn't even heard him move. Dragos, his dad, was a huge man but moved with a supernatural stealth he'd never seen anyone else do. Everyone said Drake would look like him one day but he didn't think he'd ever be that big.

His father's long, dark hair was pulled back in a leather tie, his expression calm as he stared at the fire. He didn't say anything for a long moment, making Drake's panic swell even higher. He was so going to get into trouble even though what he'd done had been in self-defense.

"Babies are time consuming the first year," his father finally said into the relative quiet.

Drake didn't understand what he was trying to say. He frowned, watching the flames flick higher. "I know." His sister was barely a year old and kept his mom busy because she was already shape shifting. It was funny to see such a tiny dragon flying around. She wasn't much bigger than a baby pig in her animal form.

"Eventually things will return to normal and your mom will have more time for you." Taking him by surprise, his father put his arm around his shoulders and pulled him close. He wasn't affectionate. Not like Drake's mom.

Drake's frown deepened even as he leaned into the embrace. He still didn't understand what his dad was trying to say but he liked the hug even if he would never say so. "Mom's busy with Keelin and I love my sister. I don't mind sharing Mom." Besides, he had his own friends and his younger brother. At eight years old Drake was busy. "I . . . punched Cody *today. Hard. And I kicked him and breathed fire at him, but I was careful not to burn him. It was just a warning." Normally he didn't let his cousin's taunting bother him but today Cody had been picking on someone weaker than him and Drake hadn't liked it.*

His father was silent which meant he was weighing his words. But he didn't drop his hold. Finally he spoke so softly Drake almost didn't hear him. "Good."

Drake blinked, sure he'd heard wrong. "What?"

His father heaved a sigh. "I'm glad you stood up to him."

Drake straightened at the note in his father's voice. It sounded like pride. "I'm not in trouble?"

His father snorted and pinned him with an intense silver gaze. "No. You don't go out of your way to hurt others so if you punched your cousin I know it was in self-defense." His jaw tightened for a moment and his gaze flashed molten silver before returning to a duller gray. "You're from a strong line and you're naturally bigger than most of the other boys your age. Some males feel the need to prove themselves and want to start fights. It's a natural thing, but I'm glad you're not like that. True leaders know how to control themselves. They earn loyalty and respect by leading by example, not by bullying."

This was not at all what Drake had expected. "But we're family. Shouldn't we stick together?"

A ghost of a smile pulled at his father's normally hard lips as he nodded. "We should. And when you grow older things will be different between you and Cody. Better. Until then, always stand up for yourself without fear of repercussion from me or your mother. But never hurt someone if you don't have to."

"Okay, but I don't like fighting. I'll probably just walk away if he bothers me." He still didn't understand why his cousin liked to fight and tease him. It didn't matter anyway. He'd recently made a new friend. A secret friend. One he wasn't going to tell even his parents about. If Cody tried to antagonize him, he'd try to find a way to ignore him. Unless his cousin picked on others.

His father sighed again. "You . . . have a kind spirit, Drake. You're a better man than I'll ever be and you're only eight."

His dad's words stunned him, but he wasn't sure how to respond. His father was the best, toughest man he knew.

"What is it? I can hear the wheels in your head turning from over here," Victoria murmured, her voice dragging him back to the present.

When he focused on her he saw that she wasn't looking up from where she was poring over an ancient text his brother had given to her. He loved the sight of her so intent on something.

Wearing dark jeans, a plain white T-shirt that dipped into a V showing off the necklace he'd given her, and her favorite green cardigan, she was the most beautiful thing he'd ever seen. After last night in the pantry they'd both crashed for a few hours even though he'd wanted to do more. But first he wanted to talk to his brother more about mating. Originally he'd thought he'd just go with his instincts but after the way he'd bitten Victoria, he wanted to discuss that with Conall. In private. Because the last thing he ever wanted to risk was hurting her.

"I had another memory. This time of my father," he rasped out.

Her head snapped up, her eyes widening. "That's great. Do you want to . . . share it with me?" There was a hesitancy in her voice he didn't like. He didn't ever want her to feel that way with him.

"It was a short one, in a study or library, when I was about eight. Keelin wasn't very old. My father was an intimidating, big man, but he told me that I was already a better man than he'd ever be." Saying the words made Drake's throat clog with emotion. He still wasn't certain why his father had said it, but it warmed him from the inside out.

Victoria seemed to understand Drake's internal struggle because she didn't respond, just sat there patiently, her expression kind.

Still unsure of the emotions running through him, he cleared his throat and decided to change the subject. He wasn't ready to talk about his parents just yet. The sensation of remembering an actual memory with his father was too jarring. Drake nodded at the file he'd set aside. "Just finished the clan leader's file."

She paused for a moment, as if she wanted to say something about what he'd just told her, but instead said, "And?"

"There's not much on Bran Devlin. Or any of them. They had an alliance with my clan for thousands of years, their land bordering ours when I was young, but we had almost no interaction." He'd discovered from his brother that they were originally from Scotland and Ireland, with deep Celtic roots, though they'd intermarried and inter-mated with other supernaturals more back then. Things had apparently changed in the last thousand years, with dragons keeping more to themselves.

"That's normal though, right? My pack didn't even know dragons were real until you. So doesn't it make sense there's not much on them?" She hadn't looked at the files Drake had been dissecting, but he planned to have her read them too. Victoria was sharp and he wanted her insight.

His frown deepened. "Maybe. But most of this is just notes compiled from conversations or texts between Keelin and Fia or others in the clans."

Now Victoria's eyes widened. "Wait, like a dossier?"

He paused, trying to remember the definition, then nodded. "Yes. It's my understanding from Conall that most clans have something like this. They keep records of even innocuous things."

"Like freaking spies or something," Victoria murmured, her eyebrows drawn together.

"Exactly like that. And the clan leader was missing for a couple decades. There are no notes about where he was or what he was doing until a year ago."

"When the former leader and his mate died, right?"

Drake nodded. "Yes, his parents. That's why Bran Devlin came back, but there's no information on where he was before then."

Victoria shrugged. "Ask him."

That seemed too simple and it would require seeing the male in person. Of course that didn't mean he had to invite the Devlin clan members into the village. He could go see them offsite and away from Victoria. Except she wouldn't like that. Not his sweet and fierce female. She would completely balk at him going to meet them without her. "Maybe I will. There's something else..." He picked up the file for Gavin Devlin and flipped it open as Conall walked in.

His brother was dressed sharply this morning in what Drake guessed was a custom made suit, white shirt and silver tie. From what he was coming to learn about this world and the wealth of his clan, the material of his clothing looked expensive.

"Morning." Conall smiled warmly at Victoria.

The sight eased something in Drake's chest. He'd been worried about his siblings and their reception of Victoria but so far they seemed to all like each other. Victoria was hard not to adore though.

His brother continued. "I know it's early but clan members have started arriving. They would like to meet you, but I understand if you're busy or still not ready."

Drake looked at Victoria who just shrugged. "I'm fine with it if you are."

"Have I ever met Gavin Devlin?" he asked abruptly. He wasn't sure how he felt about meeting others just yet.

Conall stiffened at the name, no doubt because it was Fia's mate. "No. You're the same age and our land bordered each other but you never interacted. Our parents were too strict for that."

"Why?" Victoria asked.

"Our mother was very overprotective. So was Gavin and Bran's. Female dragons can be temperamental."

Victoria snorted, the sound making Drake smile. "All females can be. So where are you going all fancy?" she asked Conall teasingly and Drake knew she was trying to alleviate the tension in his brother.

The tenseness in his brother's shoulders eased, Drake's healer's magic working. "Just a meeting regarding land. We're looking to purchase more and the owner wants an in-person discussion." He glanced back at Drake. "I can cancel though."

"No." Drake's answer was immediate. He didn't want his family changing their schedules or lives for him. He liked that no one was smothering him. It was making adjusting to his new clan easier. Even if he didn't know if he'd stay. He hadn't broached the subject with Victoria yet because he wasn't sure what her answer would be. He'd live with her pack forever if it was what she wanted. "And we'll see my clan members now. But not in here." He didn't want to move the files and he didn't want anyone to know what he and Victoria were doing. Not when he wasn't sure who he could trust. It didn't matter that his brother had told him he'd checked out everyone in their clan, Drake wanted to personally meet everyone and get a feel for them. Maybe meeting his clan members would trigger something in his memory, like when he'd met his two cousins.

"There are half a dozen waiting in the sitting room in the front of the house."

"Is that the room with the uncomfortable furniture?" he asked.

Conall let out a sharp bark of laughter, the sound taking Drake by surprise. His brother nodded. "That's the one."

"Give us ten minutes. And . . . when you're back would you mind meeting with me in your office?" Drake asked.

"I'll contact you as soon as I return." Conall ducked out of the library, thankfully not questioning what Drake wanted to discuss. Victoria placed a ribbon bookmark in the pages of the book she was reading and stood, rounding her desk as she came to lean against Drake's. Her scent intensified the closer she came, making his brain short-circuit for a moment.

Drake opened his mouth to speak but all thoughts disappeared as she inched down the desk until she was directly in front of him, placing both her feet on his chair on either side of his thighs. With her legs spread like this, images of last night flickered through his mind like snapshots. Not that he'd actually stopped thinking about her taste and how she'd come against his mouth.

"You sure about meeting with everyone?"

He nodded, grabbing her hips and earning a yelp of surprise as he pulled her to straddle him. "Are you trying to get me hard before we go meet everyone?" he murmured, brushing his lips against hers as the room lit up in a soft, golden glow. The oversized windows of the room had the drapes pulled back so if anyone was flying nearby they'd see it.

"No. I've just gone too long without touching you this morning." She slid her fingers into his hair and leaned close, moistening her lips.

"I agree," he murmured, even though they'd been together the past couple hours in the same room. After going hundreds of years at a time without touch, and even when he did touch, it had been mostly in violence, the feel of her soft hands on him pushed back the darkness inside him. Clearing his throat before she would have kissed him, he said, "I need to tell you something." *No!* his dragon side shouted at him. *She doesn't need to know everything.* But she did. Deep down Drake knew that. And he had to trust her to accept him.

She paused, her eyebrows knitting together, probably at his grim tone. "Okay."

He was probably making a mistake, but she deserved to know about his darker side. If she was truly to be his mate, she needed to know everything about him. Even if his deepest fear was that she'd reject him when she learned the truth. Reaching out, he loosely gripped her neck, rubbing his thumb along her jawline as she watched him with a mix of lust and curiosity.

"In Hell I used to fight. A lot. After hundreds of years alone and in my dragon form I was going insane." Some nights when he stared at the ceiling in his room, he wondered if he'd just completely been consumed by the darkness and all this was a fantasy. If it was, Victoria was the best damn thing he could have ever imagined.

"When I returned from isolation into the land of the damned I started engaging in brutal, bloodthirsty fights. Not because I was forced to, but because I *wanted* to. I liked hurting other beings, craved it, fucking relished in it." He had, the blood and violence making him feel alive in the worst way possible. "For so long I felt like I was wasting away into this dark abyss of nothingness and all my rage and anger came spilling out with a brutal vengeance." When his gaze fell to his hand, a hand that had once been stained with endless blood, touching Victoria's gentle neck, he dropped it, letting it fall to his side.

Victoria cupped his face, her hands gentle as she held him. "I don't even know if there were any innocents in Hell, but did you ever hurt any intentionally?"

He shook his head. The males he'd fought had been demons or other beings cursed to Hell for violent crimes in their previous life. Usually vamps. Fucking hedonistic bastards.

"My sweet Drake," she whispered, leaning forward to brush her lips over his. Teasing her tongue against the seam of his lips, he gave her entrance, meeting her tongue with his tentatively, not understanding why she was being so kind.

His hands settled on her hips, barely holding her out of fear she'd bolt. When she started peppering kisses along his jaw, heading to his ear, his hold on her hips tightened.

"*Victoria.*" He stressed her name, making her pull back.

"What?" The word came out breathless.

"Don't you have something to say?" *Like he disgusted her?* He'd just admitted to not only taking part in violence, but enjoying it. She was a healer, the exact opposite of him. What if she feared him now? Panic slid down his spine at the thought, like a blaze of needles slamming into him all at once.

She paused, her wolf flickering in her gaze. "If I find who put you in Hell, I'm going to destroy them." The savage edge from his healer punched through his chest. "You were an innocent child sacrificed because of . . . I don't know why yet, but I *will* discover why. You had no one and you did the best you could. I hate what happened to you but I could never judge you for any decisions you made. Not knowing who you are now. And you're definitely not the same male you were then. Did you think I would?" Her eyebrows drew together, just the woman looking at him now.

He nodded, not trusting his voice. He'd feared just that. Had tried to prepare himself for her revulsion. The very small civilized part of him wanted to tell her that she shouldn't want him, should run from him, but his primal side won out. If she accepted him, that was it.

"Oh, Drake. You are mine. Every single part of you." The words were a soft whisper as she wrapped her arms around his neck, burying her face against his neck as she held him.

Mine. He understood what that meant. She was his too. For someone who'd never had anything close to resembling love in his life for far too long, her words undid him. He returned her embrace, holding her tight to him, her touch grounding him, telling him that he might just have a real future with her. One with dreams and a mate who loved him despite everything he'd done.

Victoria stood in the foyer with Drake, saying good-bye to the last group of dragon shifters who'd stopped by. Her arm was wrapped loosely around his waist as they smiled, her face hurting from all the talking and smiling they'd done for the past eight hours. Jeez, had it really been that long? And she'd been the only one smiling. Drake tried, but it came off as more of a baring of teeth.

"No more visitors," Drake growled, his body tense.

It was close to five that evening and she found herself agreeing, even though everyone had been incredibly welcoming. She didn't want to smile at any more strangers, didn't want to make small talk. Plus she was starving. "Agreed. Think we can raid Conall's fridge?" she asked, turning in his arms.

Nodding, he bent to nuzzle her neck, sending a shiver down her spine. "I didn't like those males looking at you," he murmured against her ear.

A laugh escaped. "I'm pretty sure I wasn't the only one being checked out." Most of the shifters had just been curious but Drake had been on the receiving end of more than a few appreciative female looks. Not that she blamed the females. He was stunningly masculine. And all hers.

He just grunted and nipped at her earlobe, his teeth pressing down as his hand slid to her butt.

Maybe she wasn't hungry after all. "Forget food, let's—"

The front door swung open and Keelin stopped, her face turning red. "Sorry, I uh…" Two males were behind her, making Drake's glow dim immediately as a growl built in his throat.

He definitely didn't like sharing any part of Victoria with others.

Victoria smiled at Keelin. "We were about to head back to the guest house." A tiny lie. Victoria still wanted to look over some of those notes and especially that book Conall had let her borrow. "But we've got time to visit." Even if she really didn't want to.

Keelin looked at Drake and must have seen the exact opposite expression on his face because she winced. Before she turned to the two males, however, she pasted on a smile and motioned them in. "We won't keep you two long, I know you're exhausted. Nevin and Cody wanted to meet Victoria."

Victoria smiled at the familiar names. Drake had mentioned he'd met two of his cousins when he'd dropped by Conall's.

Victoria listened as Keelin explained how the males were related through which sibling of their parents. It seemed as if Drake's mother had two sisters but from the way Keelin spoke, only one was alive. Alma. Victoria was going to ask Keelin about that later.

Cody was on their father's side and Nevin on their mother's. Victoria was pretty certain Drake had memorized everyone's names and faces today, and she was trying to do the same. Even though she didn't know what the future held for her and Drake, she knew that his clan was going to be a part of their lives and she wanted to make an effort to get to know everyone.

"You're really a wolf shifter," the male named Cody said after introductions and brief small talk. He watched her curiously, something about his tone making her hackles rise. She couldn't decide if that was condescension that laced his words.

She raised her eyebrows at his obvious statement. Family or not, she had no problem standing up for herself. "And you're a dragon." How was she supposed to respond to that?

Drake stiffened beside her and she was certain she scented fire burning in his throat. She resisted the urge to smile at his overprotectiveness and instead squeezed him so he wouldn't do something he'd regret. Like setting a relative on fire.

The other male, Nevin, smiled apologetically and looked back and forth between the two of them once, his gaze landing on Drake. "We're both pleased to meet your mate," he said to Drake before looking at Victoria. "I hope you enjoy the time you're here." Something about his words were odd, but she just smiled back.

"Thank you."

Drake didn't respond and wasn't even trying to smile now. Crap, she had a feeling he was at his breaking point of pretending to be civilized.

"It's just a shame your parents aren't awake yet," Cody continued, his voice sincere.

"Yes it is. But I have a feeling they'll be waking soon." Keelin sounded strained by that thought and Victoria guessed it was because of her relationship with her mother.

Since she'd never had one she couldn't relate, but she could sympathize. Being smothered was beyond annoying.

Before Victoria could say anything Drake tightened his grip on her. "I apologize for my rudeness, but my mate is still recovering from her poisoning." Three lies. One, he wasn't sorry. Two, they weren't technically mated and three, she wasn't recovering. She was more than fine.

But Victoria wasn't about to correct him. Not when she wanted Drake alone time.

"So we will be heading back to our place, but please feel free to visit later this week." Drake's words were so polite and civil but the growly edge to his voice definitely wasn't. Oh yeah, he was at the end of his rope.

To give the males credit, they simply nodded and left, with Keelin shutting the door behind them. "I'm so sorry about the last minute drop in. I know you guys want some down time. Aunt Alma probably left food in Conall's fridge if you want to hit it up before heading back to the guest house."

Perfect. Victoria smiled. "We will, thanks." She should probably invite the female to stay and eat dinner with them, but selfish girl that she was, she held her tongue.

Keelin nodded and cleared her throat almost nervously. "So, have you decided about seeing Fia and the others?"

It had only been a day but Victoria guessed Keelin was asking because she was friends with the female.

"What is your personal opinion of the Devlin clan?" Drake asked.

Keelin seemed surprised by the question. She looked past Drake for a moment and Victoria realized why.

"Conall's out," she said quietly.

Keelin's gray eyes flashed with guilt. "I feel weird saying anything, but personally I really like those I've met
from their clan. Gavin loves Fia and dotes on her in a
way Conall never would have. And I know you're not
asking that outright, but I'm telling you anyway. They
never would have worked long-term. Fia is beautiful
and a little fragile—I'm not talking physically—and she
needs a certain type of mate. It's not right or wrong,
we're all different. Conall might not realize it but he
needs a strong mate, not someone needy.

"So if you're inadvertently asking what I think about
Conall's ex, that's my personal opinion. They're both
better off without each other and personal stuff aside,
the Devlin clan will make a strong ally. Considering
what happened with the Veles clan, I think we need one
now. I also think we need more interpersonal communication between our clans and other supernatural beings
period. We've been living in shadows for too long."

Victoria's eyes widened and shot a glance at Drake.
That was the most she'd heard Keelin say at one time
since they'd met. Her stance on coming out to other supernaturals was also interesting and one Victoria agreed
with. The more they all supported each other, the better
it would be for everyone. Because one day humans were
going to discover their existence. It was just a matter of
time.

"Would you mind looking at some files Victoria and
I have been reviewing on the Devlin clan? I want to set
up a meet with them tomorrow and I'd like your opin-

ion on those you know. I'd also like you to go to the meet with us."

For a fraction of a second, Keelin's eyes widened, but she nodded, clearly pleased Drake had asked her. If Victoria had to guess, the female's parents had not only sheltered her, but smothered her. They probably wouldn't have ever asked her to attend something like this.

"I'll help any way I can," Keelin said.

"I'll grab us some food." Victoria leaned up and kissed Drake.

Keelin started to protest that she'd do it but Victoria cut her off. She wanted the female to spend time with her brother and it was obvious Keelin was knowledgeable on clan dynamics. Right now they needed more information. Because the Veles clan wasn't going to forget what had happened, even though they'd been the ones to attack. And Victoria wanted every single ally they could get.

CHAPTER TWENTY-ONE

Easing down the interior stairs of the guest house, he paused when he heard two familiar females talking. The house had been empty for a while so he'd taken advantage to search through the wolf shifters' rooms for anything he could use against them. He didn't know that he would need to, but he liked to be prepared.

Hurrying down the last of the steps, he headed in the direction of the voices. Outside the swinging door of the kitchen he paused by the wall. He let his camouflage fall so he wouldn't have to drain the power it took to maintain it. Lowering his heart rate and keeping his breathing steady, he leaned in and listened.

"You should come tomorrow," Keelin said.

Greer, their healer, snorted. "No thanks."

"I'll never understand why you and Fia don't get along. And don't deny that's why you don't want to go."

"No, I don't want to go because I wasn't invited. Not seeing Fia is icing on the cake."

Keelin made an admonishing sound before continuing. "I can't believe Drake asked me to go."

He frowned. Where was she going tomorrow? If Keelin was meeting with Fia it meant she'd likely be meeting with the rest of the visiting Devlin clan.

281

"Why can't you believe it?" Greer asked.

Now Keelin snorted. "Conall would have never thought to ask me."

"That's because he still sees a little girl when he looks at you. Drake doesn't have those blinders and clearly he recognizes your value in going. You don't need me with you."

Keelin was silent, or he couldn't hear her response if she made one.

Greer continued. "What else is going on with you?"

"Nothing." Keelin's answer was quick. Too quick. He knew her well enough to read her.

"Come on. You've been acting differently the last few months. Are you . . . seeing someone?"

"No. I just want a change, that's all. When we discovered Drake was alive it almost feels like, I don't know, I don't want to waste any more time not living the way I want. I let my mom dictate too many terms and I'm over it. This new world is amazing and I want to see more of it."

"What kind of change are you thinking?"

Keelin laughed. "That's just it, I have no idea. I want to travel a bit for sure but other than that, I don't know. I guess I need to spread my wings, no pun intended."

"Good. I hated that you went into Protective Hibernation when your parents did. You deserve to live a little. Or a lot." Greer's voice was teasing.

Keelin made a soft sound that might have been a 'yeah' or something else. He couldn't tell and he didn't care. He wanted them to return to talking about where they were going tomorrow.

Greer continued. "So what are you thinking, hooking up with that sexy wolf shifter? That shifter Gabriel is hot." She made an appreciative sound at the mention of the male. "And I'm ninety-five percent sure he's not together with Rhea. They seem like just friends."

He rolled his eyes at Greer's words. She might be a healer and respected by their clan but she was a bad influence on Keelin. He stayed away from her as much as possible.

"Yes, he's good looking, but he's not my type. And I don't even know if I want to hook up with anyone. I just want to get away from here where I'm not constantly under the watchful eye of an entire clan. It's annoying."

"Well breakfast tomorrow with the Devlin clan won't exactly be getting away but it's wonderful that Drake's included you. I'm so glad he's back. And it seems like most of the clan is happy about his chosen mate."

He tuned the rest out. Breakfast tomorrow. It would either be here or at the lodge where Conall had put up the other clan. He guessed the lodge. It would make more sense than allowing them into the village.

It would also be a lot easier for him to target that wolf shifter, Victoria. He hadn't liked the way either she or Drake had looked at him earlier. Supposedly the male didn't remember anything, but that could change. Instead of trying to target Dragos through the wolf shifter, he could simply go after her and frame the Devlin clan.

Simple and neat. And Dragos would have a new target to focus all his attention on. It would give him time to go after Dragos again too. He could strike when the male was weak and mourning.

He turned away and crept toward the front of the house. He needed to leave now before anyone caught him.

Killing that male would solve all his problems because he couldn't keep living in fear that his sins would be found out. Even if they had been justified. Dragos's parents deserved to lose their oldest son and he was going to make sure the male was gone before they ever woke from their Protective Hibernation.

That would be the sweetest justice of all. For them to awaken and learn they'd lost their son for a second time.

CHAPTER TWENTY-TWO

Slipping his cell phone into his pocket, Bran strode into the sunroom from outside using the side door. He wasn't surprised to see Fia frowning at the setup of the long table, hands on her hips.

"It's going to be fine," he muttered, her tension rubbing off on everyone in the cabin.

"It needs to be perfect." She didn't look up at him as she rearranged a little bouquet of small, yellow flowers on one end of the table by moving it half an inch.

"The flowers are . . . pretty," he gritted out the word. Fucking pretty? He felt bad about the way he'd snapped at her Sunday night even if she had deserved it. The female hadn't spoken to him since, which was sort of a relief, but her cold shoulder meant Gavin was pissed at him too.

"Really?" She looked up, her expression more stressed than normal.

Shit. He was an asshole. She was just trying to make things nice for the other clan. He should be thanking her. "Yeah, yellow is . . . bright." Males didn't give a shit about flowers and he doubted Dragos's mate would care either, but he was wise enough not to say that.

She bit her bottom lip as she glanced back at the immaculately set table. Instead of meeting the Petronilla clan members on their land, they'd opted to meet here. The lodge had catered a large breakfast and the private cabin Conall had put them in was big enough for four families.

This was basically neutral ground. Made sense to Bran and he preferred it that way. He didn't want to be deeper into their land than necessary. Even if he did want them as allies. He leaned against the sturdy chair at the end of the table. "So have you forgiven me?"

Fia sniffed and looked at him, her lips pursed. "Maybe. If you behave yourself this morning."

He snorted. No other female in his clan talked to him like this. The truth was, even though she drove Bran crazy most of the time, she loved his brother. And she was like an annoying little sister. "Behave myself?"

"No surliness. This is important to . . . me. So please, I'm asking you to be civil."

He frowned at the way she'd paused. There was something he was missing; had felt the strangeness for the past few months, but he couldn't put his finger on it. "You do know I'm clan leader?" he asked mildly.

She sniffed again and turned on her heel before marching from the room. She hadn't said but he could tell that he was forgiven. She wouldn't have spoken to him at all otherwise. Freaking females.

Rubbing the back of his neck, he started to follow and find his brother when a soft knock at the glass door drew his attention.

A short female with a furry, hooded jacket pulled up around her face stood there. She smiled and half-waved, her silver eyes flickering under the bright morning sun. For a moment he couldn't draw breath as he stared at her. Her smile was blinding, the type of smile females like her did *not* reserve for him. Unlike most male dragons, he didn't look like them. He wasn't what Fia called GQ attractive. He looked like a fucking thug and he couldn't see out of one eye. Dragon females prized whole, beautiful males. At least in his experience. Yeah, she wasn't looking at him.

He glanced over his shoulder. Nope. He was alone. Turning back, he found her now frowning at him. She pointed at the door and made an unlock motion with her hand. Like he was a fucking moron who couldn't figure out how to open the door. He would be insulted except he was acting like one.

Gritting his teeth, he strode to the door and opened it.

"Hi. I'm Keelin," she said, pushing the hood back from her face. The small wisps of blonde hair he'd seen peeking out tumbled around her face now. Behind her, her footprints indented the light dusting of snow on the wooden stairs that led to the ground below. The sunroom looked out over the mountain, the view stunning. But nothing compared to the female standing in front of him now. When she raised her eyebrows, he figured he should stop staring and formulate a response.

"Bran," he rasped out.

"I know. I've seen your picture. Are you going to invite me in?"

As he stepped back, the petite female breezed past him, her scent making him think of raw, primal fucking under a moonlit sky. The abrupt thought made him draw up short. His dragon rippled beneath the surface, savagely curious about the female. What the fuck was wrong with him? He loved women. Loved everything about them. Their soft curves, the way they moaned when he made them come. That was just sex though. And his dragon never gave a shit about any of them. This was . . . odd. And unwelcome.

Rolling his shoulders, he shrugged off the strange sensation. He knew she'd recently come out of Protective Hibernation. Must be why her picture wasn't in their files of the Petronilla clan. Why the hell hadn't Fia told him about Keelin? "Where are your brothers?"

She shrugged and unzipped her jacket. "I came early. Figured Fia was freaking out over breakfast and could use the help."

He snorted and felt his heart stutter when she gave him one of those blinding smiles again.

The female laughed once, the throaty sound a punch to his solar plexus. "So I was right to come early? Is she having a meltdown?"

Before he could respond, Fia appeared in the doorway and started squealing over the blonde female who just smiled and gave her friend a big hug. There was a whirlwind of high-pitched, excited shouting, all from Fia, before the two females hurried from the room.

Bran rubbed the back of his neck as he stared at the empty entryway. *Fuck him.* Keelin's sweet scent lingered in the air, making his dragon angry, his talons raking against his insides demanding he go after her.

Right the fuck now.

Females were too complicated. He'd seen his brother become pussy whipped over one. Not something he wanted for himself. But . . . he rubbed his neck again. He wasn't letting that female just walk away. Something intrinsic inside him flared bright, telling him he didn't have a choice in the matter.

Victoria gave Drake her hand as she slid out of the back of the SUV. She didn't need the help and he knew she didn't, but she loved touching him. Unfortunately they weren't touching enough. Last night she'd been so sure they'd take things to the next level, but Drake had been all about oral exploration only. Which was amazing but she wanted more.

So much more. She wanted all of him. To feel that thick length of him pushing deep inside her, to score her nails down his back as they both came, to experience his canines marking her skin again.

Ahead of them, Rhea, Gabriel, Conall, Lennox and Cody were all walking toward the huge cabin where the Devlin clan was staying. She wasn't sure what she thought of the dragon Cody, but Keelin—who'd come an hour earlier—had told Victoria that he was a warrior and well-trained. And Conall had wanted him to come with them as part of their protection.

Victoria squeezed Drake's hand and stopped walking. He instantly tensed, scanning their surroundings and looking for danger. "What is it?" he murmured.

"Nothing bad. I just want to talk to you in private. Will you tell the others we'll be inside in a sec?"

He nodded and called out to his brother, who paused in concern, then continued along the stone walkway that wrapped around to the back of the cabin. They were using the back stairs as their entrance instead of the front door. She wasn't sure why but didn't really care.

Once everyone was out of sight, Drake's big hands settled on her hips. He pulled her close, the feel of his thick length resting against her abdomen making her shudder. "Are you nervous?" he asked quietly.

"No. And this is may be terrible timing, but . . . why aren't we taking things further in the bedroom?" Monday night in the pantry had been hot and last night had been more of the same, except in their bedroom instead of the kitchen. But he hadn't wanted to take things further and she'd been too nervous to ask why when she'd been naked and vulnerable.

His gray eyes went silver as he swallowed hard. "Are you not pleased with what we've done?"

She blinked in surprise. He'd made her come three times last night with his hands and wicked tongue. "No, I mean, yes. I'm very pleased." That being an understatement. Another shiver rolled through her, her nipples hardening against her bra as she thought of everything they'd done only hours ago. How he'd had her get on all fours then slid underneath her and had her sit on his face. It had been beyond erotic. "I just . . . something's holding you back." And she really hoped it wasn't her.

Maybe now that they were surrounded by his dragon clan he realized the differences in their species and was having second thoughts about actual mating. That thought made her throat tighten, unwanted emotions bubbling up.

His fingers clenched harder around her hips and he was silent for a few long beats, making her think the worst. "I've never been with a female." His words were so quiet she almost didn't hear him.

"I haven't either. With a male, I mean. With *anyone*. Not completely." Sure she'd fooled around with that guy in college but that had been short-lived thanks to the obnoxious Guardian.

Drake's head tilted to the side a fraction, his eyes going supernova as he watched her. "Really?"

She nodded, swallowing hard. "Really. I wasn't waiting for any reason other than Gabriel and the rest of the pack made it impossible for me to, you know." But now she was glad she hadn't been with anyone. She and Drake could learn everything together. She just hoped that was the only reason he was holding back.

"I was worried I might hurt you during sex. I spoke to Conall this morning and he told me . . . he explained that . . ." To her surprise, his ears tinged crimson.

When it was clear that he was struggling for words, she smiled. "He basically told you dragons aren't into weird shit and you have nothing to worry about?"

Breathing out a sigh of relief, he nodded. "Yes, but I will bite you."

Something she already knew since his brother had told them in the cabin and Drake had nipped at her more than once. "You've already bitten me." And it had been hot. Her nipples tightened even more and the soft glow Drake had been emitting went pure gold, the snow around them glistening under the effect.

"When we mate it will be deeper and will mark you for life." His words were tentative.

But they were music to her ears. "Good." She wanted to be marked by him, wanted the whole damn world to know she was his. And vice versa.

His gaze went molten as he watched her. "It's only been two days. Barely."

"It's been more than that if you think about it. I've wanted you since pretty much the moment you went all growly and sexy in that graveyard." Which was a little weird to think about but she didn't care. Drake was an amazing male. And four months of waiting was long enough.

"I do not growl."

She bit back a smile. "You just did."

Leaning down, he brushed his lips over hers but pulled back way too quickly. "You *do* have terrible timing. We should just leave now." His voice was low, sexy, his intent clear.

Laughing, she pushed against his chest and stepped back. "No way. And you might want to..." She motioned to the glow around them.

Because of the bright morning sun she didn't think anyone could see the glow. The cabin was too far away from the rest of the lodge, one of the exclusive areas where those who paid a boat load could walk out of their cabin and pretty much ski right down the mountain. This high up and with so many trees blocking them she figured they were safe but still. They didn't need to walk into the breakfast with him lit up like a Christmas tree. Then everyone would know what they'd been doing out here. Not that she was ashamed, but still.

"Terrible, terrible timing," he muttered, wrapping his arm around her shoulders as they headed up the walk.

Slipping her arm around his waist, she held on tight. She wasn't exactly nervous, but okay, maybe a little. This was a new world and now they were about to meet new dragons. The back part of the cabin had a huge upper room with all glass windows that glinted under the sunlight. A wide set of stairs led to a door where Conall was waiting, his body tense.

"Is everything okay?" she asked as they started up the stairs.

"Yeah." His voice said otherwise. His tone also didn't invite further questioning.

It had to be weird for him to be around his ex, so maybe that was why he was on edge. But she wasn't going to say one word about it.

"Let's get this over with," he muttered, opening the door and heading in first. It was a sign of respect to go first, to enter a room before them to take on any potential danger in their stead.

As they stepped inside a bright room where a beautiful table was laid out, all conversation stopped and everyone turned to stare at them. Next to her Drake stiffened, his grip tightening. She knew this was hard for him, but he was doing it because it would be good for their clans to become allies.

"Drake, Victoria, this is..." Conall went on to introduce them to members of the Devlin clan. There were five in all. The leader, his brother, his brother's mate and two warriors.

Victoria had seen a couple dragons with Devlin coloring in the sky earlier and asked Drake about it but he hadn't been able to see them until he touched the blade she had strapped on underneath her long jacket. He'd been insistent she wear it today as extra protection. Apparently, according to Conall, blades forged with dragon fire had all sorts of magic associated with them. Including giving the owner of the blade the ability to see past dragon camouflage. Which was why they almost never made them.

Not even for themselves. It was too dangerous. Someone else might accidentally get a hold of it.

The blades could pretty much kill *anyone*. Of course, not all dragons could even make the things according to Conall. It took skill and very specific knowledge, most of which was only passed down through royal lines. He'd been shocked to see Victoria carrying one that first time they'd met in Bo's club because of what it was and because Drake had actually made one. Neither he nor his sister had ever tried. That knowledge that the blade could kill anyone had freaked her out, but had made Drake even more insistent that she wear it today. In one of the ancient texts Conall had lent her—from his personal family library—there was a whole section about ancient weapons made from dragon fire and she'd just started reading it.

Right about now, with everyone staring at them, she wished she was back in his library reading it or anything else.

Normally Victoria was good at breaking the ice in social situations but she felt tongue-tied with so many people looking at them. It was beyond disconcerting.

These people weren't her pack or even Drake's clan. And her own two packmates looked tense and ready to draw their weapons. Actually, everyone looked as if they were ready to draw their weapons except the female named Fia. She just appeared stressed as she looked at the big table, tension lines marring her beautiful face.

Thankfully Keelin stepped forward, the petite woman dwarfed by most of them in the room. She held up a tray of flutes filled with something orange and fizzy. "Fia made mimosas if anyone wants them." Her smile was warm and genuine and dissipated some of the tension as everyone started taking the drinks.

"What's a mimosa?" Drake murmured.

She leaned up on tiptoe so she was close to his ear. "Champagne and orange juice, you'll like it."

He brushed his lips over the top of her head before they moved farther into the room. Everyone started pairing off and talking quietly and it was clear that Fia and her mate, Gavin, wanted to talk to Drake so Victoria steered them toward the other end of the long table. Light streamed through the room, bathing everything.

As they reached the other couple, Fia gave them a shaky smile, her knuckles white around the champagne glass. Victoria hoped she didn't break the thing.

"I can't believe you're back," the female said, true joy in her expression now.

In that moment, Victoria decided she could like her if her sincerity was real.

The male nodded, his expression almost searching as he looked at Drake.

Drake just stood there stiffly, so Victoria squeezed his side. "It's a beautiful place for Drake to come home to," she said when it was clear Drake wasn't going to respond. There, that was generic enough.

"Are you staying then?" Gavin asked, his stare intense as he watched Drake.

Okay, that was a little weird. Drake shrugged. "I don't know."

"We live in the mountains too. Oregon though," Fia said. As the female started to chat, clearly nervous, Victoria sneaked a peek around the room. Bran, the clan leader, was staring at Keelin—who was chatting with Lennox—as if he wanted to devour the female. Much in the same way that Drake looked at Victoria. Well that was interesting. *Aaaaand,* Conall had noticed too because he looked as if he was about to breathe fire at the other leader. Conall took a step in Bran's direction but then Rhea moved next to him, two drinks in her hand and a smile on her face. Conall's expression immediately softened. Crisis averted. For now.

Victoria looked back at the other two, still listening as Fia nervously chattered on, and froze when she saw a dragon flying straight for the display of windows as if it was about to dive bomb them. It took less than a second for her to realize she saw it because the hilt of her blade was touching her skin.

"*Dragon*," she screamed, the word barely out of her mouth before Drake tackled her. Fire and glass exploded all around them as her back slammed against the wooden floor.

Another blast of fire illuminated the room, the heat licking around her but not touching her skin, as if a small dome was above her and Drake. It was breathtaking and horrifying as the orangey flames danced above them.

Just as quickly the inferno fizzled. Drake jumped to his feet. Victoria did the same, quickly scanning to make sure everyone was alive. The windows and most of the ceiling in the sunroom were gone. Gabriel was covered in soot and burned in a few places, his clothes nearly fried off, but he was already healing at that rapid Guardian rate. It looked as if Conall had covered Rhea because she was unharmed.

At once, everyone jumped into action, but she couldn't move. Victoria's vocal cords froze for a fraction of a moment as her gaze trailed back to the sky. *Oh my God.* "Ten more headed this way!" she shouted, pretty sure the others couldn't even see the newcomers as they descended toward them, their yellowish-orange bodies a blaze of color against the brilliant blue sky.

CHAPTER TWENTY-THREE

Drake ripped open Victoria's jacket in one jerk. Buttons flew everywhere but he ignored everything and grasped onto her blade. The instant his hand made contact with the hilt, he saw what she saw.

Ten dragons, clearly of the Veles clan if their coloring was any indication, flying directly for them and two circling back from their first attack. Withdrawing the blade, he pushed her to Gabriel. "Keep her safe," he ordered, not bothering to see if Victoria argued. Gabriel would die for Victoria, would sacrifice himself faster than anyone else in this room to keep her alive.

Not waiting for the others, he raced toward the shattered window, using the jagged edge as a springboard to propel himself through. His dragon burst free as he soared through the air, the change sharp as his shift took over with a brutal intensity he'd never before experienced.

The blade still clutched tightly in his talons gave him an advantage he planned to use. Calling on his fire, he flew right at three dragons, knowing they didn't realize he could see them. He didn't bother with camouflage because he wasn't going to need it. Letting his stream of fire go, he arched it perfectly, scorching over their faces in one long torrent of pale bluish, almost invisible flames.

Their heads burst into flames as hideous screeches filled the air, their bodies plummeting toward the trees below.

His fire had never burned so hot before but the need to protect Victoria and his clan seared bone deep, something dark inside him breaking free as he dipped down toward the trees, following the falling dragons and avoiding the others coming his way.

Behind him he heard others coming as backup but ignored them, focusing on the three flapping and flailing in their descent. He trusted his brother to have his back and for some reason he trusted the male, Gavin, though he had no clue why. The unbidden thought fled his mind as quickly as it entered.

On a burst of energy, he flew at the closest dragon before it hit one of the tree tops, savagely biting down on its neck, ripping through the tendons and muscles, breathing fire as he tore through its spinal cord.

Tossing the head away, he brought his wings in tight and dove through a cluster of foliage, avoiding branches as he flew with vicious speed.

Just as the trees started to thin he spotted two naked human males on the snowy ground below, stumbling against the snow as if they thought they could run from him. Fools.

There was nowhere they could hide now. His brother had told him that a dragon's essence protected them to an extent from another dragon's fire for a limited time during battle. But these three hadn't been able to protect themselves and he wasn't sure why he'd burned right through their bodies so quickly.

Calling on the rage that drove him to protect Victoria, he let loose another stream, the fire ripping from his body and hitting its target. The male on the left incinerated, a scorching black pocket of charred remains staining the white snow.

He slowed his descent and forced the change to his human form before he hit the ground. He barely felt the cold as he rolled onto the snow, blade clutched in his hand. A power like he'd never experienced before flowed through his veins, jacking him up on an adrenaline so intense it was as if he'd had a pure shot of energy injected directly into his heart.

Swiveling toward the other male, the darkest part of him smiled at the sniveling excuse for a dragon in front of him. His face and upper body were burned beyond recognition, his skin peeling away as he tried to run, but he couldn't find purchase against the snow, his screams agonizing.

Drawing the blade back, Drake sliced through the male's neck, a clean stroke separating head from body. Before the head hit the snow Drake lit it on fire, turning everything to ash.

Without pause or taking time to enjoy his kills, he shifted forms and took to the sky. He felt invincible, as if nothing could stop him as he burst through the treetops once again.

One Veles dragon remained.

The last fire-and-sun-colored dragon was flying away, high up the mountain. If Drake had been in human form, he'd have laughed.

No one could escape him now.

A dark hunger fueled him, the need to destroy this beast who had come after his mate pushing him faster and faster until everything blurred around him. In his peripheral he was vaguely aware of his brother in pursuit not far behind him, but Drake ignored him.

Ignored everything but his target as the male suddenly dropped, trying to use the trees as cover.

That intense burn built inside him again. On instinct he let the stream of pale, blue flame go. It incinerated the trees, carving a clear path to the screeching shifter who had nowhere to go.

Dropping through the smoldering ashes in a freefall, he aimed directly at the male, not surprised when the dragon rolled midair and shot fire at him in harsh, orange flames.

Drake flew through it, the fire barely grazing him as he opened his jaws wide and leveled a blast hotter than anything he'd delivered so far right at the dragon's underbelly. He cut a path straight up the male's body, the beast splitting wide open before bursting into ash and nothingness.

Though Drake tried to slow his descent he was going too fast. Before he would have slammed into the earth face first, he rolled, letting his shoulder and back take the brunt of the hit as he tumbled on his side.

His wings protested as he rolled to his back, but he didn't try to fight it, instead embraced the jerky movements until he slammed into a tree. It shuddered from the impact, snow dusting his entire body.

As he tried to clear his mind, Conall landed beside him, almost a mirror image of Drake in his dragon form, though perhaps a fraction smaller. When his brother shifted to human form, Drake did the same. It took longer this time, as if his beast wanted to hold on to him.

Breathing hard, he stood, picking up the fallen blade as adrenaline still jagged through him. Before he could speak another dragon landed with a hard thud, snow flying everywhere. His body was a bluish-green with pale, blue wings that glittered like jewels. The sapphire eyes told him it was Bran even before the male shifted, letting his primal side know this male wasn't a threat.

"The females?" Drake asked, looking between them.

"Safe," Bran said. "Gavin told me. We're telepathically linked."

For some reason, that knowledge sounded familiar. He brushed it off though, only caring that Victoria was safe. He wouldn't rest easy until he saw her with his own eyes, but some of his tension eased. "The warriors are all dead?"

Bran's expression darkened. "Yes. I've already dispatched our warriors to destroy the rest of the warriors in their clan. This kind of attack in broad daylight will not be tolerated."

Conall's eyebrows rose the slightest fraction as he looked at Bran. "If you require backup, our warriors are available."

The other leader nodded. "They're closer to my people in distance. It will be done by tonight."

A dark part of Drake was angry at the knowledge. His dragon wanted to destroy them all, wanted to bathe them in fire and watch them burn. The sudden craving for violence made him pause, reminding him of his time in Hell. Time he wanted to forget. He didn't want to be that male.

"Both our sets of warriors are headed to the cabin, but we need to talk," Bran continued.

"About what?" Conall's voice was neutral enough, but there was an underlying edge to it.

Drake didn't want to sit around and talk; he needed to see Victoria, but he remained where he was.

"What the hell was that?" the other leader asked, his focus on Drake.

Drake frowned. "What was what?"

"The blue fire," Bran said.

Drake didn't know so he shrugged. "What did it look like? Fucking fire."

Bran's jaw tightened. "It basically incinerated those dragons."

"Yeah and you're welcome." What the hell was this questioning bullshit? He took a step forward, ready to hoof it back to the cabin, but stopped at his brother's expression. Conall seemed concerned by it too.

Bran rubbed the back of his neck. "I don't know what you remember about, well anything, but we've all got a basic essence that protects us from other dragons' fire. It won't last forever under an attack. Eventually it wears down and we can be burned by an opposing force, which is why we normally just rip off our opponents' heads. What you did . . . I've never seen it. And I've never heard this was a Petronilla trait." He sounded as if he was choosing his words carefully.

"It's not," Conall said, even though Bran hadn't specifically asked.

Drake didn't think there was a right answer even if he had one for what he'd done. All he knew was that Victoria had been in danger and he'd reacted. It had been different than before at the cabin in Tennessee. This time there had been a bigger threat and something dark inside him had flared to life with the intensity of the sun. He'd felt unstoppable. But that wasn't something he was sharing with an opposing clan leader. "I have nothing more to say. If you want to try to stop me from getting to my mate, go for it. Otherwise, I'll meet you back at the cabin."

Without waiting for a response, Drake ran through the snow up the hill, uncaring that he was naked. His body burned hotter than normal, the cold not affecting him at all. As he reached the top of the hill, Victoria was at the bottom of the lodge's stairs, Gabriel behind her, two blades in the Guardian's hands.

Everything faded away when he saw her, long, black hair free around her face and shoulders, her green eyes shimmering. Shit, were those tears? He raced toward her, dropping the blade in the snow before he caught her midair when she jumped at him. She wrapped her legs and arms around him as she buried her face in his neck.

"I saw you go down in those trees and..." Her voice caught on a sob, his neck wet from her tears. Shit, she was shaking too.

He held her tight, rubbing his hand up and down her spine as he tried to comfort her. The feel of her so close, wrapped around him soothed him on the most primal level.

But it also made him feel as if he didn't deserve her touch. He'd just destroyed three dragons and felt no guilt. If anything he was amped up for more bloodshed. "I'm okay," he murmured. And she was too. The only thing that mattered.

When he met Gabriel's gaze, he nodded at the Guardian in silent thanks for protecting Victoria. He knew that Gabriel would have preferred to be fighting, that staying back would have tested every warrior bone in his body. Gabriel nodded once in acceptance, but there was something in the male's gaze that gave Drake pause. It was respect and something else.

Something he didn't know if he wanted to define because it made him question his choice to bring Victoria here at all.

She shouldn't be here. Not when he had no clue if the Devlin clan would even be able to finish off the Veles clan. No, she shouldn't be here at all. Not when next time he might not be able to protect her. According to what his brother had told him, these types of attacks were not common in the dragon world, especially not in the middle of the damn day. And he didn't like that all this was happening now that he'd returned to his clan.

When Gabriel stepped forward, closing the distance between them instead of giving Drake and Victoria space, Drake knew something else was wrong.

"We have a problem," Gabriel murmured, low enough for only Victoria and Drake to hear. "We need to head somewhere private. Now."

Victoria dropped her legs from around him and by her fierce expression he knew she was aware of whatever Gabriel was referring to. Her mouth pulled into a thin line as she glanced up at the blasted out sunroom. He handed her the blade he'd made her. Instead of sheathing it, she held it tight in her grip.

"This way," Victoria said, motioning toward the woods on the side of the house where a gray and brown wolf stood keeping guard.

The intelligent, amber eyes would have told him it was Rhea even if he hadn't seen her in wolf form before.

She looked at them, then turned tail and trotted out of sight.

Drake glanced behind him to see Conall and Bran heading up the hill. He nodded once at his brother and motioned with his hands that he was going to talk to the others. Conall nodded back and Drake just ignored Bran. He didn't need to tell the other leader anything.

Drake wanted to check on his sister, but with Conall there he wasn't worried about her. Ten minutes later the three of them met with Rhea deep in the woods. As she shifted to her human form, Gabriel tossed her his shirt. She didn't seem to be concerned with her nakedness, but put it on anyway.

"Nice kills," Gabriel said before anyone could talk, looking between Rhea and Drake.

Drake's eyebrows raised as he glanced at the female shifter. "You killed one?"

"Hell yeah."

That was impressive. He'd ask Gabriel for details later. "What's going on?" He wrapped his arm around Victoria's shoulders.

Rhea raked a hand through her wild hair, her jaw clenched tight. "There was silver in the mimosas. I scented it."

Ice congealed in his gut. "You're sure?" Drake knew Victoria hadn't drank any. The Veles clan had attacked before either he or Victoria had tasted any.

She nodded. "Yeah. Before I could say anything, shit went haywire."

"Did either of you drink any?" Drake asked.

Rhea shook her head and Gabriel snorted before he said, "I'm not drinking anything called a fucking mimosa."

"Did you scent any?" he asked Victoria.

She shook her head. "No. Gabriel couldn't scent it either after Rhea told us. But she's sure it's in there."

He frowned and glanced at Rhea for an explanation.

"Colloidal silver is difficult to detect, period. Even to wolf shifters. Put it in something like orange juice and champagne and it's guaranteed to hide the very faint scent of it. But I'm a tracker." She shrugged, as if that should explain everything.

"And?"

"I have a stronger sense of smell than pretty much all supernatural beings, including our Alpha. Spiro's a tracker like me too," she said, referring to one of the Stavros packmates. "It gives us an edge when hunting."

Drake frowned, digesting the information. "Silver won't hurt dragons."

"Exactly," Victoria murmured.

So either she or all three of the wolves were targets. But he was betting it was just her. "You've been targeted." A deep, ugly rage began to unfurl inside him. Whoever had done it, would die.

Her eyebrows drew together as they did when she was deep in thought. "It would appear so. It's possible that Gabriel and Rhea were targeted too, but that doesn't make sense. It would be easy enough to put something in those mimosas that wouldn't hurt most who drank it, to target one or a few individuals. If I had to guess, I'd say someone wanted to hurt me to hurt you."

"It's possible someone from the Petronilla pack told the Veles clan where you were in Tennessee," Gabriel continued. "Who else other than them and us knew you were there."

"Bo," Victoria said.

"I don't think he'd do anything against our pack," Gabriel said.

Drake nodded. He remembered the way the male had protectively stood in front of Victoria at his club, the action almost instinctive. And what motive would the half-demon have? "Agreed."

"And now someone wanted to poison Victoria or all of us the same day the Veles dragons attack your clan and the Devlin's," Rhea added.

"The poisoning seems like overkill though, if the Veles clan thought they could surprise us with an attack." Drake wondered if the two events were separate. Because how would someone from the Veles clan get in the cabin to poison them? Especially when they'd just arrived this morning. "Someone in the Devlin clan or my clan tried to poison you. Where are the drinks now?"

"Keelin poured some into a Mason jar so we could test it," Victoria said.

"Shit." Drake rubbed a hand over his face. Shit, shit, shit. "The female Fia made the drinks. And she was nervous."

Victoria nodded. "Yes, but it would be so stupid to make the drinks if she intended to poison someone. She doesn't strike me as stupid. I think she was simply nervous to see you after so long."

"Shit," Drake said again. He didn't want friction with the Devlin clan, not when they could be powerful allies, but he also didn't want to endanger his clan or Victoria. She was the most important thing of all.

"That about sums it up," Gabriel muttered. "What are you going to do?"

Instead of answering the Guardian, Drake turned Victoria in his arms, placing his hands on her shoulders. "I think you need to head back to Biloxi with Gabriel and Rhea. Too much is going on and I need you safe. I'll come for you once everything is sorted out." He was going to find out whoever was behind the poisonings and if need be, finish off the Veles clan. He couldn't risk another attack on Victoria. What if he wasn't there to protect her again? Next time the guilty party might succeed. If that happened . . . no. He couldn't imagine a world without Victoria in it. He *wouldn't*.

Victoria gently cupped his cheek with one hand and placed another palm on his bare chest. She smiled sweetly at him. "Hell. No."

CHAPTER TWENTY-FOUR

W hat. The. Hell.

Dragos had destroyed four Veles dragons in minutes with a pale, blue fire. Everyone in the village was on lockdown and they were all talking about the powerful display the male had made. And some were wondering if he should be leader. He was the eldest so it made sense he would be, but it hadn't seemed as if he was interested.

Those fucking Veles dragons shouldn't have attacked and he wasn't sorry they were dead.

He was also glad he'd found out about Dragos's ability. He wondered if it had something to do with his time in Hell, but that didn't make sense. Whatever it was, he didn't care. It was clear that he could never take on the male one on one.

So he'd have to move on to his next target: Keelin. She was so naïve and trusting she should be easy enough to subdue. That wasn't the hard part. Cornering her alone was.

Arya, her mother, would never recover if Keelin died. Never. Maybe the bitch would go mad, just as she'd accused his own mother of doing. He rolled his shoulders, as if it could lift the agonizing memories of losing both his parents.

According to the *great* Arya and the older Dragos, his mother had gone mad. Or feral, as other supernaturals liked to call it. She hadn't though. She'd just been more in touch with her dragon than most.

So what if she'd killed a few humans or livestock? Thousands of years ago they'd been respected and feared. Still myth in most parts of the world except in certain areas. Where dragons had thrived, the people had thrived also. They'd been protected. In exchange for that protection his mother had taken what she wanted for their clan.

It had only been fair after all.

It was unfortunate they didn't live like that now. They were fucking dragons in a world full of weak humans. He and the other supernaturals should be ruling this planet.

His inner dragon clawed at him, its talons scraping and raking against his insides, whispering that he undergo the change, that he take whatever he wanted. The darkest part of him smiled, imagining what it would be like to reveal himself to humans, to go on a rampage destroying anything he wanted. His own clan or other clan leaders would try to kill him and maybe succeed, but by then it wouldn't matter. They'd be revealed to the world and fire would rain down everywhere. It would be a fucking bloodbath between humans and all supernaturals.

His soul sang at the possibility of that type of freedom. To not have to hide who he was. To anyone.

His phone rang, the low tune bringing him back to reality. He frowned at his inner dragon's darker thoughts. He couldn't reveal himself to humans. That would be foolish. A dull throb ached at the base of his skull.

He couldn't end up like his mother and inadvertently, his father. Because his father had died when his mother had been taken down, as bonded mates did when they lost their other half. No, he would avoid their fate. He'd go into Protective Hibernation to protect himself before his inner dragon wrestled too much control from him. The thought of sleeping for a couple hundred years was exactly what he needed. No one would be able to find him then.

First he was going to kill Keelin, but he wouldn't just kill her. No, he was going to make sure his clan remembered him before he went into Protective Hibernation. He'd make sure that when Arya finally woke up, she woke up to Hell. Perhaps he'd be able to take the shifter bitch too. His poisoning attempt had failed because of those inept Veles dragons. Now it appeared he'd have to be more hands-on.

Tonight if possible.

"You can try to stare me down all you want. You're not going to win this stupid argument. And it *is* stupid." Victoria crossed her arms over her chest as she glared at Drake, refusing to get up from where she sat behind the desk in Conall's library.

After shit had gone haywire, as Rhea liked to say, they'd all returned to the village and the Devlins had moved to another location, though they were still in the area. Their precise whereabouts were unknown to the Petronilla clan as of now. Only Victoria, Drake, Gabriel, Rhea, Keelin and Conall knew about the attempted poisoning. And of course the guilty party—or parties. Drake and Conall wanted to keep the knowledge of the poisoning quiet until they discovered more clues. Any freaking clues at this point. Sure it might be the Devlin clan, but that just seemed so freaking obvious.

And stupid.

So for now Victoria was scouring books on various dragon histories. Conall's library was extensive and she was determined to find out what had caused Drake to emit that pale, blue fire with seemingly impossible heat. He'd confessed to her that he had no idea how he'd done it, only that he'd felt different when he'd shifted earlier, more savage. It had seemed like he wanted to say more, but he'd held back.

"Wanting to keep you safe is not stupid." Drake mirrored her pose, his big arms crossed over his chest as he leaned against the front of another desk. The muscles in his arms bunched, flexing tight as he stood there.

Her gaze strayed over every inch of bared flesh and she was barely able to contain the growl of need rising up inside her. In the woods he'd been absolutely beautiful and naked and it hadn't mattered that he'd just killed four dragons. She'd simply wanted to jump him once she'd seen he was unharmed even though they'd had no privacy. Until now.

But things between them were awkward and even though she still wanted to jump him, they needed to hash things out. "I don't need or want to be locked up tight and kept safe from the outside world. I'm a capable shifter. Treat me like one."

"You're capable, but a dragon could still kill you," he snapped, his eyes glittering bright silver.

"Maybe. Maybe not."

"No maybe. They could fry you in seconds." His face twisted in agony as he said the words, his pain making her want to comfort him.

But she stayed where she was. She wouldn't let him put her in gilded cage, no matter how good his intentions. "I've got your dragon's essence, remember."

His jaw clenched tight, his expression darkening to the point she could actually envision steam coming out of his ears. "That's not a long-term solution. Until this shit is figured out—"

She shoved up from the desk, shaking as she stood. "Just *stop*. I'm not leaving you to deal with this by yourself. If you think I would ever entertain that idea, you don't know me at all. If you want me as a mate, we'll be equals and I'll never stick my head in the sand to leave you to deal with anything alone. That's not how partnerships work!" She shouted the last part, unable to stop the rising pitch of her voice because damn it, if he thought she'd ever leave him, it sliced her up.

Victoria rounded the desk and stalked toward him when he didn't respond. He just watched her with a simmering mash of emotions. Anger for certain, but there was a lot of lust in those bright silver eyes. Hoping he'd see reason, she stood in front of him and laid a calm hand on his chest, which was unfortunately covered with a shirt. "Drake—"

He crushed his mouth to hers, the dominating move taking her by surprise. She was still mad at him and kissing wasn't going to solve anything but . . . Oh, god, he tasted so damn good.

Arching into him, she wrapped her arms around him, sliding one hand behind his neck and cupping his head.

He moaned into her mouth, the savage growl making her nipples painfully tighten. She needed more of him. So much more.

Her body hummed with energy. Unable to take not touching more of him any longer, she slid her hands under his shirt and shoved it up. Taking her cue, he grabbed the hem and yanked it over his head, moving back a fraction as he did.

Her hungry gaze raked over the hard lines and striations of his incredible body. His breathing was as erratic as hers, the rise and fall of his broad chest making heat pool between her legs as she imagined kissing every inch of it.

Before she could move, he came at her like a male possessed, grabbing her hips and lifting her so that she had to wrap her legs around his waist. Not that she was complaining. She craved this closeness. After she thought she'd lost him in the woods, she needed reassurance that he was here. Alive.

And all hers.

Before she'd blinked her back was flat against the desk and Drake was covering her, his huge frame dominating everything as he slid his hands into her hair, holding her head in place as his tongue tangled with hers.

The way he kissed her was raw, like he was fucking her with his tongue. At that thought, she spread her legs wider, welcoming the feel of his hard length pressing insistently against the juncture of her thighs. Too bad they both had pants on.

Her fingers dug into his back hard as she arched into him again, writhing against him so he knew exactly what she wanted. She didn't care if their first time was on this desk. She just wanted Drake.

His kisses grew more intense as he reached between their bodies and unbuttoned her jeans. After tugging the zipper down, he slid his hand down her panties and cupped her mound, sliding a finger deep inside her. Slowly he began thrusting in and out of her, her inner walls clenching around him with each deeper push.

"You're so wet," he growled against her mouth, moving to trail kisses along her jaw. "I want to fuck you right here."

"Do it," she rasped out, nipping his earlobe between her teeth as she raked her fingers down his back. His muscles bunched under her touch. She slid her hands under the waist of his jeans and gripped his taut skin.

"Not . . . here." He pulled his finger out of her before sliding two in and pushing deep.

She let out a groan at the way he stretched her. It wasn't enough but at least he wasn't completely stopping. "Why not?"

"Fuck my fingers," he whispered darkly. "Come on them." A possessive growl.

His words sent a spiral of need through her as she rolled her hips against his hand. When he started strumming her clit with his thumb she completely lost it. Hadn't even realized she was so close to orgasm until he tweaked her sensitive bundle of nerves.

Body bowing tight, the unexpected climax ripped through her, shattering her nerve endings. "Drake." She couldn't hold back the shout of his name as she moved against his hand.

He buried his face against her neck, raking his teeth against her pulse point as her inner walls convulsed around his fingers.

Letting her head fall back against the desk as her orgasm peaked, she saw that the room was lit up like a Christmas tree. She wasn't sure how long she writhed against him but eventually her climax faded, leaving her loose limbed and emotionally exhausted.

Wrapping her arms around his back, she held tight. When he withdrew his fingers from her, her body immediately mourned the loss. "Thank you," she whispered, not trusting her voice more than that.

He leaned back to look at her but was still covering her with his body. She savored the feel of his weight on top of her, the security of Drake. Lifting his hand he licked the first then second finger he'd just had buried inside her. The way he watched her as he did it was so primal a shiver snaked through her.

"Love your taste," he murmured, his gaze pinned to hers.

She started to respond when a knock on the door made her jump. Drake made an annoyed rumbling sound in his chest and glanced over his shoulder. "Who the fuck is it?" he shouted, his words more of a growl than anything.

"Conall. Bran called. Might have some information for us. He's waiting at the gate."

"Give me a sec." Drake cursed under his breath but pushed up from her. As he did, he helped her sit even though she didn't need it. "I just want you safe," he said as he slid off the desk and grabbed his discarded shirt.

"I know you do. I want you safe too. But I don't want to lock you up somewhere."

"I don't want to lock you up either," he snapped as he once again covered that beautiful body with his shirt. "Going back to stay with your pack is just good sense."

Frowning, she zipped and buttoned her pants. "So I don't have good sense?"

"I didn't say that. It's just smarter if you put distance between here."

"Says *you*." Her ire rose again, swift and sharp. She faced off with him, her hands on her hips.

"Damn it Victoria!" Before he could continue, Conall, Keelin, Gabriel and Rhea strode in the room, all carrying manila files.

"Your argument will have to wait." Gabriel's voice was completely unapologetic. "Conall's got more files on everyone who was at the cabin this morning. And on Petronilla clan members who your immediate family has had issues with, no matter how small. I also called Finn and he's calling in a favor to Bo. He's going to see if the half-demon has heard anything through his supernatural grapevine about anyone having a beef with your clan. Other than the Veles clan." His voice was wry as he said the last part.

Victoria was glad she was dressed but knew the others must scent what she and Drake had been doing minutes before. Her face flushed but she ignored it as Conall looked at her.

"Victoria, if you wouldn't mind, I'd like you to keep researching Drake's . . . ability," Conall said.

She nodded. That was fine with her.

"What else did Bran say?" Drake asked.

Conall shook his head. "Nothing. Just that he wants to see me in person."

"I'm going with you," Drake said immediately, then paused, tilting his head in Victoria's direction, but refusing to look at her. She could practically feel the wall he was erecting between them even after what they'd just shared. All because he wanted her to leave. "The house is being guarded, but keep your blade on you."

She gritted her teeth at his coldness. "Of course." She had it sheathed and strapped on against her calf so that it touched her skin at all times. Hidden and accessible. Victoria looked at Drake, willing him to meet her gaze as he headed to the door with his brother, but he wouldn't look her way.

His refusal to even look at her was a punch to her senses. The way he was completely shutting her out, as if he was encasing himself in this icy wall she couldn't breach. Like all shifters, she needed physical touch, especially from her mate. Or future mate as it were. Especially in a situation like this.

As the door shut quietly behind them, her eyes started to burn with tears so she moved back to the desk she'd been at and started to read the same bit of text, not wanting anyone to see her crying.

How freaking pathetic.

The room was impossibly quiet though, as if the others were afraid to breathe too loud. And she felt all their eyes on her. For a few minutes she just stared at the page in front of her, but everything was wavy and unreadable through her tears. She blinked quickly and when a drop fell onto the text, she stood. Keeping her head down, she rounded the desk.

"He just wants you safe," Gabriel murmured.

The fact that Gabriel of all people was saying that, made her want to cry even more. Without responding, she hurried from the room, and headed in the direction of the front of the house. There was a guest bathroom next to the kitchen and she desperately wanted privacy right about now.

Shoving the bathroom door open, she angrily swiped at her falling tears. She shouldn't be crying right now, she needed to be doing research. Throat clogged, she started to turn on the faucet when the door cracked open. She turned, ready to tell whoever it was she wanted to be alone when Keelin tentatively stepped inside.

"Hey," the female murmured. "Males can be dicks sometimes."

To hear the proper female say dick made Victoria laugh, the unexpectedness lifting some of her tension and drying her tears. "No kidding."

Stepping fully inside, Keelin leaned against the double-sink granite counter. "Conall's always been protective and my parents stupidly so. Must be a trait that runs in the family."

Victoria leaned against the counter too. "I don't mind the protectiveness, I just can't stand him shutting me out and insisting I actually leave." She would swear that it almost physically hurt. She absently rubbed the middle of her chest.

"I know. I think he's just trying to deal with everything in his own way. After being locked away for so long, you belong to him for lack of a better phrase. I can't imagine that he's ever had anything that belonged to him. Not that I think you're a possession, but you know what I mean."

Victoria *did* know what Keelin meant. But it didn't make her feel any better. "Yeah, I guess." But she and Drake needed to talk later, when they had some privacy. This kind of thing with him shutting her out would never work. Not for a real relationship. And she was in this for the long haul. But, she couldn't think about any of that now. Research was the only thing that might distract her and it was certainly better than talking about things she didn't want to focus on. "Thanks for checking on me. I'm okay, I swear. Let's just head back to the library."

"Okay." But instead of moving toward the door, Keelin pulled her into a tight hug, the small female's grip strong.

"Crap, now I'm going to cry again," she muttered, returning the other woman's embrace. She hadn't realized how much she'd needed the tactile sensation until now.

Laughing lightly, Keelin pulled back. "Things will be fine once you two talk."

Likely true but it didn't make Victoria feel much better at the moment. Nodding, she followed the other woman out, but froze when she saw a familiar male pointing a gun right at them. It registered that he had a suppressor on the weapon. Icy fingers clenched around her chest. Before she could move or think about reacting, he pulled the trigger, his aim dead on. A bullet slammed into her stomach.

The sound of a puff of air filled the room as pain rippled through her, her nerve endings on fire as she tumbled back into the bathroom. Her back hit the cold tile as she tried to scream for help. Everything funneled out as Keelin fell next to her, her eyes wide open in shock and horror as the female groaned in pain.

Victoria tried to roll over, to find purchase on the ground, but the male shot again, hitting her in the stomach a second time. Raw agony bloomed inside her. She opened her mouth, trying to find her voice but all that came out was a low moan. "Drake," she whispered his name or tried to. She needed to warn him, to keep him safe but could barely keep her eyes open.

Blackness edged her vision as the shockwaves of pain washed through her like a blowtorch. Her throat tightened, making it impossible to scream. Her wolf begged to take over but she overpowered her inner animal, embracing the pain and taking it as her own.

She couldn't shift. Not now. That blade attached to her calf was a strong weapon and she needed it. Her animal side seemed to understand her need because it abated as she started to fade, the pain like razorblades sweeping across her middle. The creeping blackness consumed her as she fell into unconsciousness.

CHAPTER TWENTY-FIVE

Bran straightened as an SUV jerked to a halt in front of the locked down village, clasping the file he had in his hand against his side. He'd wanted to see Conall in person because he wasn't sure who he could trust. Not with the information he'd found. He wasn't going to pass it off to anyone and he wasn't emailing the male. This intel was going directly from him to Conall.

Conall and Drake exited the vehicle at the same time, both moving like warriors on a mission. If he was going to pursue Keelin—and he planned to—he would have his hands full with her brothers. Not that she should be his concern now. But she was. Something about her had affected him and he wanted—needed—to know more about her.

The gate opened as the two males reached it. Bran guessed someone was guarding it from a location not visible to outsiders and opened it when anyone wanted to leave. He didn't wait for them to reach him, but strode over the asphalt, his rubber soled boots silent.

"The rest of the Veles warriors have been eliminated, including the clan leader," Bran said. A small part of him felt guilt that the female mates of the warriors also died but the clan had declared war, knowing what would happen to them if their attack failed.

"You could have told me that over the phone." Conall's gaze flicked down to the file in Bran's hand for a moment.

"We received interesting intel from one of the Veles warriors before he died. My warrior agreed to put an end to his suffering for any information about why they attacked and how they knew where to attack Drake the first time. Their leader received an anonymous tip on where to find Drake the first time. That was all the warrior knew, but he gave me the date and time the call was made so I had a contact retrieve the leader's phone records."

"Contact?" Conall asked.

Bran nodded. That was all he was saying on that subject because he wasn't telling anyone he'd called his former boss in black ops for a favor. Getting phone records was fucking child's play for his old team. "Yeah. Cross-referenced all the calls with any connection to any known dragon clans. The call was made from a burner cell and pinged off a tower down in Biloxi." Which would have left them screwed in locating whoever had bought it because the male had purchased the thing in cash. "But the guy turned the damn thing on which makes it traceable. Tracked the signal back to an address in your village. It's in the file."

Conall's and Drake's eyes flared silver, the deadliness rolling off them both a palpable thing. After seeing

Drake in action Bran was tempted to tell his old boss about the male's abilities, but wouldn't. The guy could be a valuable asset in the protection of all supernaturals, but after being locked up in Hell, the male deserved a break. And to live in peace with his mate.

"Just thought you'd want to know," he continued. He didn't have the name of whoever lived at the address because the Petronilla clan purchased everything through a corporation and no one's names were listed. Would make it impossible to plan a specific attack unless you knew where someone lived. But he had no doubt that Conall knew the name and address of every one of his clan members.

Jaw tight, Conall flipped open the file and his eyes burned supernova before returning to gray. He nodded once at Bran. "I'll need to verify this, but thank you."

Drake was simply silent, his dragon visible in his silver eyes and pushing at the surface. Not that Bran blamed the guy. Anyone stupid enough to fuck with a dragon's mate deserved to die. Bran just nodded at Conall and started to leave. He knew the male would be in touch soon enough. They had more to talk about after Conall cleaned house. Like creating a solid alliance between their clans.

As he reached the driver's side door, he paused and gritted his teeth. Looking back at the males who were already heading back to the gate he cringed at his fucking stupidity, but he couldn't stop himself. "Conall."

The male stopped and glanced over his shoulder. "Yeah?"

"Is . . . Keelin being protected?" Fuck his pride, he had to know. Needed to know she was safe. If the Petronilla clan had a traitor in their midst, the female could be a target considering she was part of their royal line.

Drake's eyebrows rose just the smallest fraction, but Conall's expression didn't alter. "Yes." He turned away without another word.

Good enough for Bran. Hell, it'd have to be. As the gate started to close, he slid back into the driver's seat and reversed. He hated the thought of not being able to protect Keelin himself, but knew there was no other option. For now.

Joy spread through him as blood slowly pooled over the bathroom tile, but there was no time to enjoy the beautiful sight of Keelin and Victoria bleeding.

He had to move quickly.

Conall's house was under watch, but he'd used a combination of his camouflage and knowledge to gain entrance. Even with the guards, the home's security system had been armed. Except there were two small windows not linked to the rest of the system. The stained glass windows had recently been installed and he knew Conall hadn't had the system updated yet. He'd been too busy searching for his brother.

All it had taken was camouflage, patience and skill. He might not be as strong as Conall or Drake, but he was gifted in other ways. The stained glass windows were two of the highest windows in the house so he'd had to shift to his human form at the last minute, mid-air, and clutch onto the frame, balancing himself before popping the window free. Not all dragons could do that.

He'd been feeling smug at his genius but he'd never imagined he'd see his target ducking into one of the bathrooms as he'd come downstairs. He'd wanted to know what the hell everyone was doing here. Conall had put his home on lockdown with the shifters and his sister in it.

For all he knew they were on to him. His dragon pushed roughly against the surface, begging to be freed, to take over completely. He shoved it back and stayed on task.

The wolf shifter was bleeding faster than Keelin so he grabbed a towel and tied it tight around her middle to staunch it. He didn't want her dying or losing too much blood. Not when he could still use her. She didn't move or utter a sound as he shifted her body. Good.

Keelin's eyes were closed but she was moaning softly. That wouldn't do. He needed her quiet and he needed to get out of here unseen.

Unfortunately he'd have to set off the alarm to do it. The only good thing was, the guards would be looking in the house for the break in, not for someone escaping. He'd be gone by the time they discovered the blood.

There was no shower curtain in the bathroom and he needed something to help him transport the females. Blood pounding in his ears, he cracked open the door. The hallway was empty.

Using stealth, he hurried down the hall toward the main sitting room. There was a huge afghan throw in there that would be suitable for his needs. On silent feet he hurried to the room but paused when he scented one of his clan mates.

Peering inside, he saw Cody, his cousin by marriage, standing by one of the windows, hands shoved into his pockets. Right next to that damn blanket. He didn't want to hurt Cody, but it looked as if he had no choice. There wasn't time to race around looking for another blanket. He had to be out of here in the next sixty seconds.

Moving quietly he went to one of the open displays of swords over the fireplace mantel and gently lifted it. His steps were silent as he navigated around the couch, but his blood rushed impossibly loud in his ears.

His cousin suddenly stiffened, faintly inhaling. He must have scented his presence. As Cody started to turn, he dove the last few feet, sword raised, and plunged it into his cousin's back.

The male let out a grunt of surprise, quickly followed by a shout of pain as he stumbled forward, catching himself on a high-backed chair before he fell to his knees, gasping.

Ignoring Cody, he snatched the blanket. "I'm sorry," he muttered. It wasn't as if his cousin would die from the wound. But it would give him enough time to get out of the house undetected.

Racing from the room, he didn't bother with camouflage now. He'd need to save all his energy for when he made his escape.

Back in the bathroom he found nothing had changed except Keelin was now unconscious too. Even better. But he needed to make sure she was alive. Her and the shifter. At least for now. Tossing the blanket out on the ground, he rolled them into it then tied it securely at both ends so that they were wrapped up tight. Wasn't perfect but it would have to do.

Now came the tricky part.

He'd have one chance to do this right. First he dragged the females to right below the bathroom window. Unlocking it, he took a deep breath then slid it up.

The alarm blared.

His heart pounded wildly in his chest, a shot of energy slamming through him as he grabbed the bundle and shoved them through the opening. They were on the first floor so the drop wasn't far. Quickly following, he jumped through and didn't bother shutting the window. One of the guards or even Conall himself would soon figure out where he'd escaped from with the females.

The scent and pools of blood on the tile guaranteed that. It wouldn't matter by then, if he played this right.

Not bothering to strip, he underwent the change, letting his clothes and shoes shred on the icy ground. The blare of the alarm seemed intensified as he shifted to his dragon form. Though his adrenaline was high and his concentration was shot he managed to force a faint camouflage in place as he took flight.

He held the bundled females in his talons close to his body, hoping the lower half of him hid most of the blanket as he flew north, heading straight for the mountains and thousands of acres of untamed land.

Soon both females would be dead, but he wouldn't let their lives go to waste. Not when he could open another Hell Gate using all Keelin's blood. When he opened the Hell Gate this time, he wouldn't be closing it afterward.

CHAPTER TWENTY-SIX

"Whose address is it?" Drake asked as he and Conall slid into the SUV.

"Cody. He's our cousin from our father's side of the family. He's a little old school, not into inter-species matings, but…" Conall's expression tightened as he sped up. "Text Lennox, tell him to meet us at Cody's house. They're tight."

Fighting the rage that a family member might truly be involved in all this, Drake pulled out his phone and typed in the message. "You think Lennox's presence will help?"

"If Cody sold you out to the Veles clan, he's dead. But I want to give him the benefit of the doubt. We're family." His brother shook his head, as if he couldn't believe Cody was guilty. "And if he was smart enough to use a burner phone, it doesn't make sense he'd turn it on in his own home."

Drake was glad he didn't have strong ties to the rest of the clan right now. "Whoever the guilty party is, I will eliminate them." That way his brother wouldn't have to kill someone he was close to.

Conall didn't respond. When Drake's phone buzzed with an incoming text he glanced at it and froze. At the same time, Conall's phone buzzed with an incoming call.

"Head to your house. Now." Drake stared at his caller ID, his heart caught in his throat. He'd expected a text from Lennox, but it was Gabriel. "Keelin and Victoria have been taken."

Taken.

His heart froze for a single moment before rage and terror splintered through him. He had to actively control his beast not to take over and start burning everything in sight. A cracking sound rent the air and he realized he'd broken the plastic handle off the side of the door. Releasing the crumbled pieces, he dragged in a breath, forcing himself to remain calm.

Conall cursed as he took a right at the next corner and pulled out his own phone. Drake stayed silent, listening as his brother spoke to one of the guards who was supposed to be watching the house.

"Hurry!" he roared as Conall took another turn. The truth was, they were almost there and his brother was driving at break neck speed, but Drake was too far over the edge.

Conall shoved his phone in his pocket. "There's blood in the bathroom. Victoria and Keelin's, according to their scents. Cody is in the living room. He was stabbed."

Victoria was bleeding. A scream ripped from his throat and fire coated the dash and glove compartment, the stench of melting plastic an assault on his senses.

"Keep it together," Conall snapped.

His brother's voice helped him rein in his beast. Barely. "Who took them?"

Conall gritted his teeth. "Not sure yet."

"Why the hell had Cody even been at your house when it was on lockdown?"

"He came by because he wanted to see what he could do to help. One of the guards left him alone in the sitting room and went to ask Keelin if Cody was allowed entrance. When he returned, Cody was trying to pull one of my swords out of his back. That's when the others realized Victoria and Keelin are missing. And . . . found their blood." Conall let out a savage curse, his knuckles white against the steering wheel.

Drake only cared about the wounded, missing females. "We're going to find them." Or Drake would die trying. But not before he ripped apart every inch of this planet to find Victoria. Fire burned in the back of his throat again, clawing, hungry to make whoever had dared to take his mate pay. He needed her safe, in his arms. With him.

He never should have left her, even under guard. This was his fault. Guilt threaded through every fiber of him. How could he have left her? The passenger window shattered as he slammed his elbow into it. If they didn't make it soon he was going to massacre the entire SUV.

Conall didn't respond, just took the last turn onto his street, the SUV slightly fishtailing as he revved the engine. He jerked to a halt directly in front of the iron gate in front of his house. Drake was already out of the passenger side before his brother had shut off the engine.

He raced through the open gate, his heart pounding out of control. Gabriel stood in the open doorway. The male's expression was murderous as he turned and motioned for Drake to follow.

Inside the foyer the male named Cody was sitting on the wood floor while Greer was tightening a thick, multi-layered bandage around his middle. If he'd been stabbed in the back he was already healing with a swiftness that told Drake he was old.

"What happened?" Drake asked as Conall stepped up next to him. He couldn't scent Victoria's blood, but soon enough he'd need to see where it was. To smell it, to track her . . . to save her. Because he refused to believe she was gone for good.

"I was in there." He tilted his head in the direction of the sitting room. "I was just waiting when I scented him. I started to turn and the fucker stabbed me from behind."

"Who?" Conall's voice was a jagged-edged sword.

"Nevin." Cody winced as Greer pressed her hands on either side of his back and abdomen, a soft blue glow emitting from her as she started using her healing gift.

Drake's cousin. The tall, blond male. If Cody was telling the truth, Drake was going to kill Nevin as soon as he got his hands on him.

Drake focused on Cody even though he wasn't sure the male was telling the truth. For all he knew Cody was lying and was involved in all this. Unfortunately Drake didn't know enough about his clan to know what the male's motives could be. He might have memories of fighting with Cody when they were children, but that didn't make the male a killer.

"You're sure it was him?" Conall asked.

Cody nodded. "Pretty sure. I know his scent and I could almost swear I heard him say 'I'm sorry'. But I didn't *see* him."

"His scent is in the bathroom along with Victoria and Keelin's," Lennox said. "He had to have taken them. The bathroom window's open. It's what set off the alarm. If I had to guess he flew north. Even if he was camouflaged it would have been difficult to conceal them if he flew over the village. North is the only direction that makes sense if he wanted to escape unseen." Fists clenched at his sides, his body vibrating with rage, he stood off to the side with Gabriel and Rhea.

They all looked ready to wage war.

Somehow Drake shoved his beast back down. The darkness inside him wanted out but the moment he let it free he'd lose all ability to reason. He couldn't go on a rampage. He had to remain calm and sane.

For Victoria.

He closed his eyes for a moment and all he could see was her beautiful face, her long, black hair falling softly over her shoulders, her sweet, open smile as she teased him.

She was depending on him. It was the only reason he hadn't demanded to see the bathroom yet. He couldn't see her blood and remain sane. Swallowing hard, Drake turned to his brother. "Why would Nevin target the females? What's the first thing that comes to mind?"

Conall started to shake his head but let out a savage curse. "It was long ago. *Thousands* of years ago. Our mother killed Nevin's mother—one of her sisters—because she'd gone mad. She was far beyond saving and had started killing humans. Eating them as if they were sacrifices to her. It was before we were born, but I know the story. We all do. No one blamed our mother though. It was a just kill and it grieved her to do it. It could be why he targeted Keelin. And it's possible he was behind your disappearance."

Drake didn't care so much about the why of it, he just wanted to know where he'd taken the females. Because it was clear the male was guilty. Without Victoria, Drake might as well throw himself back in Hell. Because that's what life without her would be. He looked at Cody, fighting to keep his inner dragon contained. It was growing more difficult and he knew his dragon showed in his eyes by the way Cody flinched back from him. "Where would he have taken them?"

Fear bled into the male's gaze. "I don't know."

Drake couldn't scent a lie but it was difficult to distinguish anything due to how out of control his emotions were. Right now fire burned in his throat, the need to destroy anything and everything to get to the woman he loved was a live, dark thing inside him.

As he looked at his brother, a vivid memory shattered through him like giant shards of glass slicing through his flesh. His throat tightened under the onslaught. He pressed a hand to his chest as the scene played in his mind like a movie.

Drake looked at the note his cousin had sent him. He and Cody had been fighting over something stupid again. He couldn't even remember what this time. Drake wasn't sure why his cousin was such an asshole sometimes but the male liked to push his buttons. Cody was a couple years older too, he should act better. At least that's what Drake's mom said.

Now Cody wanted to meet him. Drake would rather go play with his brother but he knew it would make his mother happy if he made things right with Cody. She always said family had to stick together.

Stripping, he took off his tunic and pants and bundled them into a tight ball before shoving them in his small pack. He went to the open window of his room in the clan's castle and hoisted himself up to the edge.

Camouflaging himself, he tossed his pack out the window then jumped, shifting mid-air as he'd been practicing. The rush was exhilarating as it overtook him, his wings snapping out in the cool dawn air. Swooping down, he snatched his pack in his talons before it hit the grassy earth below. Then he twisted his body, angling down along the rocky ledge of the cliff that bordered one side of the clan's castle.

His cousin wanted to meet close to the border with the Devlin clan's land. Drake knew he wasn't supposed to go there, but he did it anyway.

Maybe he should have told one of the warriors where he was going, but he was twelve—nearly a man—and didn't need a chaperone everywhere he went. Besides, he'd be fine with Cody. His cousin might be a jerk sometimes, but they were family and could protect themselves.

Miles later he reached the designated clearing. The big lake he and Cody liked to play in glistened under the rising sun, calm and beautiful. The sight always made him happy. It was early and no one was around. Not even Cody.

Unless he'd cloaked himself too.

Landing near the lake, Drake let his camouflage fall. He dipped his snout in the water and immediately pulled it out, giving his head a shake. Too cold for now.

Shifting back to his human form, he hurriedly dressed and looked around the clearing. Dew shimmered over the grass like shiny jewels and he loved the feel of it under his feet.

The sound of wings flapping behind him made him turn. Less than a moment later a giant dragon appeared. Not Cody. He and his cousin were about the size of adult rhinos and this male was huge, like his dad.

Drake smiled when he realized it was Nevin, his other cousin. Nevin was at least a decade older than him and Cody but sometimes played with them. He was handsome, according to pretty much every female, and Drake's mother said he had a natural charm that would land him a good mate soon.

Drake didn't know why anyone would want to mate, but his mother assured him he would understand one day. He frowned as Nevin reared up and swatted at Drake with his paw.

On instinct, he ducked and rolled out of the way as alarm punched through him. What was happening? Confusion made him hesitate and he wasn't fast enough. Nevin's talons sliced through his back as he flew through the air, landing with a thud twenty feet away.

His ears rang and pain shot through him but he shook it off and shoved to his feet. That was when he noticed a strange female on the dragon's back. She wasn't part of the clan. There was a strange energy hovering around her, her dark aura setting off alarms in Drake's head.

Something was wrong. So very wrong. He needed to run.

Without thinking he shifted forms, the abrupt change shocking to his system as his dragon took over in a ripple of sensation. Nothing mattered other than getting away.

He didn't know why Nevin wanted to hurt him, but his predator side screeched at him to flee. His heart pounded wildly as he took to the air. Another surge of panic slammed through him, making his flight clumsy. His cousin breathed fire at him so he banked right, planning to dip behind Nevin who still hadn't moved from the ground.

As he did, the woman threw something at him. It looked like a shimmering cobweb as it flew through the air, spanning out in a snare that caught his wings.

Pain immediately erupted through his system, as if a thousand daggers had been embedded in his wings.

Screaming, he let loose a stream of fire as he fell to the ground. Before he'd even hit, he shifted back to his human form almost against his will. He had no control. As he cried out, blackness swept through his system like a wave, dragging him into unconsciousness.

He wasn't sure how much time had passed, but when he opened his eyes he was naked and chained to an altar of sorts, his arms above his head and his ankles strapped down. Dripping water sounded somewhere in the distance and candles flickered everywhere. Based on the damp smell he was in a cave, he was sure of it. He blinked slowly, trying to get more of his bearings as a dull throb ached through his entire body.

Poison.

He'd been poisoned. Maybe from the weird cobwebbed net. It must have been spelled.

Full blown panic raged through him, the shot of adrenaline welcome, but he couldn't speak, couldn't summon the strength to try to break his bonds. He tried to open his mouth, but nothing would come out.

"Ah, you're awake precious boy." A sickly sweet female voice spoke somewhere to his left.

Drake turned his head and saw the same woman from before striding toward him. She had on a thick-looking purple robe with the hood pushed back. Her dark brown hair fell around her face in ropes that looked like snakes. He blinked, wondering if he'd imagined it, but it was still the same creepy sight when he opened his eyes again. His heart hammered against his ribs.

"I'm truly sorry you'll be awake for this, but maybe it is best." She lifted one of her hands, revealing a dagger as she glided toward him with a graceful gait that seemed almost inhuman.

But she was human. He could sense it. Confusion filtered through his pain. "You're human," he rasped out, surprised his voice worked.

"I am." She smiled, her eyes like dark endless pools of blackness, sending a shudder through him. "And you are going to give me so much power."

At that she smoothly slid the blade deep into his abdomen, smiling evilly as she did. Agony burst inside him, a starburst of colors exploding in his line of vision as he watched blood drip off his stomach onto the slab altar under him.

When he struggled against the chains, she laughed, the harsh sound echoing around the cave. Forcing himself under control, he stilled, knowing he wouldn't be able to break the chains. Not until the poison had worn off. Unfortunately he didn't know if he would have enough time.

He was young, but he wasn't stupid. There weren't many reasons to capture a dragon shifter and it didn't take long to figure out that this crazy female probably wanted to open a Hell Gate.

His throat clogged with tears and he prayed for his mom and dad to find them. His dad was more vicious but his mom was a better hunter. There was no one as good as her. She had to find him. Had to save him.

His tears dried as he scented his cousin Nevin nearby. He didn't have much mobility so he couldn't look around. "Nevin?" Drake called out, his voice raspy. He didn't understand why his cousin was here, why he would do this to him.

Boot steps echoed around the cave and a moment later his cousin stepped into his line of sight, sidling up to the woman who was now licking the bloody blade. Revulsion tore through Drake, dulling some of his pain.

"Why are you doing this?" he croaked, unable to comprehend why his cousin would hurt him.

Nevin's greenish-gray eyes darkened, his face twisting into a mottled rage Drake had never seen on anyone before.

"Because your mother killed mine. Now I'm taking what matters to her most."

"But . . . we're family." His voice broke on the last word, the betrayal slicing through him bone deep.

"You're no family of mine," Nevin snarled. *"And you're going to suffer far more than my mother did before she died. An eternity in Hell."*

Drake blinked as the memory faded as fast as it had come. Seconds had passed though it felt like an eternity. He focused on his brother. "We should keep him secure while we search for the females." After what he'd just remembered Drake was ninety percent certain Cody wasn't involved, but he still wanted the male locked down. When Conall nodded he continued. "How fast can we get a search party together?" Without knowing Nevin's goal it was impossible to know where he'd gone. But the male wouldn't be able to fly too far carrying two females.

Cell phone in hand, Conall was texting. "Already on it. Every capable clan member will help."

"I'm calling the Devlins." Drake wasn't asking for permission as he pulled his cell phone out. He'd seen the look on the leader's face when he asked about Keelin. Like a male ready to claim a female. Bran Devlin would help without question. Right now they needed all the help they could get.

It didn't matter how far away Nevin had taken Victoria. Drake would get her and Keelin back. No matter the cost.

CHAPTER TWENTY-SEVEN

Head pounding as a dull throb splintered through her abdomen, Victoria remained still as she struggled to regain consciousness. The faint scent of sulfur and blood teased her nostrils and she heard muttering.

A male's voice. His words were incomprehensible.

She remembered being shot. *Twice.* Then she'd forced her wolf back from taking control over her body so she'd remain in human form—because she needed her blade. Even as she fought the pain, that knowledge was clear in her hazy mind.

Fighting the panic welling up inside her, she cracked open her eyes. Blinking in the dimness, she immediately knew she was in a cave. Shadows played off the stalactites above her, the icicle-shaped points ominous looking.

She was lying on her side on a gold-colored blanket. A white towel was wrapped around her middle, the majority of it stained crimson from her blood. Her gunshot wounds were already healing though, the bullets likely having been pushed out already. Without touching her abdomen or removing the towel she couldn't be certain, but as a healer she healed faster than others of her kind, despite her young age.

Another jolt of panic punched through her as she remembered Keelin. Where was she?

"Why are you doing this?" Keelin rasped out, her soft voice echoing in the cavernous space somewhere close by.

Even though Victoria couldn't see Keelin, a small dose of relief filled her that the female was alive. Victoria was afraid to move too much until she'd taken complete stock of the situation. Lying on her side, her head was next to a stalagmite formation, blocking her from seeing anything past it. Taking a steadying breath, she called on the part of her that made her a healer. A warmth from deep within spread out directly from her middle, immediately easing the throbbing in her belly and making it easier for her to breathe.

"Because your family deserves to die!" Nevin screamed, his rage-filled voice making Victoria cringe. She remembered the male was one of Drake's cousins. Somehow related to him on his mother's side.

"Did you sacrifice Drake when he was twelve?"

"Of course I did, stupid girl." He started muttering again under his breath, the words not making sense. Or maybe they were. It almost sounded like he was speaking another language. Maybe Latin based.

Taking a chance, Victoria slowly pushed up, thankful she was able to remain quiet. Discomfort shredded through her, but that was the least of her worries. Ignoring the pain, she peeked around the edge of the stalagmite and her throat tightened in horror. Keelin was stretched out face up on a stone slab like an offering, her hands bound above her head with some kind of chains. Her clothes had been cut away and too many slices to count were all over her body, the blood flowing freely down the sides of the slab.

As horrible as that was, the sight of the partially open Hell Gate two feet from her supine body was a whole lot worse. Victoria had seen one exactly like it in New Orleans months ago. It explained the sulfuric stench.

A huge black area of viscous-looking material floated in the air, about two feet off the ground. Dark mist swirled around it and just like in New Orleans, this gate was only open a fraction in the shape of a crescent moon. Smoke curled out of the crescent opening, like the fingers of the dead reaching into the land of the living. That smell it emitted made her nauseous.

Similar designs to the ones she'd seen in New Orleans were painted in blood on the ground around the makeshift altar and on the uneven cave walls. The male was clearly doing a ritual spell. He was hunched over a big text he'd placed on the end of the altar near Keelin's feet, his eyes glued to it as he read. He was either doing an Akkadian ritual spell like that psychotic vampire from New Orleans or some other spell. Either way it didn't matter because the bastard was trying to open a door to Hell. She didn't care why, she just knew she had to save Keelin—and avenge Drake. This bastard was going to pay for taking away Drake's childhood and so many precious years of his life.

A burst of rage swelled through her like a tsunami, muting most of her pain. This male was going down. And she'd likely only get one chance to take him out.

"But why? He was only twelve. He trusted you, looked up to you." Keelin's voice was fading, weak with pain and fatigue, spurring Victoria into action.

Slowly, ignoring the cramping pull in her abdomen as she sat up, she started sliding her pant leg up. Clasping the hilt of the blade forged in dragon-fire strapped there, she clutched it tight and slid it out of its sheath. The towel around her middle was awkward but she left it in place, not wanting to move too much.

Nevin turned from looking down at the book to Keelin, but his back was still to Victoria. The blond male was shaking, as if he was close to losing control. "Dear Aunt Arya killed my mother so I took what was important to her. Stupid male should have stayed there forever. Now I'm going to sacrifice you and release Akkadian demons onto our land before I escape into Protective Hibernation. By the time your whore mother and worthless father wake up from their Hibernation you'll be dead and with any luck so will your brothers."

Keelin laughed, the sound weak as Victoria stood up. "You're a fool. Even if you release demons the clan will destroy them all. And it doesn't matter where you hibernate, someone will find you."

He grunted and turned back to the book. "Not if they don't know where the gate is. They'll just keep coming and coming and the pack will be too busy trying to kill demons to worry about me. That little shifter bitch is going to be the perfect treat for the escaping demons. And no one will find me." He laughed then, the maniacal sound like something out of a cheesy movie or cartoon.

What a freaking psycho. Raw violence was against her intrinsic healer nature but now she felt practically savage. He'd shot her and Keelin, kidnapped them, but more than anything, he'd dared to hurt her mate. When Drake had just been a boy unable to protect himself. She was going to relish killing Nevin.

Victoria took a step forward, careful of where she placed her foot. Her movements were silent, though her heart pounded out of control. She couldn't afford to alert Nevin. Heart racing, she took another step. Then another.

Keelin's gaze flicked in her direction for a fraction of a moment but quickly reverted back to the crazy dragon shifter staring at the big book.

"The only thing I regret is that I won't get to see your mother's face when she returns," he muttered, scratching his head like an animal with fleas. He let out an angry growl. "But I must hibernate . . . The symbols are painted, the blood is flowing . . . What am I missing?"

"So you sacrificed him simply for revenge? You're pathetic, going after a boy like that," Keelin rasped out.

"Of course not!" He screamed, back to making that horrible screeching sound. "His sacrifice was supposed to give me unimaginable power. I was going to take over the clan and kill your parents for taking away mine. But a fucking witch betrayed me."

Victoria figured Keelin was trying to keep him distracted. Perfect. She was only ten feet from him now, dagger poised. So close she was almost in reach. As she started to take another step, the ground beneath her rumbled and the cave shook.

A stalactite fell from the roof, crashing near the altar, the splintered rock spraying everywhere. Managing not to cry out, Victoria caught herself before she fell to her knees, but Nevin turned, his greenish-gray eyes filled with dark hatred when he saw her there.

His gaze landed on her blade and he let out an ear-piercing screech that ricocheted off the cave.

Victoria lunged for him, blade ready to strike when he let loose a bright stream of orange flames. She instinctively ducked though she had nowhere to go. Instead of being burned, the fire flowed around her, the flames engulfing her in a bubble but not touching her skin.

Drake's essence.

The male screamed even louder, his fire shooting off like a blazing roman candle as he threw his head back and spread his arms out wide. Victoria braced herself, feet wide apart as she withstood the onslaught. She had no idea how long Drake's protection would hold up under the attack.

The only thing she knew was that she needed to get close enough to kill this male. And get him away from Keelin.

Victoria let her claws extend on her blade-free hand. She started walking backward, taking slow steps as if she was trying to flee.

Nevin growled and his flames stopped as he stared at her, his eyes wild with rage and deep emptiness. "I'll wear down your protection eventually. Or maybe I'll just cut your head off." Again with the crazy laugh as he jumped at her, breathing fire.

Victoria dove to her left, rolling behind a giant stalagmite for cover as fire burned around her. Part of the rock crumbled under the intensity of the blaze, but her protective bubble held.

She stood, ready to run again when the flames fizzled and she found Nevin a foot in front of her.

On instinct, she slashed out at him, the blade slicing against his cheek before she jumped away again, putting five feet of distance between them. She might be younger than him, but she was nimble on her feet. Growing up in a wolf shifter pack had taught her a lot of things. While she might be a healer, she still knew how to attack and retreat and wear down her opponent. Then when the time was right she would attack, attack, attack, until this male was destroyed.

Nevin screamed again, his body trembling as he shot fire in an uncontrolled arc over her head. He knew his flames couldn't touch her so the energy seemed like a wasted effort. It was almost as if he'd lost his mind.

Whatever was wrong with him, she took advantage of the situation when he let his head fall back and screamed even louder. The cave rumbled ominously, rocks raining down on them. She ignored everything but the male in front of her.

This was her chance.

Diving at Nevin, she covered the last couple feet and sank the blade into his chest, striking his heart dead center. The blade sank deep, the thudding sound terrible as the hilt rammed into his ribs. The flames immediately died around her, the male's wide eyes flaring to a bright silver tinged with black flecks, as if the darkness in him was eating away from the inside out.

Baring her teeth, letting the rage flow through her, she twisted the blade, shredding his heart. She felt like a female possessed. As the brightness from his eyes faded, she withdrew the weapon and raised it above his head. Arching her arm down hard, she sliced through bone and tendons, severing his head. Blood arced away from her in a crimson spray as the separated body fell forward.

The ground rumbled again, nearly knocking her off balance.

Before Nevin's head hit the ground she turned to find Keelin staring at her from the altar, eyes wide. "We need to get out of here," she rasped, her voice still weak. Too weak.

Victoria nodded and went to the female's shackles. After a brief touch on the chains she was grateful they weren't silver. "How hurt are you?"

"I'm okay. The gunshot wounds have healed but he injected me with some sort of poison. It's dulling my strength and . . . hard to talk." Her voice was too faint.

"Don't talk then. I'll get you out of here." Then she would figure out where the hell they were and get Keelin to safety. She yanked on the manacle and breathed out a sigh of relief when it broke away. After breaking off the other one, she slid her arms under Keelin's back and legs and lifted her off the altar. Holding the female close, Victoria winced at the pull against her abdomen. Even though she was healing quickly it still freaking hurt.

A quick look at the Hell Gate told her that it was still opening. Unfortunately Victoria had absolutely no idea how to close the thing.

Stepping over Nevin's body, she snagged the blood-stained throw and wrapped it around Keelin's shaking body.

"I'm going to get us out of here then start healing you. We'll get help soon. Can you stand for just a sec?" She hated to put the female down but needed to do one thing first.

Keelin nodded, her skin tinged gray. Victoria placed her on her feet and only let go when the female held on to the cave wall for support.

Though she hated to touch Nevin, she quickly searched his pants pockets and patted him down for a cell phone or another way to communicate. Cursing when she found nothing, she grabbed the book on the altar and hurried back to Keelin. Victoria knew she might have to figure out a way to close the Hell Gate and this book was the best chance they had. If that maniac had used it to open the gate, they could use it to close it.

Hopefully.

"I can walk out of here," the female murmured.

Yeah, that wasn't happening. "Just hold this." She gave Keelin the book then lifted her in her arms. Then she grabbed one of the LED lanterns Nevin had waiting here. Right about now, Victoria was seriously thankful for her shifter strength. Even in the midst of healing she was still stronger than any human.

"I smell snow," Victoria murmured as she slowly made her way through the cavernous opening. They had to be close to an exit. Hope soared through her at the thought of freedom.

The cave rumbled again but she kept her footing and increased her pace. She was trying to be careful since Keelin was injured too, but decided a little pain was worth getting out of here sooner.

Less than a minute later they reached the mouth of a cave. Victoria stepped out onto a thirty foot ledge, into the freezing night air. A blanket of stars illuminated the sky. Her heart caught in her throat. The cliff dropped straight down farther than she could see. Even in wolf form she couldn't walk down that type of angle. It was a straight freefall.

"Keelin—"

"I can't shift yet," she rasped out, clearly knowing what Victoria planned to ask.

Well, hell. She set the female on her feet and tucked the blanket tighter around Keelin's shoulders. They might not be able to escape yet, but she could start healing the other female. "Let's get you into the mouth of the cave." It would keep the chill off Keelin. Later she'd worry about the fact that a Hell Gate was inside that cave. One problem at a time.

Keelin nodded and they both started back across the ledge for the mouth. The ground shook again, worse than before. As the ledge floor fell away beneath Victoria she shoved Keelin forward.

A scream tore from her throat as she tumbled backward off the cliff, her stomach jumping into her throat as she fell into darkness.

CHAPTER TWENTY-EIGHT

Victoria's scream died in her throat as a huge rush of wind swept under her, making her tumble midair. A muscular arm snagged around her waist and she found herself slamming hard against . . . Drake. In dragon form.

She stared up from Drake's scaled back at Gabriel who'd just grabbed her midair. "You all right?" Gabriel shouted over the sound of wind rushing over them. The Guardian sat on Drake's back, holding on to the ridged scales down the middle of his long body.

She nodded, not bothering to talk. For a moment she buried her face against Drake, not surprised how smooth his skin was. He'd saved her.

Holding on tight to the pale diamond-toned ridges, she turned her head toward Drake's. His head was turned back to her and though she could only see his profile, she knew all his focus was on her as sure as she knew her name. Wind rushed over her face and body as Drake flew down the mountain. "Drake! We need to go back and get Keelin!"

In response, he let out a loud growl.

Thankful he understood her, she laid flatter against him, hugging him tight as his jade-colored wings flapped rapidly, taking them higher and higher. Her stomach dipped at the sharp climb. It was exhilarating and terrifying at the same time. She'd never flown with him before, but once all this was over she wanted to do it under different circumstances.

As they reached the opening of the cave relief slammed through Victoria to see Keelin deep in the wider mouth of the cave, huddled next to a huge boulder. Her pale, blonde hair stood out like a beacon.

With surprising agility for such a large shifter, Drake landed in the mouth of the cave in seconds. The moment she and Gabriel slid off him, Drake shifted to his human form with a rapid fluidity that still amazed her. Gabriel hurried toward Keelin as Victoria threw herself into Drake's arms, more thankful than she'd ever been to see him. Her throat was tight, making it difficult to breathe as she held him close. She couldn't stop the shakes racking her body.

He returned her embrace, his big body quivering. "You're alive." She could barely hear his whisper.

She buried her face against his neck, her trembling starting to subside as she took comfort in his steel embrace. They needed to close the Hell Gate and get out of the cave but she needed to hold him for just a second first. Needed to know this was real. "You found me," she managed to rasp out, tears clogging her throat. She didn't bother hiding them. She'd been keeping it together until falling off the cliff. She might be supernatural with extra healing abilities, but she wasn't sure she'd have survived the fall.

Knowing that she could have died, wouldn't have gotten to see Drake again, to kiss him, and finally make love to him . . . She stopped her mind from going there.

He pulled back, but remained close, his bright silver eyes pinned to hers as he cupped her face in the gentlest hold. "I will *always* find you." The deep vow pierced her.

She opened her mouth to respond but the cave rumbled again. She clutched on to his forearms to steady herself. Panic slid through her veins, an icy reminder of what they needed to do. "Drake, your psycho cousin started to open a Hell Gate. He was using Keelin's blood to do it and the process has already started. You're the only one I know who can close it." He'd done it in New Orleans when none of them had known how. From what Victoria knew about sacrifices and spells, she guessed that because of the strength of Keelin's dragon blood things were moving at an accelerated rate.

"Stay here . . . Never mind, come on." Drake grabbed her hand and they raced past Gabriel and Keelin. "Keep my sister out here," he threw over his shoulder as they hurried deeper into the cave.

Drake held Victoria's hand tight, knowing she'd never stay put and they couldn't waste time arguing. His female would never leave him to face this alone.

Or anything else. And it was one of the reasons he loved her. When he'd seen her falling from that cliff he'd lost a century of his life. He'd never flown so fast or pushed so hard. His heart was still pounding erratically at the sight and he wasn't sure he'd ever get over the terror that he might have lost her.

"Nevin sacrificed you. He was behind it all," she said as they hurried. "I killed him."

The raw satisfaction in her voice shocked him, but he didn't stop now. There was no time. Not until the gate was closed and Victoria and his sister were safe.

Keep my mate safe and claim her. The two primal thoughts were the most prominent that raced through his mind. As he and Victoria spilled into the heart of the cave, his heart stuttered at the sight of Nevin's decapitated body on the ground and the rapidly opening Hell Gate above it.

Victoria had killed the traitor. For him. He'd never be able to thank her for what she'd done for him, for slaying the bastard who'd taken his childhood away.

But he sure as hell was going to protect her now.

"Stay behind me," he ordered as he jumped over a fallen, shattered stalactite. Too many emotions swelled inside him but he had to keep everything locked down until Victoria was far away from here.

Needing the spilled blood to close the gate, he started toward the altar when a snarled, claw-tipped reptilian hand appeared from the viscous hole. Fuck.

"Akkadian demon. Get out!" he ordered Victoria as one of the ancient demons crawled through the door.

He knew they could glamorize themselves in this realm if they chose, but right now the thing staring at them was seven feet of nightmare. Short horns topped its head and his body was covered in thick, reptilian looking skin. Both hands and feet were clawed, like monkeys. Its eyes glowed eerily yellow as he snarled at Drake.

It raised a fist in the air, his reptilian face twisting oddly as it shouted, "Freedom." The creature spoke in ancient Sumerian, but Drake understood perfectly well.

"Not for long," he growled, opening his mouth and letting a burst of fire annihilate the demon.

It burst into flames as the thing screamed in agony. Drake was aware of the pounding of boots echoing off the cave walls, but ignored the sound since he knew it was Gabriel.

When the demon turned to ash, Drake stilled his fire and turned. Victoria was still there, her blade in hand, along with Gabriel, two blades in hand.

"I'll handle this!" he shouted at them. He just needed to close the gate and he didn't need their damn help.

He *needed* Victoria safe and away from here. It was the only way he could focus.

"Fuck you," Gabriel snarled. "If you're her mate, you're fucking *pack*. End of story so shut up and let's close this damn gate."

Victoria nodded once, her expression beautifully fierce. "What he said."

Throat tight, he stared at Victoria for a moment before turning back to the gate. He didn't want to look at the fallen body but he couldn't help it. His gaze snagged on Nevin's decapitated head and stayed there.

Nevin's lifeless eyes stared up at him from the rocky ground, the sulfuric scent around them as disgusting as the dead male. Drake started to shake, wishing he'd been the one to destroy the monster who'd stolen everything from him. Killing one Akkadian demon wasn't enough to stop the rage burning through him like an out of control volcano. His shaking worsened and he tried to order his body under control, but couldn't tear his gaze from Nevin's head.

He only stopped when he felt Victoria's soft hand on his forearm. "We need to close it and you're the only one who can do it." The trust in her expression filled him with warmth despite that they were standing in front of a Hell Gate with more demons ready to escape at any moment.

The black viscous-looking hole was halfway open, gray smoke spilling out faster each second that ticked by. It was starting to coat the altar, floor and Nevin's body. Though Drake hated to do this, he knelt down in front of the altar and coated his hands in Keelin's spilled blood. It was fresh enough that he could use it to reverse what a monster had started. He began smearing it along the edges of the gate. Before he could tell them to stop, Victoria and Gabriel started doing the same on the opposite side of the gate.

When a rush of smoke shoved through the hole as if it was tangible, shoving into all three of them and making them stumble back, all the hair on Drake's body stood on end.

No.

Diving for Victoria, he wrapped his arms around her and tackled her, throwing them behind a huge stalagmite. "Take cover," he shouted at Gabriel.

The other male jumped with them, using the natural formation as a shield. "What's happening?"

Ignoring him, he looked at Victoria, his focus laser sharp on her sooty face. "Demons are coming. At least fifty of them. I can scent them. I'm only going to have one shot at this. There are too many for all of us to take in hand to hand combat but I can incinerate them. I need you to trust me. This isn't about not wanting your help." He looked at Gabriel then. "Pack trusts each other, right?"

Gabriel muttered a curse but nodded.

"Good. Stay here and let me handle this. Do *not* move away from Victoria, her essence will protect you." He gritted his teeth at the newest rumble, knowing what was happening, and looked back at Victoria. "I'll never say this again, but . . . wrap your arms around Gabriel, keep him close." At that he jumped up to see a mix of demons, mainly Akkadians. He didn't care what type they were.

They were all going to die.

Over twenty were in the huge cavern with more spilling out. They all turned to look at him at the same time, their creepy yellow eyes glowing brightly.

"Dragos," one hissed angrily.

That's right, stupid fucker. His most primal side relished that the demon knew who he was. Taking a deep breath, he let free the same energy he'd felt while killing the Veles dragons. The energy inside him burned so brightly, the need to protect his mate an all-consuming thing with a life of its own.

Unable to stop himself even if he'd wanted to, that bright supernova flame tore free from his throat, the burn liberating as he ashed every single demon, swinging his head back and forth, cutting them down like they had no more substance than paper. He kept his focus tight, directing his energy only to the demons. Even if Victoria was protected, he wasn't risking Gabriel either.

Screams filled the air and some demons raced for the Hell Gate, desperate to return to their prison, but none escaped his wrath.

For long seconds he felt like that beast he'd become in Hell. As the demons burned and screamed around him he relished their deaths and his darkest side dreamed of bathing in their blood. Until Victoria's sweet image flooded his mind and all that rage and anger dissipated as if it had never existed.

The demons were dead. His mate was safe. That was all that mattered.

Silence reined as his fire dimmed, pieces of ash floating aimlessly in the damp cave. He turned toward his mate, adrenaline jagging through him as intense as his fire had been. Before he could take a step in her direction, Victoria popped up from behind the stalagmite, Gabriel next to her in a defensive stance, weapons drawn.

Her eyes widened as she took in the ash floating everywhere, but she didn't say anything other than to ask if he was okay. When he nodded, she just rounded the barrier with Gabriel and hurried to the altar. There was no time to waste, something he was glad she realized because he still wasn't thinking clearly. He just wanted to pull her into his arms, but there would be time for that once the gate was closed.

Working together the three of them finished coating the edges of the circle in blood and Drake chanted the same ritual he'd done in New Orleans. He hadn't remembered four months ago but he now knew exactly why the Hell Gate spell was imprinted in his memory. When that witch and his treacherous cousin sacrificed him, he'd memorized the spell she'd chanted, determined to eventually escape and get his revenge.

The ground rumbled beneath them, as though the demons and other creatures sensed what he was doing and were furious, but he continued. The faster he spoke, the faster the gate closed.

Smoke billowed out, the sulfuric scent intensified and faint screams of terror all too familiar to Drake drifted out until it slammed closed. The black circle still hovered, however. He didn't bother telling Victoria to stand back this time. His essence protected her, would never harm her.

He breathed out a long stream of flames, covering the black hole until it completely disappeared from sight, vanishing as if it had never existed. He'd fill in the cave later, but for now this would do. After he was finished with the gate, heart pounding out of control, he turned to look at Victoria and went to pull her into his arms but stopped. Blood covered his hands and he never wanted to taint her. Taking away his choice, she threw her arms around him, plastering herself to him.

Drake was vaguely aware of Gabriel leaving them, but he didn't care. All his focus was on his brave mate.

Crushing his mouth to hers he forgot everything, the blood and their surroundings, as her tongue fervently danced with his. She pressed so tightly against him it was like she wanted to climb inside him. He couldn't wait to slide into her and claim her fully. On a broken sob she pulled back. "It's really over?"

Throat raw and tight, he nodded. "It's over. And I remember . . . everything." After that initial memory back at Conall's house, he'd thought the rest of his memories would come back slower. But in his rage-filled haze searching for Victoria and Keelin over miles and miles of terrain, everything else had all come crashing back, like watching a film about someone else's life. He'd learned a hell of a lot about his past and who he'd been. Young, innocent, naïve and full of life. But he'd tell her about everything else later. Now, all that mattered was that his psychotic cousin was dead. "Nevin was working with a human witch but that was so long ago the female would be dead by now."

"Oh, Drake. I'm so sorry your own family member betrayed you." She tightened her grip around him, her eyes glittering with tears as her fingers dug into his back.

He wanted to swipe them away but didn't want to get blood on her face. "I'm not. Everything that happened led me to you." And he'd endure Hell again to be with her.

When she buried her face against his chest he swung her into his arms and strode from the cave. Away from his past and into the future. Growling softly, he tucked his face against the top of her hair. Her sweet scent overrode everything around them. "You're mine," he murmured quietly.

She shivered in his arms and burrowed deeper. As soon as they were alone, he was going to officially claim her. He'd almost lost her today. It wasn't going to happen ever again.

CHAPTER TWENTY-NINE

Drake took the interior stairs of the guest house two at a time, hurrying to get back to Victoria, as he balanced the covered tray of food in his hands. They'd already showered—separately since he'd insisted, much to her annoyance. Even though she said she was completely healed from the gunshot wounds, he hadn't wanted to risk inadvertently hurting her. Before he'd let her shower though, he'd run his hands over her skin, checking everywhere to make sure she wasn't hurt and just not telling him. He only wished he could rip that bastard Nevin limb from limb for daring to hurt Victoria like that.

After she'd gotten out of the shower she'd sent him downstairs to grab food and hot chocolate for her. But he was under the impression she'd been trying to get rid of him. He wasn't sure why.

After they'd found Victoria and Keelin, Drake had brought her and Keelin back to the village. Many of the dragons were still out searching but Greer was with Keelin, who was going to be fine, and Conall was out rounding everyone up and letting the clan know the females had been found. Drake knew he should probably be out with his brother helping, but to hell with that.

He needed to take care of Victoria, to make sure she was truly okay. He was going to make sure she rested.

Then he was finally claiming her for all eternity.

As he reached their room, he nudged the cracked door open with his foot. Two steps inside, he nearly dropped the tray.

On her knees at the foot of the bed, Victoria was completely naked, her perfect body on display for only him. Long black hair fell in soft waves over both breasts, her pale pink nipples already tight and waiting for him to tease. His gaze trailed down the pale column of her elegant neck, over her full breasts and down to the juncture between her legs where a small triangle of dark hair covered her mound.

All thoughts of waiting dissipated. He was finally going to sink deep inside his mate and fully claim her.

Without taking his eyes off her, he kicked the door shut then set the tray on the floor, letting it go without paying attention to where he set it. The silverware and tray rattled loudly but he ignored it as he stalked toward Victoria. His heart was an erratic tattoo against his chest and it was all he could do to drag in a full breath.

Tearing his T-shirt over his head, he tossed it away as he approached her. When he reached her she held out a hand, placing it against his chest, her green eyes startlingly bright against her face. Just the feel of her touching him made him shudder. He'd almost lost her.

"Are you ever going to try to send me away again?" A soft, demanding question.

"I'd rather cut off a limb." She'd never listen anyway. "We're a team."

She nodded once, her dark hair swishing seductively around her face, her expression softening. "Always."

"*Forever,*" he growled.

Her eyes heated at that and her fingers dug into his chest. With her free hand she reached out and cupped his hard length over his pants. He rolled his hips against her hold. Soon there would be nothing between them.

Though he wanted to devour her, he managed some semblance of control as he slowly lowered his head toward hers.

Victoria had other ideas, sliding her hand up his chest and around the back of his head, tugging him down so their mouths meshed in a frenzied mating.

Instinct took over. He grabbed her hips, flipping her onto her back, his chest covering hers as she moaned into his mouth. His entire body was pulled taut as she wrapped her legs around him, arching into his body.

On his darkest nights he'd never imagined that someone as sweet and giving as Victoria was out there for him. It had simply never occurred to him that there could be anyone for him. And definitely not someone like her. Until that day in the graveyard when he'd caught her scent and it had been over for him.

Now that crisp mountain scent of hers intensified as she reached between them to unbutton his pants. Tearing his mouth from hers, he placed his hands over hers.

Holding her wrists, he gently guided her arms above her head.

"This first time . . . don't touch me yet." His words were a harsh growl. He couldn't have her hands on him without completely losing it. He needed her to climax first, needed her to experience pleasure before he did. Because he had a feeling his first time in Victoria's tight heat, he wasn't going to last long.

Her eyes darkened with lust as she nodded.

With shaking hands he finished what she'd started and shoved his pants off until he was standing completely bared to her.

She pushed up on her elbows, her eyes shining with the same bright love he felt for her. "I love you, Drake. Every part of you. And I want to be your mate."

His chest was tight as he looked down at the female who'd completely stolen his heart. He tried to speak but his fucking voice just wouldn't work. Not now. Over a thousand years of emotions were rushing up all at once, making it impossible.

But he could show her how he felt.

Lowering himself on top of her, he savored the way she let out a soft sigh of pleasure and plastered herself to him. She wrapped her arms and legs around him, sliding one hand through his hair and the other down to his ass. "I know you said no touching but..." Smiling wickedly she gripped him hard and rolled herself against him, her unspoken demand clearer than anything she could have said.

Though every primal part of him demanded he thrust deep into her and claim everything, he was going to make sure she came first. He'd read enough on sex to know that it could hurt females the first time and he'd die before doing that to her.

As their lips melded again, he teased his tongue against hers and reached between their bodies. He wished he had more hands so he could touch her everywhere at once. Cupping her mound, he shuddered as he slid his middle finger over her slit.

He could scent her need, but she was so damn wet. All for him. That knowledge made his cock pulse even harder. He dipped one finger, then two inside her, moving in and out of her in a slow, torturous rhythm he'd learned she liked. Her breathing grew more erratic and she bit down on his bottom lip impatiently.

Always so impatient.

Part of him wanted to drag this out, to bury his face between her legs and taste her again on his tongue, but he couldn't tear his body from hers. The skin on skin contact was too perfect.

He pulled his fingers out and she groaned in protest until he guided his hard length between her wet lips. First he stroked himself against her teasingly. Never before had he let his cock get so close to her like this. Because he'd known he would have no restraint.

His balls pulled up even tighter as he nudged against her entrance, barely pushing inside her slick body. The friction was already driving him insane but he didn't slide any deeper. If he did, he was going to lose it. Instead he bent down to one ripe breast and sucked her tight nipple into his mouth.

"Drake." She grabbed on to his head, holding him tight. As if he planned to go anywhere. No way in hell.

Swiping his tongue over the tight bud, he simultaneously tweaked her clit with his thumb and forefinger.

She made a garbled moaning sound as he gently started rubbing her sensitive bundle of nerves in a tight circular motion. The faster he rubbed, the more erratic her breathing and heartbeat grew.

"I'm close," she rasped out, starting to writhe against him.

He switched breasts, giving equal attention to the other tight nipple as he pushed deeper inside her. He hadn't moved far but her inner walls clenched around him, the convulsing sensation letting him know just how close to coming she was.

Pressing down on her nipple with his teeth, adding an extra bite to his teasing, he growled victoriously against her breast when she arched up and shoved it into his mouth as if she couldn't get enough. She cried out his name like a prayer. "Now," she demanded.

He hesitated for a moment but she rolled her hips and impaled herself on him. There was a slight giving sensation before he buried himself to the hilt inside her. Pure pleasure shot down his spine at the erotic feel of her inner walls gripping him tight but he didn't thrust even though every instinct demanded he do so.

He continued rubbing her clit and pulled back so he could look at her. Every breath he dragged in was unsteady as he grasped onto the last shred of his control.

Her eyes were heavy-lidded as she watched him and stroked her fingers down his chest and over his forearms as if she couldn't get enough of touching him. As her inner walls began to convulse tighter and tighter around his cock her head fell back and she completely closed her eyes.

Her mouth parted and she came on a silent cry, her body bowing tight as her orgasm crashed through her.

Seeing the pure ecstasy on her face, knowing he'd caused it, set something free inside him. Burying his face against her neck he began thrusting in long, hard strokes, her slick sheath squeezing him tight, her erotic scent making him crazy.

His canines descended the harder he thrust. It felt so good to be inside her. He knew Hell existed and this was true Heaven. With Victoria.

When he scraped his teeth against the sensitive place where her neck and shoulder met she groaned out his name and squeezed even tighter around his cock.

He could stay here forever. Wanted to be lost inside her sweet body as long as she let him.

As her orgasm started to ebb, he let go, allowing himself to completely relinquish control. His climax built and built, the sensation shoving out to all his nerve endings as her sheath gripped him tight.

Shouting her name he released himself inside her in long, fierce strokes, marking her with his seed. Letting instinct rule him, he bit down on the skin between her shoulder and neck, sinking deep into her flesh as he claimed the female he couldn't live without.

Her fingers dug into his back and for a moment he tensed, worried he'd hurt her, but the sounds of pleasure emanating from her immediately released that fear before it took root inside him.

After riding out his orgasm he licked away the blood from where he'd bitten her, not surprised when the small wounds immediately started healing. Feeling lightheaded, he nuzzled her neck, wanting to stay locked inside her for the rest of the day. Week. Months. Forever.

"That was amazing," Victoria murmured, her voice thick with pleasure.

He grunted because that was all he could do. He'd finally claimed Victoria. His female. For always.

Though he didn't want to separate their bodies, he leaned back and slowly pulled out of her. She winced slightly but tried to hide it.

He stretched out beside her, placing a hand on her flat abdomen. His mate was so soft and delicate, yet strong in ways that continued to amaze him. "Did I hurt you?"

Her smile took his breath away. "Not even a little bit. I might be sore though."

He didn't want to leave her for even a moment, but...
"Give me just a second. I'll be right back." He dropped a
kiss on her lips before hurrying to the en suite. Moving
quickly he grabbed a washcloth and rinsed it with warm
water.

Back in the bedroom he kneeled in front of her and
gently wiped between her legs. When he saw tears in
her eyes, all the breath in his lungs escaped in one
whoosh. "Victoria." Her name sounded guttural.

"Happy tears," she quickly said, her voice watery.
"Turn around."

Confused by her request, he let the cloth drop and
did as she said. Her soft fingers trailed over a small section on his upper spine. "When wolf shifters, or were-
wolves as the older generation says, mate, it's for life.
But with . . . destined mates, a tattoo-like symbol ap-
pears on their bodies after they officially mate. You have
one." He could hear the emotion in her words, the way
her voice shook. "It's a black wolf. Just like me."

Another swell of emotion pushed up inside him. Her
mark would be on him forever. According to his brother, other supernaturals would be able to scent their mating anyway, and know they were taken, but the mark
was something he hadn't realized he'd needed. He was
glad he had a symbol of her on his skin. She'd be with
him wherever he went.

Turning, he pulled her into his lap, needing to hold
her close. Though he was almost positive the tears in
her eyes were joyous, he needed to know for sure. "This

is a good thing?" he asked quietly, tightening his grip on her. He would never get tired of holding her, loving her, and taking care of her.

She nodded, wrapping one arm around the back of his neck and cupping his cheek with the other. "So good and very rare. I should have one too." She leaned forward, her breasts brushing his forearm as she moved.

His heart caught in his throat as he saw it. "It's me," he managed to squeeze out, the outward symbol of their bond affecting him soul deep. A small, pale glittering dragon with flashing jade wings sat perfectly in the middle of her upper back. More intricate than any tattoo.

When she leaned back to look at him, he covered her mouth with his, needing to taste her again, needing this female like he needed his next breath. He'd meant what he'd told her in that cave too. For this female, for even this one moment, he'd go back and do everything in his life exactly the same.

Making it through Hell to get to Victoria was worth every second he'd been locked up. Now every day with her would be his reward. He didn't care if he ever made it to Heaven. Victoria was his Heaven.

CHAPTER THIRTY

One week later

"You're sure about this?" Conall asked Keelin, looking warily at her plethora of suitcases in the foyer of her home.

Drake just wrapped his arm around Victoria's shoulders and pulled her close. He was definitely staying out of this. Drake and Victoria were headed back to Biloxi to pack up Victoria's things. His mate had surprised him when she'd said she wanted to live in Montana indefinitely. He knew how much her pack meant to her and he'd never planned to push the issue. But when Victoria got something into her head, he'd learned that nothing he said could convince her to change her mind. Then, surprising everyone, Keelin had announced that she'd be moving to Biloxi indefinitely. Gabriel had worked everything out with Finn and his sister would be staying in Victoria's old room.

His sister nodded in that regal way of hers. "Yes. I need to get away from the clan and live my life on my terms. No one hovering constantly and no one telling me what to do. It's time I spread my wings—pun intended. And I'll be back all the time now to see Drake and I know Victoria will be back to see her pack. The Stavros pack took care of you and if you two trust them, I trust them to give me support if I need them." She beamed at him and Victoria, but her smile grew brittle when she glanced past them to the opening front door.

He'd noticed that she'd been jumpy ever since they returned and Drake wondered if fear was part of her reason for leaving. It didn't matter that Nevin had been working alone in his madness or that she was completely healed, a trusted family member had betrayed them all.

They turned to see Gabriel, Rhea and surprisingly Gavin and Bran Devlin, stride in. Drake thought the Devlin brothers had left this morning and had already said his goodbyes. When Drake had regained his full memory he'd discovered why Gavin seemed so familiar. They'd been friends when they were children. Best friends.

When he was just eight years old Drake had gotten himself snagged in jagged tree branches jutting out from the side of a cliff. He'd been too young and too panicked to free himself and Gavin had discovered him. He'd helped him get free and they'd kept their friendship secret because of their families. Deep down Drake didn't think their clans would have actually cared but they'd been children and keeping secrets had been fun. The only person Gavin had ever told about his friendship with Drake was Fia. It was why she'd been so insistent on coming to Petronilla land. For her mate's happiness.

Dropping his hold on Victoria, he pulled Gavin into a brief hug. They thumped each other on the back in the way he'd seen Gabriel and Finn and other Stavros packmates do, the action warming something long buried inside him. He'd worried that his friendship with the other male would bother Conall because of their history, but his brother had made it clear he was happy Drake had a friend. And Drake believed him.

"I thought you already left," he said, pleased to see the male just the same.

Gavin's mouth pulled up a fraction. "Fia decided to get some more shopping in before we left. And I wanted to see you again."

"We're going to see you in just a couple weeks," Victoria said teasingly as she sidled up close to Drake, wrapping her arm snug around his waist. Her scent teased him as it always did, making him wonder if they could sneak in a quickie before their plane ride. He and Victoria had gotten very creative the past week, finding time for each other anywhere and everywhere. She was just as insatiable as him.

"Yes, well, I suppose I don't need an excuse to see my oldest friend." The male's voice was oddly tight.

Friend. The word brought up all those damn emotions again.

"I knew I liked you," Victoria murmured, her gaze trailing to where Bran was lifting two of Keelin's suitcases.

Victoria was so observant of everyone and everything. She was still doing research into what had given him the ability to incinerate those dragons and then all those demons with that pale, blue fire. His mate had been in abject danger and his beast had simply reacted, calling on all its strength. That was all he needed to know, but she was determined to find out how he'd done it. He was just thankful he'd been able to protect his mate.

Drake followed Victoria's gaze to Keelin, whose face was flushed red, whether in embarrassment or annoyance that Bran was helping her, he couldn't tell. But she didn't try to stop Bran from picking up her bags. Drake knew the male had been by to see Keelin every day since the females had been found, but he wasn't sure what was going on between them. If anything.

Though a primal part of him wanted to rip apart any male who looked at his sister, Keelin was grown and capable. Something Victoria liked to remind him of. Plus, he actually approved of Bran. The male was capable of protecting her and had stepped up to help them with no questions asked and no strings attached when they'd needed help searching for the females.

"Hmm." His mate slightly shook her head and made a knowing sound before turning back to Gavin. "I've never been to Oregon before. We can't wait to visit you guys."

He laughed lightly. "We're excited to have you. Fia's already making plans for us so you don't have to worry about anything."

As they continued talking Drake noticed Rhea pull Conall aside, but their voices were too low for him to hear anything. That was saying something considering his supernatural hearing. He'd asked his brother if anything was going on between him and Rhea but Conall had shut down. Even if he was still learning a lot about this new world, Drake knew that a female was the one topic he shouldn't push his brother about.

Standing in his sister's home, with his arm wrapped tightly around Victoria, the mate he loved more than anything, surrounded by friends and family, it was hard to believe how much things had changed in just four months.

From literal Hell to a small slice of Heaven. His time in the underworld had taught him to savor the smallest pleasure. Now he had the rest of his life to make the most of the new blessings he'd been given. He wasn't going to waste one second.

Thank you for reading Taste of Darkness. I really hope you enjoyed it and that you'll consider leaving a review at one of your favorite online retailers. It's a great way to help other readers discover new books. I appreciate all reviews.

If you liked Taste of Darkness and would like to read more, turn the page for a sneak peek of Bound to Danger, the next book in my Deadly Ops series. And if you don't want to miss any future releases, please feel free to join my newsletter. I only send out a newsletter for new releases or sales news. Find the signup link on my website: http://www.katiereus.com

BOUND TO DANGER

Deadly Ops Series
Copyright © 2014 Katie Reus

Forcing her body to obey her when all she wanted
to do was curl into a ball and cry until she passed out,
she got up. Cool air rushed over her exposed back and
backside as her feet hit the chilly linoleum floor. She
wasn't wearing any panties and the hospital gown
wasn't covering much of her. She didn't care.

Right now she didn't care about much at all.

Sometime when she'd been asleep her dirty, rum-
pled gown had been removed from the room. And
someone had left a small bag of clothes on the bench
by the window. No doubt Nash had brought her something to wear. He'd been in to see her a few times, but
she'd asked him to leave each time. She felt like a
complete bitch because she knew he just wanted to
help, but she didn't care. Nothing could help, and being alone with her pain was the only way she could
cope right now.

Feeling as if she were a hundred years old, she'd
started unzipping the small brown leather bag when
the door opened. As she turned to look over her shoulder, she found Nash, a uniformed police officer, and
another really tall, thuggish-looking man entering.

Her eyes widened in recognition. The tattoos were
new, but the *thug* was Cade O'Reilly. He'd served in
the Marines with her brother. They'd been best friends
and her brother, Riel, named after her father, had even
brought him home a few times. But that was years ago.
Eight to be exact. It was hard to forget the man who'd
completely cut her out of his life after her brother died,
as if she meant nothing to him.

Cade towered over Nash—who was pretty tall himself—and had a sleeve of tattoos on one arm and a couple on the other. His jet-black hair was almost shaved, the skull trim close to his head, just like the last time she'd seen him. He was . . . intimidating. Always had been. And startlingly handsome in that bad-boy way she was sure had made plenty of women . . . Yeah, she wasn't even going there.

She swiveled quickly, putting her back to the window so she wasn't flashing them. Reaching around to her back, she clasped the hospital gown together. "You can't knock?" she practically shouted, her voice raspy from crying, not sure whom she was directing the question to.

"I told them you weren't to be bothered, but—"

The police officer cut Nash off, his gaze kind but direct. "Ms. Cervantes, this man is from the NSA and needs to ask you some questions. As soon as you're done, the doctors will release you."

"I know who he is." She bit the words out angrily, earning a surprised look from Nash and a controlled look from Cade.

She might know Cade, or she had at one time, but she hadn't known he worked for the NSA. After her brother's death he'd stopped communicating with her. Her brother had brought him home during one of their short leaves, and she and Cade had become friends. *Good friends.* They'd e-mailed all the time, for almost a year straight. Right near the end of their long correspondence, things had shifted between them, had been heading into more than friendly territory. Then after Riel died, it was as if Cade had too. It had cut her so deep to lose him on top of her brother. And now he showed up in the hospital room after her mom's death and wanted to talk to her? Hell no.

She'd been harassing the nurses to find a doctor who would discharge her, and now she knew why they'd been putting her off. They'd done a dozen tests and she didn't have a brain injury. She wasn't exhibiting any signs of having a concussion except for the memory loss, but the doctors were convinced that this was because of shock and trauma at what she'd apparently witnessed.

Nash started to argue, but the cop hauled him away, talking in low undertones, shutting the door behind them. Leaving her alone with this giant of a man.

Feeling raw and vulnerable, Maria wrapped her arms around herself. The sun had almost set, so even standing by the window didn't warm her up. She just felt so damn cold. Because of the room and probably grief. And now to be faced with a dark reminder of her past was too much.

ACKNOWLEDGMENTS

As always, thank you to Kari Walker for too many reasons to count. I appreciate you reading the early version and offering your insight. Carolyn Crane, thank you for all your thoughts on this book, specifically regarding Drake. Deborah Nemeth, editor extraordinaire, I'm incredibly grateful for your insight. Joan Turner, thank you for catching all those pesky little errors during the final read through. Jaycee with Sweet 'N Spicy Designs, as always, your design work is beautiful. For my readers, I owe a big thank you for all your continuing support. I'm blessed to have such wonderful readers! Lastly, thank you to God.

COMPLETE BOOKLIST

Red Stone Security Series
No One to Trust
Danger Next Door
Fatal Deception
Miami, Mistletoe & Murder
His to Protect
Breaking Her Rules
Protecting His Witness
Sinful Seduction
Under His Protection

The Serafina: Sin City Series
First Surrender
Sensual Surrender
Sweetest Surrender

Deadly Ops Series
Targeted
Bound to Danger

Non-series Romantic Suspense
Running From the Past
Everything to Lose

Dangerous Deception
Dangerous Secrets
Killer Secrets
Deadly Obsession
Danger in Paradise
His Secret Past

Paranormal Romance
Destined Mate
Protector's Mate
A Jaguar's Kiss
Tempting the Jaguar
Enemy Mine
Heart of the Jaguar

Moon Shifter Series
Alpha Instinct
Lover's Instinct (novella)
Primal Possession
Mating Instinct
His Untamed Desire (novella)
Avenger's Heat
Hunter Reborn

Darkness Series
Darkness Awakened
Taste of Darkness

ABOUT THE AUTHOR

Katie Reus is the *New York Times* and *USA Today* bestselling author of the Red Stone Security series, the Moon Shifter series and the Deadly Ops series. She fell in love with romance at a young age thanks to books she pilfered from her mom's stash. Years later she loves reading romance almost as much as she loves writing it.

However, she didn't always know she wanted to be a writer. After changing majors many times, she finally graduated summa cum laude with a degree in psychology. Not long after that she discovered a new love. Writing. She now spends her days writing dark paranormal romance and sexy romantic suspense.

For more information on Katie please visit her website: www.katiereus.com. Also find her on twitter @katiereus or visit her on facebook at: www.facebook.com/katiereusauthor.

Made in the USA
Charleston, SC
09 November 2014